I0823415

Bloodfire, Baby

Bloodfire, Baby

A Novel

EIRINIE CARSON

DUTTON

DUTTON
An imprint of Penguin Random House LLC
1745 Broadway, New York, NY 10019
penguinrandomhouse.com

Book design by Laura K. Corless

LIBRARY OF CONGRESS CATALOGING-IN-PUBLICATION DATA

Names: Carson, Eirinie author
Title: Bloodfire, baby : a novel / Eirinie Carson.
Description: New York, NY : Dutton, 2026.
Identifiers: LCCN 2025039030 (print) | LCCN 2025039031 (ebook) |
ISBN 9798217044825 hardcover | ISBN 9798217044832 ebook
Subjects: LCGFT: Gothic fiction | Novels | Fiction
Classification: LCC PS3603.A7756 B58 2026 (print) | LCC PS3603.A7756 (ebook)
LC record available at https://lccn.loc.gov/2025039030
LC ebook record available at https://lccn.loc.gov/2025039031

Printed in the United States of America
1st Printing

The authorized representative in the EU for product safety and compliance is Penguin Random House Ireland, Morrison Chambers, 32 Nassau Street, Dublin D02 YH68, Ireland, https://eu-contact.penguin.ie.

For Larissa, who started it all

i am accused of tending to the past as if i made it,

as if i sculpted it

with my own hands. i did not.

this past was waiting for me

—Lucille Clifton

After

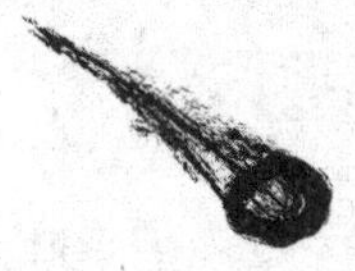

You have to understand that the universe is imploding, the planet is dying, we've been told this so many times and I know I know I know that this is the end because surely, at the end there is so much blood. Surely at the end I am on my hands and knees cleaning, trying to gather it all, put it all back but I've killed her, there's no reversing this. Hell and brimstone, cleansing and renewal. This is what was preached to me. And briefly, I promise it is briefly, I think: What would have happened if we hadn't had a baby? What would we have done, who would I have been? If this hadn't been a thing, if this hadn't been an aim? What else. What else. I don't take it back, but I want to know the other possibilities, how else could this have ended?

The planet is dying and if you look at my Instagram, if you check my stats, you'll know I did my best to reverse it all. I did my best to be honest and true, to prevent Armageddon, but I have been alone too long. I have been struggling too long, and I don't know how I am supposed to keep this planet turning. No man is an island.

I scoop and I scoop more blood than you have ever seen in your life across the floor, gathering it into my arms. It is dark and sticky and viscous, exactly like the corn syrup they use in the movies. I like the movies because in the end, you always get a summary. A tidy bow you can tie it all up with. In the end, the guy gets the girl and they have a baby and live happily ever after. In the end there is resolution, time is linear: then to now.

You have to understand that I am a person who likes rules and guidelines. Give me a path I can follow into goodness and I will take it. I built myself, brick by brick, after I left my mother's house, exchanging one set of rules for another, the ones I crafted. I didn't know the rules were actually threads across something else, across a vast interminable space that can unravel all at once.

The blood is soaking my sweatpants. It is on my face in my hair under my fingernails, I want to scream but I try to stay calm, I try to clean. Blood in vast quantities is impossible to gather, it adheres to whatever you use to clean it, a guilty conscience come to life. Perhaps if other things had happened, if we had been other people, I would never have known just how difficult blood is to get out, how it collects between your fingers, congeals into the setting of your wedding ring, how it permeates your cuticle line. I would never have known what it felt like to kill, to stand over someone you knew and realize what you had done. To push up against a hard wall, finite, fin.

I focus. Fatigue has been a constant, it has been so long since I slept but sometimes even in the depths of this sleeplessness, I can sharpen my attention like the twisting of a camera lens to see the minute details of any moment, like looking through a magnifying glass at the fibers of a carpet. I do that now, twisting within myself to look around for what is needed. I get a bucket from beneath the sink; I get newspaper and the most absorbent towels in the house, this large house that we bought before knowing what would happen here, who I would become. I soak up the blood and think of bread being wiped along the inside of a half-finished bowl, sopping up sauce.

The knife is still slippery. I cannot gain a purchase on it, it slips from my hands and I have to jump my bare, red feet out of the way to avoid it. I look up at the camera in the corner of the room and I find myself smiling at it, caught red-handed, red-footed, no denying this, no covering it up. Acceptance finally begins to cool my clammy body, my breasts slick with sweat and milk. A noise from the corner of the room, voices like distant drums, and the dark figure I have been living with appears. Even after all I have seen it watches me, shimmering in the doorway, as if trying to tell me something more, something I have missed. Its mouth (or where its mouth should be) is moving, but I cannot hear its sounds. For the first time in three weeks, I am not afraid of this thing.

I think back to being a child on summer days when the sun would stretch my shadow out in front of me, making me tall as the trees. I would try to hop into it, wanting to meet it, to align my body with its shape. The figure in the doorway is a shadow, an absence of light, hypnotizing—I can't help but stop cleaning, even though stopping seems ridiculous, like a meteor headed straight for me as I twiddle my thumbs. But what else is there to do? What else can I do but listen? My mother was right, it took me a long time to hear her but she was right, and here I am standing in front of a universe's worth of history. Nothing left to do but confront it.

Perhaps if I stretch out my hand like I did as a child, I can touch it. Perhaps I can finally bring my body against its body, both of us an outline of secrets jigsawing neatly into each other. A testimony, a confession. But I should take you back to the beginning, I want you to understand.

The floor is still wet with her blood, the whorls of the wood panels visible through a shallow, red lake as I hear the sound of keys in the door. I finally get a grip on the handle of the blade, I stand and turn like Lot's wife, bracing myself in this pool, bracing myself for my husband, who will come home now, finally and too late, and he will see what has been done.

—*

A story is made up of parts, and so is a country. There is an invisible bond always between a land and its people, a tethering like the navel string from a newborn baby. Any midwife worth her salt will tell you, you don't cut the navel string right away, you let it pulse, you let the beat of the mother's heart join the beat of the child's heart so that all the goodness can flow. But sometimes it is severed, and we must deal with the consequence, or as my mother used to say, hataclaps, because there are always hataclaps, even if it is not felt for hundreds of years.

Many years ago, before you or I were born, a ship crashed somewhere off the coast of Jamaica. It was a ship full of the enslaved, taken from their homes and led to an unknown place. Many perished, smashed against rocks, a mercifully quick death. Some drowned in the salty waters of an ocean they had never before tasted but filled their bellies until they sank to the bottom, heavy like stones. Some still were said to have found land, found mountains, found saviors there among the trees. And because we were in desperate need back then, because hope was hard to come by and harder to hold on to, tales also prevailed about the ones who Mami Wata kept, whom she took down to the depths, whom she gave fins and gills and homes in shells, because the fish are her children and the rivers and oceans her home.

Perhaps all of this is true, perhaps none of it. But if you can believe it, if you can find faith among the intangible, perhaps you can also take a step into the unknown, where all things are possible.

Before

1

I have been a mother for approximately two weeks. It is not what I imagined. When I was pregnant and thought of this postpartum time, my mind conjured myself in a sheer yet somehow demure, impeccably white linen dress, kinky hair still full and luxe from all the promised pregnancy hormones, skin shining, moisturized and rested, holding a baby who would sleep dreamlessly against my chest. I would imagine my husband, Emil, desperate to help, attentive and natural, preempting my every move, urging me to rest, canceling work to be with me. Doting and starry eyed. My boobs would go from Bs to DDs, but would remain pert like perfect fruit, grapefruits or, dare to dream, honeydews. Instead, I am feeling old and lackluster in a new bed with new sheets in our new house in a new neighborhood. The baby is screaming and I am desperate to hush her. I smush my breast into her open mouth just how the nurse practitioner taught us in prenatal classes: *Use a tight grip on baby's neck while using the same arm to hold baby close against your chest, keeping him (or her!) perpendicular. Try holding your breast like a messy hamburger!*

As hoped, my pre-partum breasts have filled out and sit precariously on my chest, although the nipples are raw and wounded, the skin chapped. I wonder, idly, through the pain, if my own mother ever experienced this, if maybe her mother told her of some remedy from back home that would soothe the agony, calm the baby. But I will never know this, because my mother and I haven't spoken for years. Neither of us seem eager to rekindle what was an all-consuming toxic fire. After I left, she never reached out and we let whatever remained of our relationship die, unstoked and unfueled. This new chapter of my life feels fresh and new and unblemished. I am putting a period at the end of the sentence that is my family. I am starting over. I can do this.

The baby is not latching and I try to swallow my frustration. My breasts are turgid, vascular melons; it is probably like trying to latch on a basketball. In all the breastfeeding classes I was a studious notetaker because I have always been a good student, good with workbooks, good with towing the line. A monogrammed Smythson notebook is sitting somewhere on my desk at this very moment, filled with detailed instructions, but the idea of picking myself and this infant up, dragging my still-sore body through this huge house to retrieve it, feels entirely ridiculous. I would laugh at the aspirations of pre-partum Sofia, if this wasn't all so agonizing.

The baby's tiny mouth searches, eyes closed, for the helicopter landing pad that used to be my areola. Once again, I mash my breast tissue, pinpricks of blood and milk appear simultaneously, and I wince, hold my breath, realign the baby's mouth. The voice of the instructor rings again, a sharp little bell inside my head. *If it hurts, you're doing it wrong, mamas!*

She latches. Relief and a searing pain overcome my body, but the relief wins. The pressure that was mounting in my boobs begins to wane, and an unquenchable thirst fills my body. The bedroom door opens and I hope for a huge icy pail of water that I can glug like an Olympian, but Emil walks in disappointingly empty-handed.

I swallow down an anger I dismiss as unfair (*He didn't know! How could he have known? He's not a mind reader*) and force a smile like the flick of a switch. I am dressed in an old zip-up hoodie, sun-bleached and worn at the cuffs, and the mesh panties the hospital handed me in bulk. The effects are a far cry from the Calvin Klein commercial I had envisioned when I thought of this moment, and for a second, sadness enters my brain. I know I should do better. I should try harder. I've seen enough Instagram posts of new parents to know that it is possible to put an outfit together, to brush your hair, or even just your teeth. One of the accounts I follow, a gorgeous brunette mom of two, had a collage of pregnancy photos. In each photo slide her tiny frame blowing up like an elegant balloon, like the white dress around Marilyn Monroe, chaste yet sexy. The next post was her post-pregnancy collage, deflating with grace, coming back down to earth, smiling in natural light with a baby on her washboard abs. Flawless. I glance over at Emil, who also looks flawless. He is wearing the Sandro shirt bought on a work trip to London, his dirty-blond hair is swept back and still wet from the shower. He looks like he smells good. He sits down near me, rubs my back as he gazes at our child. He does smell good.

"You guys are cute," Emil says, smiling, nuzzling my neck with a little more lust than is warranted, considering the outfit, and a lot more lust than I can currently handle. I should reciprocate but I lean away from him, feeling suffocated. His clean-scent smell is jarring. I am a wild animal next to him, all stale milk and sleep-warmed flesh.

"Hmm," I reply, hoping he doesn't notice the sharp bristle of my leg hair against his calves. It's been some time since I shaved. "*She* is cute, maybe, but not me."

"She *is* cute."

He leans in, kisses the top of her head.

"I am going to miss you guys so much."

My heart sinks as I remember the unforgettable fact that Emil is leaving, soon, for a work trip that I okayed as a naïve pregnant person. Emil's work as an assistant director takes him all over the country. When we first started dating, I would visit him in the hotels he was put up in, and we would roll around on pristine bedsheets knowing they would be made again the second we left the room. I would wander around unknown cities with all the time in the world while he worked tirelessly, desperate for him the minute he swiped the room key. When he was away I missed him with a fervent, unbridled passion that meant there was joy to be found in his absence. This time I knew it would be different; this time I would be alone, but not really alone.

I was always proud of this lust we had for each other, it seemed rare. It was not a lust my parents had; they had been housemates only. I had never so much as seen them hug, not that my mother had hugged me and my brother, Devon, either. We were held at a cool, reserved distance, just close enough for her to pick apart our achievements, never close enough to celebrate them. Resentment for Emil's departure wells up behind the wall I have built to keep the uglier versions of myself out, and I kill it dead. I am a new Sofia. This is a new chapter. It is perfect. I will not sully it with thoughts of my mother. Deep breath, in through the nose out through the mouth, like they taught in prenatal yoga. Goddess pose. I smile as I switch the baby from my right to my left breast, quieting the sense of panic that creeps up my throat, making it deflate along with my throbbing boobs.

"We'll miss you too. But it's not that long, right?"

"Three weeks," Emil replies flippantly, not making eye contact with me, preoccupied with closing the clasp on the chunky gold chain around his wrist.

"Three?" I reply, a little too loud, a little too Mom. I readjust my tone. "*Three* weeks? I thought it was just two?"

"It was," he continues hesitantly, still fumbling with the chain, "but it looks like we have some new sides to shoot so we decided to just conservatively say three. And there's Max's will to bend to, you know what producers are like. It's a smart choice anyway. Being conservative just means error will be factored into the schedule and we won't waste anyone's time."

What about my time? I think. What about me? I swallow, stare down at the living, breathing baby at my chest, the one we are in charge of, the one we must keep alive. *I. I* must keep alive. I take a breath, exhale a little too noisily. I reach over and clasp the bracelet around his wrist with ease and he finally looks at me.

"Okay," I say. "Okay. Three weeks, then."

"Well . . . just over. Three weeks and a day or two. I know it's more than we expected," Emil placates, already relieved, resuming the back rub that suddenly feels like sandpaper to me, "but I'll call my mom, we can get a nanny, Dominique is around. And I've seen you with her. You've got this. I mean, you read all those parenting books, you'll be okay, right?"

I know the answer I am supposed to give. The answer is yes. The answer is: I have my notes, I have resources and friends and co-workers with kids and an iPhone. The answer is: Of course you should go and work, of course you shouldn't stay here with me, your wife and new baby, of course you shouldn't help me unpack the boxes in our brand-new house, of course this is more important. But a small, persistent voice says no. I want to say no.

And as if by magic, as if a reminder of all I have escaped, my phone buzzes next to me and I look down at the screen, which reads *Do Not Answer.* My mother, Eddie. She hasn't called in years. She couldn't contact me even if she wanted to, I was disfellowshipped, it's forbidden. Just the sight of her number is enough to make my heart lurch downward, and a darkness I had forgotten the taste of is now in my mouth. I think to tell Emil and stop myself because this is a problem easily solved. I flip the phone over, push it away, push it away along with all the curiosity I have for what she could possibly want. I push it away along with all the noes I long to say out loud and instead I say,

"Yes. We will be all right."

While the baby sleeps upstairs I watch Emil make coffee in the kitchen, agonizingly slowly, via pour-over. There's a rhythm to it and I let myself be lulled, leaning against the counter, watching. Emil asks if I want a cup and I shake my head, content to watch him. I am so soothed that a sudden movement from outside is jarring, and I stand up like a startled deer. I catch something move behind the thick trunk of the beech tree. Is that a face? A hand? The day is bright and the beech tree provides ample shade to the house; is it possible it's just a trick of the light?

"I think there's someone outside," I venture, not letting my eyes drift from the tree that feels as if it is hiding something.

"Hmm," Emil replies distractedly, wetting down the sides of an unbleached coffee filter with a silver pot.

His noncommittal response makes me re-examine. Nothing is wrong—jazz tinkles in from the Sonos, the dappled late-morning light warms the room. This scene is perfect.

But then, behind the tree, a wisp of something, a shadow.

"Emil, I'm sure. Someone is out there."

Emil leaves the Chemex to follow my gaze, resting his chin on my shoulder from behind.

"I don't see anything, babe." He stares out the window for a few more seconds to humor me, then settles his attention back on the coffee.

There's nothing there. Just the tree, just the grass, just the breeze. Still. Seems wise to check. Keeping my pace casual, I unlock the French doors to the back and peer, left to right. Nothing. Slipping on some Birkenstocks I pad across the grass. Against my better judgment I take a step toward the tree, where something lingers against the bark. A finger? Or something shaped like one, but black like charcoal. I walk around the trunk of the tree, my left hand against it, the bark breaking away beneath my fingertips. Whatever it is, it's just out of reach, I feel the dread of being surrounded by something that somehow looms in front but also behind. I quicken my pace, rotating around the tree, until a face is up against my own, eyes wide in horror, a chain saw in his hands.

I scream. He screams.

The gardener.

"Sorry, miss. I didn't mean to startle you. Just doing some work on this tree." He swallows; I've made him nervous.

I press my hand against my rib cage, heart pounding. Emil steps out of the door in full protection mode.

"Everything okay here?"

"Yes," I say, forcing a smile, feeling foolish, I gesture stupidly at the poor worker. "I just . . . The gardener."

The gardener nods as if to confirm.

"Okay to continue?" He gestures with the chain saw at the tree.

"What's wrong with it?" I ask as Emil slips his arm around my waist.

"Heart rot." The gardener points up. "See those funny-looking mushroom things? They grow out of fallen branch holes. Whole tree is riddled. Probably will have to cut down the whole thing. Kind of like clogged arteries, no good."

"That's so sad, I love this tree." I sigh. Ever since we moved in, something about it has felt familiar, a faceless old friend looming over the house, shading the windows.

"If it's gotta go it's gotta go," says Emil, patting the trunk firmly, knowingly. He looks at me, amends, "But of course, do everything you can to save it."

The gardener does a mock salute and starts up his ladder to end the conversation. I take one last glance at the tree; it feels as if it wants me to look. I swear I saw a shadow of something. I shake my head, no. Just exhaustion, just the light. Emil and I head back to the house, locking the doors behind us. From inside I watch the gardener take limb after limb of the decaying tree and toss them to a pile on the grass below him like a funeral pyre.

Later, after I wake from a nap beside the baby (*Sleep when the baby is sleeping!*), the sky outside the nursery window is smoke-filled. The beech tree is up in flames. But wait, no, not the tree—out the window I see that the pyre the gardener has been making is alight and he stands back to watch it. The tree stands watching too, limbless. I wonder if it'll make it back from the brink, or if heart rot once settled is non-negotiable.

—*

After the final straw at my mother's apartment, the last time I saw her, I had fled from the Bay Area to Manhattan. I had no money, except the little left over from what I had quietly hidden away for the final few years in my mother's small apartment on Pierson Street, near the Kingdom Hall under the freeway. It was a difficult transition; without the organization and its rules I felt lost, out of my depth in a city that didn't care if I lived or died. But somehow I survived. I got myself a job that didn't pay for much outside of my rent on a room in the Bronx and the rice I bought for dinner from the Chinese takeout across the street. And although I was doing it, finally on my own, loneliness was a dense fog that crept up on me. My high school best friend, Dominique, never made good on all our promises to live together in New York. I worked long hours and had never learned how to be social, so my roommates thought I was odd. The events of that first winter in the Bronx were a fork in the road. I found myself starting over once more, this time even stronger, but I didn't feel myself becoming me until I met Emil, my second year on the East Coast.

It had been a late, lingering summer in the city and the sky was heavy with storm clouds. The multiple tiny desk fans we set up in our office were unable to break through the dense air. I had wrapped up my work as a receptionist early; everyone said it was too hot to finish at five so we left at one, Summer Fridays, and I stepped out of the building only to be hit with an oppressive atmospheric closeness. I knew I had to book it to the subway station if I was to remain dry.

The skies opened, releasing comically heavy large drops that immediately wet the white button-up shirt I was wearing, exposing me completely and flattening my hair. I cowered beneath an awning not half a city block from the subway station I needed, thinking about all the time I had spent making my hair big and loud, like a shout. It was my second summer in the city, the summer I started wearing my hair natural; a relief and a time saver. No more trips to the salon I couldn't afford or worse, nights at home painstakingly sectioning out my hair, layering on creamy relaxer to flatten any and all curl, leaving my hair flat, shiny, and limp. There was also something nagging, something deeper, that had begun to bother me about it. My mother had favored hair neat and tucked back, so I wore my hair flat and pinned to my scalp every day I did my field service in our neighborhood for the Kingdom Hall, trying to get my required hours up, trying to impress Eddie.

So, the day I met Emil my hair was big and beautiful and being rained on. Ruined. As I stood waiting for the shower to subside, I envisioned the efforts I would have to undergo once home—washing, drying, and styling my newly kinky 'fro would take up time I didn't have to spare. Summer Fridays were usually about finding the fun event being hosted that week, like the agency whose rooftop has an unobstructed view of Midtown, or the boozy picnic in Central Park. But I was tired, I wanted to eat the leftover noodles in the fridge and go straight to bed with one of the many books on my nightstand. I hesitated under the awning, double-daring myself to make the dash for the subway stairs, when Emil bounded past, a hefty fashion magazine over his hair like an umbrella. Our eyes briefly met and he stepped backward to me, as if in rewind, smiling from beneath the publication that I knew cost twenty-two American dollars. What it must be like to make such easy, expensive purchases! I only had enough on my MetroCard to get me home and not a cent more. His smile was perfect and I frowned at it, confused.

"Hey! Are you headed to the station?"

"What?" I replied dumbly, still not grasping the situation.

"If you're headed to the station, you can use this?"

He offered the magazine. I laughed, not sure if he was serious.

"Come on, I walked six blocks already with this thing, it's got maybe three minutes of life left, tops."

And then, without a moment's thought and against my better judgment, I hopped out from under the awning and between his arms, which chivalrously held the magazine, ensuring he would get soaked himself. We made a mad dash for the subway steps, skipping down them at double time, Ginger and Fred, laughing like old lovers, close and familiar. Once inside, the station I passed through twice a day felt transformed, the color brighter and the air warmer.

"Thank you." I panted.

"I'm Emil."

"Sofia."

He was gorgeous. Young and springy and smiling in a way that exuded affluence. Even the fluorescent lights above us hummed with approval. Emil's smile was what my mother would have called a sinner's smile, innocent, ignorant, his eyes lingered a little too long on mine and I had to look away. When I turned to leave, he gently took my hand so that I turned back, and I found my gaze in the stars of his eyes, and he said "I need to see you again" with such conviction that I was taken aback.

I hadn't made much of an effort to date, just a few fumbles with inexperienced men who talked of themselves at length and then, instead of a period at the end of their monologue came their mouth like a shark lunging for a kiss, using too much tongue or not enough.

My roommates had made me get on a dating app or two, editorializing my life and tweaking my selfies to make me look like a catch. The boys I matched with were aloof, playing endless games learned from self-titled pickup artists, leaving texts on read and pretending to be busy. Emil's candidness was refreshing. It turned me on. When my roommates would proclaim they didn't want a needy guy, I would readily agree, eager to please. But it wasn't true. I wanted to be loved, I wanted to be seen, I wanted to be needed. I smiled at him, asked when we could meet, and he picked a bar and a time without hesitation. And then two years went by, and we were engaged with plans to move back to the Bay Area.

And the part I do not mention when we are retelling this story, this story I keep for Emil as a testament to my desire is this: I headed home immediately, hurried past my roommates, slammed my door, and began touching myself urgently to a cinematic reimagining of his hand in my hand. A zoom on his eyes crinkling as he smiled at me, a slow camera push-in to his lips saying *I need to see you again*, the harsh subway station lights glinting on the thin chain around his neck and against his collarbone, golden from time spent shirtless in Washington Square Park. I saw us together; we'd make a beautiful couple; we'd make beautiful babies. I played this over and over again in my head until I climaxed, hoarse and breathless.

—*

The bay windows in the nursery let the sunlight flood in, and the room is awash in a warm, romantic light. The baby is awake, stirring in her crib while I set up the floor mat, get ready for the exercises the nurse prescribed before we left the hospital. I place the baby on her stomach for tummy time, which is supposed to strengthen her neck and make it easier when crawling comes, a warm-up before a marathon. I wait for the baby to do something, but she lies face down, mouth to the side, fish out of water, scarcely moving.

"Come on, lift your head." I try to keep my voice warm in some guessed approximation of maternal, but it comes off barking, like a dolphin trainer at SeaWorld. I have heard verbal encouragement is helpful, even if she hasn't shown any sign of understanding me in two weeks. How long are we supposed to do this? I check on my phone. The answer of a few minutes a day comes from Google in milliseconds.

I wait. She does nothing. She opens her mouth and begins to cry, forlorn. I am just out of the baby's eyesight; she probably thinks she's alone. I watch her, my knees folded on a pillow beneath me, hands primly in my lap. I could leave her here, I think. The thought comes to me like a jagged piece of glass. I could take a minute to myself. She can't do anything about it. I could leave and get in the car, drive anywhere. I squeeze my eyes tight, shut hard, till I see flashes on the backs of my eyelids. Flashes of silver, a glinting in the dark. Just as I blink the thoughts away and reach for her, Emil walks in with his toothbrush in his mouth and I snatch the baby up quick, guilt in my eyes.

He looks at me questioningly.

"Tummy time," I say, explaining. He nods a *got it* nod and leaves the room, off to floss, send his emails, stare at his phone. This is none of his business; this is women's business. My business, now.

Our meet-cute makes people sigh and swoon when we tell it, and sometimes I cling to our origin story as proof that Emil and I are meant to be. I look down at our new small baby soothed by my arms, at my faded outfit in need of a wash, and wonder if it will always be like this. If the memory of what the beginning was like, of my stomach twisting as I prepared to go on my first date with him, of cocktails in far-flung locations, of the chase, are all I have now. I know how it feels to be desperate for love, desperate for lust. To imagine hands on your body, firm and knowing, moving across your skin like you are braille. That tingle unfurling from between your legs like a new leaf, the thrill of being wanted, of feeling the want in the air. The penetration, causing you to sigh involuntarily, a silent amen.

Emil comes back in, toothbrush still in his mouth.

"Where is that duffel bag you got me?" he garbles, the word *duffel* coming out with a light spray of toothpaste.

"Our closet, bottom shelf."

He gives a thumbs-up and leaves to spit in the sink and, most likely, not rinse it out. I run my tongue along my own teeth, still slick with a nighttime slime.

When I was pregnant and my stomach rudely protruded out between me and Emil whenever we attempted to embrace, we would laugh to each other, *Something's come between us,* our own private joke. And now the bump is gone but the baby remains. I can't find my way around her.

—*

Emil and his team have prep work to do before his trip and it means his schedule is limited, but he offers to take us out, walk around, get out of the house for a while. I am not really in the mood but he convinces me, even helps me pick out an outfit—an unfussy Dries Van Noten shirt with a pair of stretch-waist denim pants, a Gucci blazer thrown over the top, preppy mom out for the day. I line my underwear with heavy-duty pads from the hospital, just in case, but you'd never know they were there. Any clue of my postpartum wounds has been carefully hidden; I look like a wife, a mother, uninjured and well dressed. We assemble the baby stroller, clean our child, and dress her in neutrals, tucking a knitted blanket around her body. Her fists are so small, like two tiny shrimp at her sides. Emil calls her Ol' Shrimp Hands, and I laugh, not because it's that funny but at the joy of finding myself slap-bang in the middle of a real-life dad joke.

The clouds part and the sun beams down on us as we walk the dreamy laurel-lined main street of our hood, filled with boutiques and cafés. Emil suggests a coffee, we stop in and order a chai for him, a decaf latte for me, a heart-shaped cookie to nibble. Emil finishes his drink and pushes the baby stroller dexterously with one hand, the other he has casually around my shoulders, which pulls us in close together, he is me and I am him, and here is our baby, brown and teeny, dressed impeccably, shade pulled over her dozing eyes. We are the perfect family, I think, and allow myself a moment of smugness. I linger to sniff some flowers at the corner stand, and Emil smiles at me, waiting patiently. A lady with a yoga mat tucked under her arm stops, lifts her Chanel sunglasses, and smiles wide into the stroller.

"What a gorgeous child!" She gasps, hand to her chest, not looking at our baby but at Emil, who smiles indulgently, his perfect teeth visible. I am just behind him, handing the vendor a twenty-dollar bill, assembling a bouquet, already able to see it sitting on the mantel in a vintage vase.

"She is, we're very proud." Emil beams, pulling me back to his side. I am tucked beneath his arm, the bouquet beneath mine. I look up at him, my beautiful man, and my life makes sense again for the first time in weeks.

"Lucky you!" the yoga lady says, to me rather than anyone else, and flicks her shades down. And she's right, lucky me. We continue our leisurely walk past the stores and loop round to do one last victory lap before heading home. Even when we pass the homeless encampment that has crept into the edges of the neighborhood despite the mayor's best attempts to beat them back, a homeless man stops his piss midstream to let us by.

Happiness is such a funny thing because rarely do you realize that in the moment you have it, except that I do, right now. I feel a little breeze of hope. I think that if he could stay, if he didn't have his work trip, we could stay in this bubble, floating above everyone. He could take her to baby-and-me classes, I could get back to Pilates. I could make him dinner before he got home, we could eat together after the baby goes down for the night, finally settling down in bed to discuss, under cover of darkness, the possibility of giving her a little brother or sister. The life that everyone dreams of is mine, right under my nose, and when he comes back, we will pick up exactly here, the perfect American family, starting out on our own. Things I never could have imagined when I was in the hospital all those years ago, staring out at Long Island Sound from the barred windows of my room.

I

I'll start it like a story.

Once upon a time, in a small country in the Caribbean Sea, a daughter was born. From her seed would grow a vast tree, reaching branches out across the ocean. Her name is unknown, so let's call her Sekesu, the woman at the roots of this tree. Sekesu grew up in a timeless place, where the moon and the sun hung side by side like sisters, and the past, present, and future existed together. The trees that protected them also created the shadows they lived in, keeping the brightness of the sun out. Sekesu's people had stories of a far land across an ocean that was once known as home, but had been lost to them. The forest people knew that the loss of the distant home was important, and they held what little they knew about the place close. They cooked in ways they could remember from before, spirits revered and tended to, even their language was peppered with that of home. They held tight to the past of Africa, the present of now, the future of some unknown.

For the enslaved who escaped from the plantations below, the only way out was up—up through the trees, up mountain paths to places where the old ways were kept alive. Hope and survival go well together. They defended their land from the British soldiers with machetes and stolen guns, and made sure they would never go back; even when the treaty of 1738 came, the forest people did what had to be done so their life might be preserved. Sovereignty was granted and in return they did the unforgivable—turned away people they were once like, they sent them back to their plantations and, in many instances, killed them. The things you will do for freedom may surprise you. It surprised them.

But in the here and now was Sekesu, who was born after enslavement in Jamaica had ended, when the air was full of uncertainty and a precarious feeling of hope. Perhaps because this was the air she breathed, Sekesu spent her childhood longing for something else, more than her village duties of cooking and feeding the children and heeding her elders, preparing plant medicines: cerasee tea for sickness, sweet basil for warding off spirits, milk with nutmeg for bad dreams. All her spare hours were spent mending clothes at the trunk of the cotton tree on the edge of her village, roots wide and buttress-like, twisting all the way up like a washrag wrung out, in which spirits were said to dwell. Laid in at the roots were hard, black stones pressed into the earth, making a mosaic floor beneath her. She would let her gaze drift off in the direction of the nearest town, willing something to happen, for someone to come out and rescue her and take her out into the sunlight. At night, she indulged her curiosity with dream wanderings that would let her mind leave the village, soar over the trees and the huts, and down into the rest of Xaymaca, astral traveling being one of the gifts from her long-dead ancestors.

Several decades after the freedom proclamation was read from the steps of the King's House in Spanish Town, when Sekesu was grown enough to go into the nearby big town to trade, she met a man who caused an explosion to occur in her chest. William was high yellow, with brooding blue-gray eyes and cheekbones that were sharp and severe. She began making excuses to go to town and meet him, and they would walk the dusty lanes together, ignoring the calls of market vendors and preachers, absorbed in each other's company. He was a serious man, and could talk with a passion about the future of their island, the hypocrisy of the British government that still ruled the island and would for another hundred years. Up in her mountain village, Sekesu had been so shielded from the rest of the island's experience that she listened, rapt.

And William was also schooled—she took him to her jungle, showed him how to find the wild yams and all their sweetness beneath the ground, showed him how to climb a coconut tree barefoot, her skirts knotted around her strong thighs as she climbed. He would laugh incredulously at her, and catch the green coconuts she tossed down to him. She felt she had found home for the first time, safe in his arms, hidden beneath the canopy.

They spent weeks this way, exploring with each other, making grand plans, until one day he did not meet her in town as planned. Sekesu didn't even have time to dwell on this disappointment as the town was alive with fear, something had happened. A riot, a market seller explained to Sekesu and the others who gathered around his stall. Buckra had been beaten outside the courthouse in Saint Thomas, and word was that some freedmen were on the run. Sekesu knew before she was told that her high yellow man was among them, and she felt immediately paralyzed by her inability to help him. But Sekesu's people had given her the gifts that could help, hadn't they? All she had to do was use them.

That night back in her village, she dreamed of William, leaving her earthly body behind to find his, lost and scared in her jungle.

When she awoke the sky was still dark, and she slipped out before anyone could miss her, running down to the place she had seen him in her sleep. William was alone and bloody and begged her to hide him. She would never forget, not even in old age, how it felt to take his calloused hand in hers and lead him silently through the jungle, his trust in her palm. He was grateful for the cave she housed him in and slept immediately like he had never done it before in his life. Sekesu came every day without being seen to bring him food and water, and sinkle bible for his injuries, burns on his hands from the musket's powder. She wanted to tell her people about him, knowing that they could help with their superior knowledge of plant medicine, with their ability to hide in the trees, but William was adamant that no one could know.

For the next few days, as he recuperated in the jungle under Sekesu's watchful eye, William spoke of a plan to rejoin his friends, to continue what they started; word was out that Buckra's retaliation had already begun. The smoke from burning homesteads below could be seen through the trees' canopy. She returned to her village at night so as not to arouse suspicion, but she was always desperate to see him, especially if she could not get away from her chores and the great round hut where most of the day's activities occurred. One such day she took a risk, but was followed by one of the younger girls who, badminding, ran back to the mountain village and told the elders.

When Sekesu and William were found, the elders talked of sending him back to the British, letting them do what they needed. There was no use hiding, he would be found and they would be held to account for their aid. Sekesu begged them to spare him, for what harm could he cause now? He had been up in the Blue Mountains this long and no one had come to look for him, and he was young and strong and could be of use. She could be the one to teach him! But the elders, who remembered just how burning the British desire for subjugation was, pushed our Caribbean girl aside, and did what was necessary to make sure he was surrendered.

She screamed in her trees, howled and clutched her stomach, calling his name as he was dragged from her. Sekesu was brokenhearted, and there was not a thing to be done about it. Of course, she was supposed to be punished too, but in her belly she carried the seed of all that would come to be, and the elders at last found some mercy. She was allowed to remain in the mountains, but for what? With who? The people who had made certain the man she loved would come to a long and agonizing death? The day William was taken from her something else came in his place, filling her chest like smoke from a fire. A shadow that was somehow familiar, that watched her daily, always just out of sight.

2

It seems important to mention that Emil is an only child. He likes to say that he's made an effort to change himself but really, my husband is just like the rest of the only children everyone knows. They never had to learn to share, never had a war buddy of a sibling to find solidarity in, to plan an escape with. He grew up in a house similar to the one we bought—large and sprawling but with a verdant lawn that went right to the edge of a cliff overlooking the coast, like an infinity pool of green sliding into a Pacific blue. He's one of those people who, when pressed on how they grew up, says *Oh, we were comfortable,* and anyone who's ever been poor knows how expensive it is to be comfortable. He is at home in our large house, while I still find myself feeling like a guest. He can spread out on a couch, take up space in a way I was never taught to. I have tried to make an imprint here; I buy flowers and change light fixtures and make decisive choices about artwork, but it still doesn't feel like mine. But Emil and I did not grow up in similar places. I am East Bay, he is North. He is right school, right hood, right family, and I am a girl from the wrong side of the Bay Bridge.

The days with the baby are long. Without a full-time job I find myself at a loss—I had thought it would be relaxing, all this free time, but the minutes tick by and are historically long. The Triassic, the Jurassic, and the Cretaceous periods thud by me as I nurse her, or rock her, or change her. The baby naps almost constantly, punctuated only by screams that shoot my heart into my throat. Emil can sleep right through them.

I set her down on the changing table, covered in a soft changing pad dotted with ladybugs. As I change her diaper I stare at her cheeks, trying to determine if they are flushed and red. Emil helicopters in as I button up her onesie with one hand and toss the dirty diaper with the other.

"I'm gonna miss youuuu!" he singsongs, rocking her, but looking at me, a private smile for the two of us.

I return it easily because they are lovely together, there is a naturalness that is hard to look away from, but I do, holding my hands up like a surgeon because I am covered in germs, I need to wash them. It seems all I do these days is wash my hands. I leave them to it, this quiet baby and this man whose hands always seem clean, and go into the bathroom to lather up. He follows me, still bopping about, making up songs for the baby, standing too close.

"You're my baby!" Emil sings to the tune of D'Angelo's "Lady": "My divine, my divine!"

"Can I have a little space?" I say, laughing for levity, although I feel crowded, face flushed.

"No!" Emil jokes, nuzzling in at my neck as I rinse my hands, bringing the baby's face up too so that when I look in the mirror all of us are in there, one two three. That's a family.

Emil and the baby trail behind me like a security detail as I leave the bathroom. He's been doing this since the baby was born, overly surveilling me, probably assuaging his guilt at leaving. Something about his closeness now and his nearing departure in a week feels like a yo-yo, and I can't seem to settle.

"I did want to talk though, babe," Emil begins, and he has the look on his face that means I'm not going to like it. He holds the baby in front of him like a shield. "I've been thinking about nannies, or like, help, ya know?"

"Emil," I say in warning, my voice a blade, "I told you I don't want that."

"I know, but I just feel like if we're thinking about it logically—" I breathe deep to prevent inside thoughts from escaping. *Don't talk to me about logic, man who is leaving his newborn baby and wife.* "—then hiring someone to, you know, do the dishes and whatnot, watch the baby so you can go on a run, makes sense . . . to get some freedom. It's no different than the gardener, or the cleaners."

"I don't need freedom from our child," I say, and I wrestle the baby gently from his arms.

"No, of course not, but . . ."

"Emil"—I am resolute—"yes, in an ideal world I wouldn't be alone, you'd be here. But this job is important and you have got to go, so I can take care of the baby. This is literally my only job right now, so can you just let me do it?"

I am so stoic, so calm, that I almost convince myself. Emil scrunches his chin, purses his lips, nodding grimly. A reluctant agreement, a truce. I worry I've gone too far. *Fine,* his face says. *Have it your way.*

Emil went to one of those public schools in such an affluent neighborhood that it might as well have been private. The type of school whose pick-up/drop-off line was an intimidating array of luxury cars, where kids played the kinds of sports that required costly equipment and after-school lessons—lacrosse, field hockey, tennis, polo. My school had a raggedy basketball hoop and our classrooms were in trailers that were supposed to be temporary while they fumigated and updated the old building. But it was a job they never got to, and so the trailers lasted my entire high school education. Emil always means well and I already feel the creeping remorse for snapping at my husband, and I try to backpedal. Emil runs his hands through his hair, the sun's rays from the bedroom window spill in and the effect is almost celestial; it catches the blond and multiplies it, he is pure spun gold, DiCaprio in *Titanic* waiting at the bottom of the staircase, and when he glances back at me a little of that old lust rears its head, not enough to do anything about, but it is reassuring nonetheless.

"Look," I say, consoling, "I didn't mean to be harsh. I just want to be good at this, I want a chance to be good at this."

Emil, ever the people pleaser, is relieved.

"I wasn't doubting you, not at all. I know you've got this, baby."

"I know."

"I just think I, *we,* have the resources at our disposal and that there is nothing wrong with giving in to a little"—there's a slight pause as he searches for the word—"ease."

Ease. Something his mother would say. His mother uses euphemisms whenever the topic of money is broached, words like *ease* and *comfort,* velvety, slinking out of her mouth, as if having a chauffeur or a private chef or a housekeeper was just common sense, nothing more.

I reach out to Emil and brush his cheek with my hand, and he gets closer because apparently even this small moment of affection turns him on, his optimism is tireless, even here. The minute I initiate this contact I regret it, I'm too tired, and by fortuitous magic the baby starts up like a fountain, crying inconsolably. I look at my husband, apologetic. *Next time.*

—*

The house Emil grew up in is referred to as the country house, and to get to it you must cross the Golden Gate Bridge, which stretches northbound across a glittering bay and is often shrouded by a dense fog. The bridge is always dotted with tourists in shorts and T-shirts making their crossings to catch a glimpse of Alcatraz Island, frozen fingers holding up iPhones to take a photo of nothing but cloud. When you emerge out of the mist there Marin is, Emil's hometown, with some of the wealthiest zip codes in the country, multimillion-dollar homes and boutiques, florists, Michelin-starred restaurants, and white white white, as far as the eye can see.

His mother's name is Buffy, which is not her real name, but the only name she has ever given me, the one she insists I call her. The first time we met she made me repeat it after her, like I was new to the English language. She lives with Emil's father, John, who is old and mostly invisible in a home that was not created with him in mind; it is Buffy's house. Nestled high in the hills, Buffy's house is lovely, pristine, an oasis away from anything close to where I grew up. The back of the house and its gardens face the water that cups the city, while the front is not visible from the road. The streets are empty, save for a few lone, immaculately dressed joggers and tall, old, shady trees. Each house is hidden from view by high hedges. If there were any foot traffic, the pedestrians might wonder who lived behind those large walls of green, but there isn't. No crime, no noise, no garbage, no threats.

Emil's parents have always been difficult to connect with. I am good with older people for the most part, good with the specific breed of white people his parents belong to. NIMBYs at best, blithely unaware do-gooding racists at worst. Liberal voters with little experience of the minorities whose rights they fundraise for in black tie, the types of people who are delighted to find me polite, charming, intelligent. As if I confirm something for them, that Black people can exist outside of the urgent bubbles of need that they pop on a whim. I represent the type of Black woman they can get behind; I seem to straddle two worlds, theirs and a second one they have mostly invented for me, a segregated place of gun violence and poverty and teenage mothers. I wonder if I were not married to a white man if they would so readily accept me; with Emil I have been neutralized, I am safe. A curiosity. A pet. An Asian American colleague of mine once told of how a white ex-boyfriend's father used to affectionately call her an Ornamental, as if it was charming, just a sweet nickname. Emil's father, John, is rarely affectionate, not even in a racist way. He is removed, retired but hardly there, fading away while golfing or at the club or whatever else wealthy old men do. Both Emil and Buffy rarely talk about him, and when they do it is like he is a roommate, with a life of his own that they know nothing about.

The only taste of mortality Buffy ever has is during the hot summers when the trees start to feel combustible. She had dodged the major fire that turned the sky black a few years ago, and because of that she has a skewed idea of herself as someone with grit and strength, when really, she is just someone wealthy enough to employ staff to wet down the sides of her house and the surrounding gardens with various hoses, stretched across her lawns like intestines. Someone wealthy enough to buy on the right side of the hill with the ocean spray and breeze. Someone wealthy enough to be able to retreat to her city apartment and wait it out in luxury. Buffy frequently talks to me as if I could not possibly have experienced anything close, when in reality she had never even asked me about the worst thing that had ever happened. Not that I would tell. Not that I could quantify.

The country house is lovely but, among her tennis club set of identically brittle women in Louis Vuitton and St. John and Cartier held up by blood thinners and martinis, Buffy is famous for her gardens. It feels like a villa in Tuscany: yards and yards of lavender beds, purples and mauves atop green stems, olive trees, and a whole pergola of wisteria that, for the few short weeks it blooms, Buffy likes to have cocktail parties beneath, the heady scent in the spring air adding a layer of intoxication to any glass of wine. Off beyond the wisteria, ivy climbs the walls of the guest house, the roof of which is made from the same Portuguese imported terra-cotta tiles as the main house. Vineyards lie off in the distance, birds twist and swoop in the pink and blue sunset sky, the air cools with a crisp wind off the Bay, and after one or two of Buffy's spritzes a flight to Tuscany or Provence would seem superfluous.

Of course, Buffy's spritzes aren't really Buffy's, they're Marta the housekeeper's, and Buffy's garden is planted, weeded, trimmed, and pruned by a fleet of unnamed dark-skinned gardeners who seem to materialize once a day to spruce things up. Years ago, on my first visit to Buffy's country house for a Sunday brunch, I stepped outside to get some air and witnessed the men, hunched over their daily tasks. I greeted them in Spanish but they didn't reply, they just looked up, nodded to acknowledge me, and continued on. When they looked at me, they didn't see a girl from the same part of the Bay as them, they saw me as an employer. And who could blame them? I was wearing a Dôen linen dress and straw hat from Celine, Hermès sandals, Celine sunglasses, and a nude lip from Tom Ford. Everything I wore that afternoon had the tags torn off that morning. I'd opened a second credit card to make my purchases, and I didn't look at all like a girl from the wrong side of town, which was why I had picked the outfit in the first place. I had wanted to fit in, to be like them, to make them think I belonged, but as I watched the gardeners harvest white roses in silence for the dinner table, snipping just so, ensuring there would be long, slender, leafless stems for the vases Marta would set out, I wondered to what exactly I was trying to belong.

—*

Our new house settles around us as the sun dips out on another day. The heavy wooden staircase that is almost as old as this country creaks and moans. I lie motionless on top of the sheets in our bedroom, listening, holding an ice pack to my crotch. The stitches still ache, my bones feel like they are forming a new skeleton now that the other, smaller skeleton is out of the way. Lying flat and still is all I want to do, it feels like I am waiting for something, something big, a transformation, a metamorphosis. The stairs groan again. It sounds like someone is climbing the stairs, heavy-footed, not my husband because I can tell, one two three four five and then the sound stops. The baby snoozes beside me. I push myself up onto my elbows, straining to hear. Six. Seven. Stops. My heart beats loudly, making it hard to keep track. Is someone else in the house? Are they upstairs? Are they making their way down the hallway to us?

I stare unblinking at the doorway, waiting for a stranger, but it is Emil's face that appears, sweaty and carrying a suitcase ready to be packed. Before I can speak he sets it down against the doorframe and, without saying a word, he snaps a photo of me sitting upright, the baby beside me. Fear leaves my body so suddenly that it seems entirely ridiculous that I was ever afraid.

Emil enters, sits on the bed softly, his chin and stubble grazing my shoulder as he holds up the phone to show me myself. The darkness of the room around me has made my hair look bold, not patchy or flattened but big, beautiful. The last of the golden light spills onto my cheeks, casting a shadow across my cheekbones, my eyes bright, my collarbone awash with an orange glow. If I am scared it does not translate, instead I look confident, protective of the bundle beside me.

"You look like a natural," Emil says, and it's true, I do.

—*

My own mother is a Jehovah's Witness and I look just like her. Same cheekbones, same hands. Her name is Edwina, but we called her Eddie behind her back, because her mother had and Eddie didn't like Nana Catherine much. It was the closest Devon and I ever got to out-loud disobedience, and besides, what else could we call her? *Mom?* She wasn't a Mom, definitely not a Mommy, and so Eddie stuck. When I think of her, I think of her long skirts, covered legs, sensible black shoes, of how she would crack her knuckles, fist to palm, going finger by finger till all four had been reset. When I look down at my hands my mind goes to her. I never crack my knuckles.

Eddie would cover her hair with a black scarf, triangular over the head and tied beneath her hair, like a simple prairie girl. By the time she met my father her religious fervor was at an all-time high. Dad was also in The Truth, but even he would have said that she took things too far. Nothing was to be for anyone but God, in preparation for the final judgment, anything else was too worldly. What use did we have for the material when judgment day could be now, or in a week, or a year? The only bedtime stories I ever got were Bible stories; my mother favored the Old Testament or Revelation and with it, a vengeful God who would only save a chosen few, stories of the final test from Satan, and of those who would be chosen to clean up the world into a paradise.

My mother, for all her dogged, unblinking religious zeal, was smart. I suppose some might argue she was too smart to throw all those brains at the futile hope of an afterlife to come, but she did. She knew the Bible stories inside and out and during chores, as I scrubbed the floor and she mended the curtains, she could monologue on and on about Bible heroes. It was clear from her storytelling that the only things she loved, truly loved, were the Bible stories. This is all I have in the way of tender childhood memories. The Old Testament became my favorite too. An invisible God always watching and waiting and judging. And if you were good enough, if you withstood, you were rewarded. She would tell the story of Jacob, in which he was shown the end of the world. I preferred Job, who only had to endure the devil's torment and never waver in his trust of God, and all his wealth and finery was returned to him. I could endure.

Other than Bible preaching, Eddie had no time for softness when the world was soon to end, she had people to save, and so the comforts of a mom were lost to Devon and me. No kiss at bedtime, no nightly tucking in of sheets, no comfort when we woke from a bad dream. Her time was spent doing field service, which meant being out on the streets with the *Watchtower* magazine, or in the Kingdom Hall cleaning, devoting her life to Jehovah and to a building empty of sentiment or beauty. She had to get a certain number of hours to be considered worthy, and we were to do the same if we wanted eternal salvation or even the temporary peace that comes with pleasing your mother, although I am not sure which I thought was more valuable. I learned quickly that I would have to soothe myself and I did this with obedience. I was shaped by my ambition to garner praise from Eddie: I completed my chores, came home on time, worked hard at school, putting goodness and godliness before all else. I listened to her sermonizing, I cooked meals for the family, I kept my room clean and spartan. Routine and order, those were my guardrails, and they worked all the way up until the end.

My father was not exempt from self-soothing—he would be out all evening, not preaching but somewhere else, with someone else, until after dinner, when he would eat his plate from the warming oven, not saying a word to anyone. We would never know more about the woman he eventually chose to leave my mother for, or the family he made with her, but I assume they were better, I assume they made him happy enough to never come back.

Eddie was a tough woman to live with, and tougher to try to love. I knew almost nothing about her except that her dedication to a life of Jehovah began when she was just a teenager. I knew her favorite scriptures intimately. Some people know their parents' histories but in my case, I knew about the temptation of the devil, the certainty of the end of days.

Outside the apartment and school, our time was spent at the Kingdom Hall. The main room was a big conference-type space, with hardbacked chairs in a shade you could call taupe, but as a child I thought of it as the color of rocks. The utilitarian carpet was gray and worn, the walls were also rock-colored and with no windows to interrupt the expanse of gray the hall had the illusion of being a cave. I vacuumed the floors, dusted the chairs, kept them in neat, strict lines. I also polished the lectern at the front of the room, which was the only thing with any flair. It had been gifted by a member with carpentry skills and was the only beautiful thing in the room. I would take my time with the lectern, saving it for last like dessert.

There was a side room where we kept all the witnessing literature, the carts and the shelves with thought-provoking questions printed in large font: CAN THE BIBLE MAKE YOUR LIFE BETTER?, WHAT DOES THE BIBLE REALLY TEACH?, and the one I always took out on field service with me: PEACE—WHEN? But Eddie let me know the answer to that one. When Armageddon came.

She believed in The Truth, which is what we called the way of Jehovah, and we were supposed to live in that truth. Living in that truth meant everything else was a lie, was sinful and wicked, bound to send us down the wrong path. But there wasn't much truth in our house, we were all pretending, doing our best to repent, to prepare, to survive. What else was out there for us, beyond the walls of the Kingdom Hall? What was the truth about the end of the world when everyone else seemed to have so much to live for?

Everything in our lives was just so, to Eddie's specifications, but meanwhile the kids at school were laying out plans for college, which cities they would escape to, imagining lives that seemed so removed from any notion of fire and brimstone. They were blithely unaware of the end of the world, and I was also beginning to feel the tingle of desire—I wanted to be clueless too. I wanted to reject everything the Witnesses preached because it was lonely, being the only one watching an approaching meteor. But still, I obeyed. Right up until the end I obeyed, because I had made a tightrope for myself by following Eddie's rules and I was scared of what might happen if I fell.

Devon didn't care. He would be out the door, slamming it behind him, and I would try to make up for his absence. Cleaning harder, reading more. It was exhausting, trying that hard. I tried to think of Job. If our lives were a tightrope, then Devon became a proficient jumper, swan-diving with ease off the high wire. He always landed on his feet, which is probably why I didn't look back when I left, to see if he made it too.

Devon escaped most of his duties as a Jehovah's Witness through sheer defiance, but I was a true oldest daughter; I made my needs small and fixated on hers, which were also Jehovah's. It wasn't until I stepped all the way away from home and from her that I, like Devon, was able to see how pointless it was. It was a realization that almost made me jump too, but eventually I decided that if the world was going to end, I wanted to find something real to hold on to. If Armageddon was coming, there was no way it was going to find me broken in my mother's home.

—*

My birthday is a few days away and then the following day, as a sad belated birthday present, Emil will be out the door, leaving me behind. Time is running out.

I've been sleeping badly since we left the labor and delivery ward. I haven't had nightmares in years, but after bringing home the baby I keep dreaming of a figure standing outside our house. It is a dark shadow that stares directly into me and when it speaks it sounds like the creaking of wood stairs. In the dream I don't look at it, I'm scared. I turn my head. It feels like something I don't want to see will be revealed if I look too long. Some nights, in my dream, the shadow leaves items at the front door, like harbingers. A dead bird. A snake, live and moving, pointed like an arrow out of the house. A black cat, watching. I dream of something standing over me, perfectly framed by the angular beams of hallway light that the ajar door is casting. Something looming, something filling me with unspeakable dread. A shadow is there, backed against the wall. It watches and though I see no eyes I feel a gaze on me. I squeeze my eyes tight against it.

Nothing but the sound of blood in my ears.

I open and shut my eyes a few times before I understand that the shadow is close to me, right above me, I can feel a coolness to the air and though it doesn't have a mouth it sounds like it is trying desperately to speak. I reach in the bed for Emil but no one is there. I'm alone. I fall back into a fitful sleep.

When I wake, and Emil is snoring softly beside me, my heart is still hammering from the dream, and in snatched moments of solitude I search online for the meanings of these objects. If you spend a childhood studying the Bible, reading the stories, figuring out the lessons comes easy, but after a few far-fetched Google results, I think better of it. I am a new mom, I rationalize, I am flooded with hormones. These dreams mean nothing, I think. Even so, an unease lingers.

Later on in the morning I prep for a diaper change and focus on the task of caring for this tiny being that has appeared, demanding and wanting. A spike of panic registers when my gaze drifts out of the window and I see a black cat, looking up at the house and sitting primly beside the night-blooming jasmine.

"What do you want to do for your birthday?" Emil interrupts as he enters what used to be yet another spare room but is now the nursery. He is folding a T-shirt destined for his suitcase, which lies open down the hall on the guest room floor. I look from Emil back to the window, but there is nothing out there but the uniform squares of lawns, gardeners making their way down our neighbors' hedges with trimmers, the jasmine flowers drooping, waiting for night to fall.

"My birthday?" I repeat, hazily, changing the baby diligently, wipes from the wipe-warmer and biodegradable diapers, small bottom lifted and wiped front to back. I had almost forgotten my birthday, a common symptom of a childhood without celebrating them.

"Yeah! Maybe a party or something? Some friends over? Dominique and the girls?"

I try to envision having people in my house while the baby is sleeping. I can see myself endlessly shushing and forcing people to tiptoe around. It sounds terrible, but I muster a mumbled "I don't know. Maybe?"

"It could be fun! Something before I leave for this trip. A little glass of wine?"

Emil grabs my waist, does a two-step, makes me do it with him. I can't help but laugh, two-stepping a conservative bop, dirty diaper in hand that is destined for the pail. It is a sweet scene: baby cooing on a changing table, mom and dad giggling together.

Emil continues, "A little music, a moment to get out of . . . just this holding pattern we're in."

I freeze, and Emil senses it, lets go of my waist. I scoop up the baby (*Support the head! Arm up the back, fingers wide!*) and turn to face him. He meets my gaze for a second before dropping it, sensing the danger.

"Holding pattern? What do you mean?"

"I just mean we've been doing the same thing every day for two weeks."

"You mean since she was born? It's called a routine. You have to have a schedule; you need to establish patterns. It's important for the baby," I say defensively. I can hear my mother's voice in my own, and though I want to silence it, it's too late and the words leave my mouth before I can help it:

"If you had come to the classes, you'd know that."

Emil's face drops and he takes a step back, looking at me now.

"Woah, Sofia? What the fuck?"

Most of my pregnancy Emil was working on a big movie he was certain would be nominated for an Academy Award, making it the one to launch his career into the stratosphere. He missed all four of the What to Expect classes at the hospital, admittedly at my insistence. I was excited for the direction his career was taking; besides, I was the better notetaker, and the plan was for me to share all I had learned with him. By the time Emil came home from work he was always too tired to hear about breathing techniques and baby washing, and we would just cuddle up on the couch instead. The movie didn't win. I hadn't been mad then, or at least I told myself I wasn't, but here we are.

A rage that is foreign to me sits behind my eyes, masquerading as a headache. I want to step away from the Edwina-shaped indentation I have just stepped into, but I don't know how.

"I'm sorry," I say, unconvincingly. I try again, reaching my hand out to hold his. "I'm sorry."

His hand feels good in mine, his nails trimmed and skin moisturized. I take him in for the first time today, and realize that in vast contrast to me, Emil is showered, fully dressed. He's probably even brushed his teeth, I think resentfully. I, on the other hand, am in a sweatshirt already stained with two weeks' worth of my own dairy, and terry-cloth shorts with the elastic waist blown out and rolled down. My hair is nappy and uncombed, and a crop of hormonal acne dots my jawline. The rage threatens to build, and I take what little cool resolve I have left and dump it onto the fury, dousing it out.

My husband wants to throw me a party and what kind of person would say no? A party could be fun, a small gathering of friends in our new house, marveling over the 60-inch, 32.2 cubic feet, built-in four-door French door refrigerator that cost us $14K, congratulating us, driving home and conspiratorially wondering how much an AD gets paid. I want to be envied, I want people to tell me that I did good, I made it, I won.

I want to feel like I won.

Normal people celebrate. In school I was the weird kid in drab matronly clothes with a lunch that was a mix of found objects Devon and I assembled in the kitchen every morning. I was teased, but only if I made my presence known, so I became good at being invisible. Until Dominique noticed me, I spent every day scrambling to appear like everyone else. Normal people have parties.

"Let's do it. Let's throw a party," I say with certainty.

"You sure?" Emil looks up, hair swept back off his face like a golden Lab, a good boy.

"I'm sure. It'll be fun," I reply, more to myself than to him.

I know I've just put out a fire, but beneath the bulk of its ashes are smoldering embers. The coals are still warm in my chest.

3

I grew up in an apartment building in a once-overlooked town to the east of the wealthy city we live in now. It was a poorly aerated apartment block where you could smell your neighbors' cooking and they could smell yours, where arguments and conversations heard through the walls became a daily hum. In the summer it was too hot and we used frozen water bottles to keep our beds cool. In the winter it was too cold, so we would turn the oven on and keep the door open to warm ourselves after school. When Emil and I bought the house on a quiet cul-de-sac on the good side of the big city, I realized I had done it. All that studying, all that striving, I was finally not just normal, I had surpassed normal and gone straight to *comfortable*. It was the first time I had had a whole house to myself. A yard, a paved driveway, a fireplace, neighbors I could wave to from a distance instead of brushing past them on the stairwell.

The house was made to be a big family home. It is a good house for a party. A large front door opens into an entryway, and a vintage table we bought at the French flea market sits in the center, an Ash Austin bowl in the middle holding bunches of keys to our various cars. The entryway holds both a central staircase and a large doorway framed in Victorian carved molding that leads to the living room, a big space with two couches, a coffee table, and a grand stone fireplace built in 1890 that is an original feature of the house. I like the kitchen best. The galley kitchen in the apartment I grew up in only had room for one person at a time, but the countertops in the new house are imported Italian marble, the giant fridge is also imported, a breakfast nook lined with wallpaper that cost almost two grand a roll; the whole house is like a movie set. It is pristine, nothing is out of place, nothing is broken. Double sinks in the primary bedroom's spacious en suite, a neat guest room with bedsheets that cost more than most people's monthly wages, the baby's room, which I had meticulously decorated in a gender-neutral forest theme, our wedding photos framed on the walls.

I look out our front windows and see neighbors in their yards, who are pleasant and will give out a wave when they see me, one of those close-fingered, high-up waves. Stiff, militant. One such neighbor is Susan Fletcher, who is old but not elderly, a thimble of a woman, the type who likes to wear a skirt suit for a fancy occasion, and everything is a fancy occasion. Her house is one of the oldest in the neighborhood with a plaque to tell you so, and it has the most beautiful front yard: wisteria, irises, lupine, hummingbird sage. I have seen her tending to it herself, weeding the beds, pruning the roses, even taking the care to sweep off all the cobwebs from the wrought-iron fence that borders her property and the sidewalk out in front.

Susan was also the first one to interrogate me behind a false politeness about my existence on this street, in this enclave. What, she asked, did I do for a living? And how long had I known my husband? I gave fleeting answers, desperate to move it along; I rubbed my belly, dropping clumsy hints to show I was desperate to get off my pregnant feet, and she had abandoned her line of questioning in favor of gushing maternal platitudes. She was so excited, there hadn't been a baby in the neighborhood for so long! How many months along was I? A boy or a girl? Were there names?

She was theatrically overjoyed. I had explained myself with my impending parenthood. I fit in. I was definable. It should have felt reassuring to be slotted neatly into a filing cabinet, all snug in my proper place, but I couldn't wait to be out of her company because I recognized this type of old white woman, and well, something didn't sit right. If Devon were to ever make good on his promise to visit, he would not be welcomed here; I knew that her questions would not be as kind for him. His dreadlocks alone would be a flag, a reason.

Susan Fletcher is a person itching for a reason. As a kid on the fringes at school, I got good at reading people. I can see what they need from me, even if they don't know it yet. Beneath Susan's mid-priced gardening slacks, her pristine two-piece suits, that soft white-gray perm that frames a face with kind eyes, there is a suspicion that even she cannot put to rest. To Susan I am Other, and she cannot forget this even though she tries to—voting Democrat, donating to the right causes, honking her horn in solidarity when she sees a social justice march. She can't help herself; she is a walking contradiction.

—*

I hurry to get ready; I am late to meet Dominique, my best friend since childhood. I haven't seen her since I was in the hospital and she brought a bouquet of wildflowers and some champagne. The sleeplessness I felt then had been novel and new—I'd have time to sleep, I had thought, when we were home and comfortable.

Emil is already at his office, having left early to hit the gym, then get a coffee at his favorite spot. I rush around, clipping earrings in, trying to find something to wear without milk stains on the front. I brush my teeth in a hurry over the kitchen sink and notice the back door is ajar. I go to shut it, look down at my feet to see a dead bird, twitching with innards spilled out, eyes white and unseeing. Something tugs at my subconscious. I've seen this before, this spill of muscle and tendon and fat. The cat I noticed earlier must be responsible, and I feel bad for the creature but what can I do? I lock the door after me and finish getting ready.

Unsettled, I undress the baby, I clean the baby, I redress the baby, I feed the baby. I clip the baby in her rocker while I grab clothes indiscriminately from my walk-in closet. Shoving my feet into pant legs, I realize too late that these are my pre-partum jeans. BC, Before Child. I had made a quiet pact to myself that I wouldn't touch that side of my wardrobe until the baby was a year old, give myself some space to recover, to readjust to this new body, but it's too late because my legs have jammed and the pants come to mid-thigh before stopping. The zipper strains against my akimbo stance, and the reality has been absorbed before I can even whip them off, shove them back into the closet. I know that I shouldn't care about my body at this precise moment, I have done enough body-positive work that I should be able to just shrug this off, but it is almost impossible not to compare/contrast. I wanted to be a mom, sure, but I wanted to be a mom as who I was, not this hybrid, not this transformation. I think of the Hulk bursting out of his clothes, seams ripping, flesh exposed. I think of the bird that is dying outside, guts spilled, feathers ruffled, flesh torn. I settle for a freshly dry-cleaned maternity dress, twee and too frilly for my mood but it'll have to do. I slip it over my head and rush to get the baby and myself out the front door.

We are met with intense traffic on the bridge from the new neighborhood to this old one, the one we grew up in and Dominique has returned to, and I just know we will be past the margin of acceptable lateness. Domi has a chic renovated old condo not far from our former middle school, and it is odd to picture her making coffee, having sex, agonizing over outfits so close to where I first watched her cough out an illicit cigarette she had stolen from an older cousin. We had this weekday brunch planned out long ago, I thought I would be punctual, thought that somehow the sage plan I had had to pre-pack the baby bag, to wash my hair the night before might shave off some time. But instead, here I am, trying to remember how to unclick the Goliath of a car seat the baby is strapped into, and I am late. I lose my nerve as I go to pull out the stroller frame from the trunk and click the car seat into it, an invention that was meant to be time-saving but I don't trust myself to put together safely. I can only vaguely remember the demonstration they gave us in the store when I was pregnant and we were playing pretend, pushing around strollers to see which ones made us feel like real-life parents. I lug the heavy thing, made heavier by the baby, down the street to the restaurant, trying not to jostle it too much.

Dominique is sitting at a table outside, long braids framing her face, one side half-tossed over her shoulder, chin in hand as she scrolls on her phone.

"I'm late," I say apologetically. She looks up at me and smiles, standing to meet us.

"That's okay!" Dominique replies. "You just had a baby!"

She seems light but something beneath her smile tells me she's annoyed, that she'd been sitting there sipping water, waiting and cussing me out under her breath. I have known this girl since elementary school, and then after that I would visit her at her job in the new Victoria's Secret that opened up in the mall, feeling sinful just standing near a cake stand full of thongs. She gave me my first one, black and frilly, which I hid from Edwina, never daring to even try it on, just fingering the lace whenever I needed a thrill. I know her, she can't hide anything from me.

Dominique leans in for a hug, somehow ignoring the hefty car seat I am carrying. I pat her on the back with one hand, desperate to set the thing down somewhere, desperate to sit myself down. I pull away prematurely, forcing a smile as I place the seat in the shadow of a fig tree, fiddle with the baby so she is shaded and facing away from the street.

"I haven't been here in so long," I say, trying to break the unusual awkwardness that has suddenly fallen between us.

"Me neither. Do you think they still do that boujie Bloody Mary?" Dominique says. I realize she hasn't even taken a look at the baby. In fact, if I am not mistaken, it seems like she is purposefully avoiding her.

"You don't take that sort of cornerstone off the menu, right?" I laugh.

"True." She pauses. "How have you been, it's been so long!"

I gesture at the car seat.

"Don't blame me."

"Oh my god, Sofia! The baby!" Dominique leaps to animation, suddenly crouched in front of the baby, whispering in hushed reverent tones. The baby looks glassily at her with that baby gaze that gives the feeling they can see more than you want them to.

"She's so beautiful! Way cuter in that outfit than that sad hospital blanket she was in. Does she have a name yet?"

"Still no name."

She tilts her head at me, the way she does when she calls me on my shit. I feel myself shrink in my seat a little; I am not ready to discuss why this baby doesn't have a name. I feel admonishment coming but Dominique catches herself.

"That makes sense, she's so new! There's time!"

She's placating me. What she's really thinking is *pick a damn name already*. I wish she'd just say it, but I am a new mother, to be handled with care.

"I know," I say, smoothing over the moment, trying to project the self-assuredness that I feel none of. "There's a shortlist, it's just . . . we're waiting for her to tell us."

It's the party line we've used since before the baby was born and I cling to it. I lean back in my seat, holding my Sea New York denim-quilted jacket closed with my folded arms across my chest. The restaurant we are at is painfully hip. It was the first fancy place this area got, and with its Michelin star it brought a bunch of cool, quote-edgy-unquote places to this side of town. When I was growing up, this part of the neighborhood had been all Asian American, blue-collar families. The hardware store across the street from where we sit is the only relic from that time. It is still the same, still has boxes and boxes of varying-size screws and nails, metric and standard, with descriptions in English and Mandarin, frowning working men agonizing over electrical boxes, beat-up work trucks double-parked loading up 4x4s, sploshed paint spills next to the paint shaker counter, the laser-sharp sound of keys being cut, Dickies and metal-toed boots walking down fluorescent-lit aisles.

Back in the day all we had was the diner down the street, a twenty-four-hour spot that must have had a roster of waitresses but it never seemed like it, it was always the same surly woman desperate for her cigarette break, rolling her eyes at your substitutions and endless coffee refills. The diner is now one of many pretentious boutiques that sells expensive Japanese ceramics, handblown glasses, gorgeous, gorgeous items that are high spec, low functionality. They kept the neon diner sign, because it is vintage, from the fifties. Tucked between the boutiques are restaurants like this one with menus devoid of pricing information, salads that are complex and tough to eat, that introduce ingredients you've been eating for years as if they were newly discovered. Collard greens explained to you as if they were from Neptune. Concoctions that fifteen-year-old me could not have imagined while in that small apartment eating the quesadillas my brother and I would make ourselves for dinner.

After Dominique and I order the lobster tacos and breakfast paella, and the drinks have come, I eye my $19 Bloody Mary warily. She catches me and as if reading my mind says, "One tiny Bloody Mary is fine, right? You know, for the . . ."

Here she gestures at her boobs, one and then two.

"Probably. It was mostly just fun to order."

"I get it. I remember when I turned twenty-one, I would order gin and tonics from the bar because I thought it sounded sophisticated. Now that is a *taste*! But you know me, I choked them down anyway." Dominique's nose wrinkles at the memory, one I don't recognize.

"Really?" I ask, surprised to find out something new about her. "I didn't know that."

"You were in New York by then." The sentence feels weighty, but Dominique expertly skips over it like a speed bump. "You never got to witness me drinking like a Victorian gentleman in my American Apparel tube dress at Casanovas. But I guess there's still time!"

I laugh, relieved that we are finding our flow, that I still have a best friend. Nothing has changed, not really.

"So . . . how's the new neighborhood?" Dominique asks innocently enough, although I know she has something more she'd like to say.

"It's good."

She raises an eyebrow at me, forcing me to continue.

"It's nice! Clean."

"Clean is eugenics, dude."

"Come on now!" I can feel her baiting me and I take it, like I know I am supposed to. "It's not that bad!"

She leans forward, butter knife in hand like a weapon. "Quick! Give me the name of one nonwhite person in Bay Cliff!"

"Umm . . ."

Dominique makes a ticking clock sound, the knife now a second hand, tick tick tick.

"Ruben!"

"Ruben?" she repeats, warily.

"Yes! He's Hispanic."

"Okay, fine. One Ruben, *allegedly.*" Dominique pauses, tilts her head, calling bullshit. "Wait, where does this Ruben live?"

"Well . . . he doesn't exactly live in Bay Cliff . . ."

I squirm as she watches me.

"Okay! He's the mailman."

"THE MAILMAN!" she erupts, gleefully. "Oof, my girl. You know that does not count."

I feel momentarily defensive about a place that is not yet my home, not really. Dominique seems to sense this and adds, "Hey, I know Bay Cliff. Whole lotta Black Lives Matter signs, not a whole lotta Black Lives Mattering?"

"That sounds about right, yeah," I admit, which feels good to say out loud. "People have been nice, though."

"Mm-hmm," Dominique says, which is a period to this whole conversation. She changes the subject, leaning in conspiratorially. "So! Tell me more about the birth!"

I smile, uncertain. "You sure you want to know?"

"Yeah, man, of course! Give me all that gory shit. Did your vagina fall off?"

"Oh my god, Domi," I laugh, and my vagina, which is still very much on, also seems to twitch in amusement. "It was good, I think. I don't have much to compare it to, but I feel okay about it. I don't think I'm traumatized or anything? I didn't tear too much but still had stitches. There was a lot more blood than I was expecting. The first time I stood up to go to the bathroom it was like the elevator in *The Shining*."

Wondering if I told too much, I involuntarily touch my abdomen, a habit of the last nine months, forgetting for a second that the baby is no longer in there. I look down at my flesh-and-blood child, wrapped in a beanie and a furry onesie with little bear ears, and I wonder whether she should even be out in the elements. Some of the parenting books say you should only eat warm food and drinks and keep the baby inside for at least the first four weeks. This side of the city is always swathed in fog, making it a good ten degrees cooler than anywhere else.

"Yikes!" Dominique says, reaching forward to take a sip of her Bloody Mary. I can't help but think Dominique's eyes have glassed over a little and I rack my brain for something funny, or interesting, or noteworthy.

Domi is one of those people who, in the highlight reel of her life, will inspire many people to predictably say *She lit up a room when she walked into it,* and it would be true. She is funny, not mean, although her brand of funny can border on sharp. Even as a teen she could make anyone feel loved and noticed, even a nobody weirdo church girl. Domi is this way because her parents cared for her in a way she never even thought about: abundantly. Their love was palpable. She was seen and held and known by her family and in return she did the same for me. I don't want to lose that now.

I straighten my spine, smile a secret smile, lean forward in a way that conveys the confidential. I settle into this pose, try to feel the truth of it, channeling Domi's ease and humor as if I am anything like her and not the tired and sore person within.

"My anesthesiologist was incredibly hot," I offer.

This is what Domi wants. She laughs and claps her hands. The baby shifts in the car seat.

"Yes! What kind of hot? Like skinny weedy nerd Matthew Gray Gubler type doc hot or . . ." she suggests, elbows on the table, eyes twinkling with mischief, hands playing with the straw in her drink.

"The other kind. Unnecessarily stacked, bursting-out-his-scrubs-type hot."

"Daaaaamn!" Dominique draws the word out, luxuriously.

"And of course, I had never looked better," I joke, "bent over like Gollum, butt out, tits hanging. Then in walks the most beautiful mountain of a man. Black too."

"*Daaaamn!*" she repeats, beaming large. I join her in the smile, it's true, that *is* noteworthy. "I need to meet this Black doctor. My *family* needs to meet this Black doctor. This Kofi-Siriboe-future-father-of-my-children motherfucker."

"I didn't say anything about Kofi, woman."

I am laughing despite myself. I didn't know how much I needed to see her until just now.

"You didn't have to! Kofi is the prototype; you say you saw some hot Black man, that is where my brain goes."

I smile at Domi, her braids flicked back off her face, gold nose piercing catching the sun that is peek-a-booing through the clouds as she lifts her head up toward it, a golden goddess. She looks beautiful, has always looked beautiful, even when we were awkward teens there was something gilded about her, something expensive. I have the strong urge to tell her something, anything. A secret, something real we can hold just between the two of us, like we used to. I want to tell her about the unsettling feeling I have had in the house, the dreams that have been coming thick and fast, but I settle for something real.

"My mom called," I say, deadpan.

"*Eddie?*" Dominique hollers, sitting up straight, pulling her sunglasses lower on her nose and looking out over them at me. So dramatic, I think. I shush her with my hands, I don't want her waking the baby.

"Eddie?" she repeats, lowering her voice slightly, but not much. She always did have a voice for the stage.

"Yup. *Mom* called."

I am satisfied by Dominique's reaction, I expected nothing less. It feels good to know someone like this, to have them know you.

"Well, shit." Dominique readjusts, leans forward looking concerned. "What do you think she wants?"

"I don't know. Nothing good." I pause, then add, "Money?" But then I feel guilty, because it is a lie. My mom is capable of many things but she has never asked me for a penny, and Dominique's face says as much.

"Maybe . . ." she starts unconvincingly. "Maybe the end is finally nigh? Maybe she's sick?"

"If she was sick she would die without telling anyone, just to spite us. You know how she is."

"Are you okay?" Dominique ventures carefully. "I know you haven't spoken to her since New York and—"

"I'm fine," I insist, cutting her off. In the Bronx, after I broke free, after the incident, I called Eddie from the phone down by my room, Dominique at my side as she prepared to get me out. After spitting out quotes about lost sheep and prodigal sons, my mother had hung up on me, leaving me in Dominique's arms, faced with a choice: Go back or rebuild. There was a third choice, but that hadn't worked out. Dominique is the only one who knows about that, and we haven't talked about it since I left St. Raphael's.

"Is she calling Devon too?" Dominique asks, changing tack.

"I don't know. I haven't even texted to ask," I admit. This is true, but so is the fact that our mother sent my brother and me running far from her once we were old enough, and the only way I can talk to Devon now is by not mentioning her. We used to be close the way that cellmates are close. We survived because of each other, tender moments in the night when we held hands as we said prayers that turned into whispers about our plans for getting out, detailed descriptions of the birthday parties we would have, the friends we would make, the places we would live. I still carry the guilt of leaving him in a literal puff of smoke as the fire my mother had started was extinguished. I knew it was my chance to get out. I hurriedly packed a bag, grabbed the money I had stashed away, and left. I never knew what he did after that night, how he got free, and I'm too afraid of dredging up the past to ask. I think of the last time we spoke on the phone, a hazy memory that must mean it's been a year or two.

"Maybe she wants to see the baby?"

"*The baby!*" Dominique exclaims, clapping her hands in triumph. "Of course, duh, that's what she's calling for! Do you think you'll let Eddie see her?"

"I thought about it, but I'm in a good place," I say firmly, thinking of the house, the baby, the man, the money. "I don't want her in my head again, messing shit up. I'm not in the mood to be lectured."

She nods, looking at me as if I am mature and sage and grown. A mother. A person capable of doing it all alone. I glance down at the baby, at the responsibility handed to me at the hospital the day she was born. I think about Emil's upcoming trip, and wonder if it is true.

By the time I have finished telling Dominique about my mother, discussed the prospect of me one day going back to work, and she has regaled me with tales of the new guy she's been kicking it with, it is two hours since the baby last fed and I feel nervous about pulling out my boob in public to feed her. I am anxious to get going but Dominique seems to be basking in the post-lunch lull, her sunglasses are back on and she does a quick glance at her phone for the time. I wait for her to have the same thought as me, that it is time to call it, but she doesn't.

"Do you want to check out that new vintage place up the street? I know they'll be charging two hundred dollars for an old Reformation dress with the label cut off, but still . . . ?"

She pushes her sunglasses up onto her head, looks expectantly at me.

"I don't know, I think I have to get this baby home."

"Woman, she's fine. Look, she's all peaceful! A cherub!" Dominique insists.

"I have to feed her. She has a schedule and I have to be really careful . . ."

"Okay, okay, okay, *Mom*. I get it." Dominique slaps down her card on the check that arrived during my deliberation. I know she's teasing but I feel like a letdown, like I am boring.

"This one's on me. I haven't gotten you a birthday gift so let's just call this a birthday lunch?"

"Domi! You really don't have to do that."

I know it is futile to argue with her about something like this, her generosity is not to be negotiated with. She waves me off with a dismissive hand.

"Speaking of things that are unnecessary . . . do you know what Emil has planned for your birthday?" Dominique asks as I scoop up my things into my purse and brace myself for my cumbersome load.

"He mentioned something about a party, I think. A small dinner or something? Why, what have you heard?" I ask, lifting the car seat onto my forearm.

"I couldn't possibly comment on that." Dominique winks cartoonishly, with her whole face. Dread clunks into my chest and I ignore it. The sun is burning off the fog, bringing an early-springtime warmth that comes with longer days the whole city seems grateful for. A bike messenger goes by, music blaring from his backpack. "Welcome to the Jungle."

"But you should probably practice your surprised face."

I do a quick charade of shock, my free hand slapped against my cheek in dazzlement. Dominique laughs and embraces me.

"It was good to see you, my babe. And you, little one. Text your brother."

She leans in and kisses a tiny baby hand. I almost buckle under the additional weight.

Dominique turns and heads off, back to her job and the afternoon latte she will definitely pick up on the way back home, back to the early-spring light pouring through her apartment windows. Back to a Negroni made promptly at five P.M. I feel for my phone in my back pocket, think of Devon living his peaceful life on the East Coast far from us, decide to let him have his peace a little while longer. It can wait. As I click the car seat back into the car, double-check that the baby's buckles and harnesses are strapped tight, I think about what a Negroni would taste like. A Negroni I can't have while I breastfeed, it seems forbidden and faraway. Equal parts gin, sweet vermouth, Campari. A heady, smoky cocktail. Bittersweet. I can almost smell it.

4

I wonder, had I grown up someplace else, somewhere that *when you have children of your own* wasn't a presumptuous line my mother repeated endlessly like a prophecy, a tagline for a movie of a life that was not yet mine, if I would have wanted to be a mother. Ironic, because maybe if she had not left me so severely lacking, I would have never reached out for my own chance at a do-over, to soothe a child with kind words instead of the hostility and judgment and the relentless Bible-learning that she had raised us with.

After I left St. Raphael's in New York, Dominique got me back to my apartment, did my laundry, and made me a game plan, and I made it my mission to remake my world. I worked at the publishing house diligently, went out for drinks on Fridays, saved the scraps of my paycheck with the hopes of one day living alone, in my own apartment. Of course, that never happened, because I met Emil. The day-to-day of life in the Bronx wasn't much different than my childhood—I still made my own lunches, I still organized my own day. I missed the gray cave of the Kingdom Hall and its routines. I reached for the Bible, as I always had as a child, but I found nothing there. I tried to pray but it felt cold so I stopped trying; instead I focused on the redemption found in a coveted pair of earrings, in tangible, real things I could reach out and touch, in boys' hands and kisses on the mouth and the neck and sometimes other places but always with an anthropologist's detachment. Necklaces with heavy gold pendants that I would cruise in the jewelry department of Bloomingdale's until I had enough to make the purchase, devil-may-care, caution to the wind, no money but somehow all of this shit accumulating in the room I rented from the couple who played banjos, both of them wailing about wells and darling Clementines late into the night, pillow over my head until the day crept in and I had to drag my sorry self to work and up and up and up, my rehearsed smile finally useful, because no one wants your sadness, no one wants your childhood bullshit, so I packed it away and circled Bloomingdale's one more time, building outfits in my head, suits for the job I didn't have yet, dresses for the dates I wanted to go on but couldn't, because there was nobody, not really. Until Emil, I was lonely.

It was a loneliness I kept to myself. I had been lonely since I was a child—even at eight years old in the cold dawn of Eddie's apartment I would dress myself, dress my brother, prepare ourselves for the world, tiny hands fumbling the buttons on the coat that was too big on Devon's shoulders. It is lonely to raise yourself, it is lonely to step into adulthood without a hand at your back guiding you, keeping you safe. When Emil came into my life I had someone, someone I let all the way in to see the soft parts of me. But there were certain things I couldn't let him see. Luckily, I had trained my whole life to put up appearances, to play pretend. It was for his own protection, I told myself, he doesn't need to know who I was, he needs to know who I am now. That's what's important.

Even now, I am playing pretend. I am not a mother yet, I am

more like an imposter, a stand-in for the real mother who will come into this house, knowing and calm, and take the screaming baby from my arms to expertly shush her. If I had not been raised with this expectation, would I have forgone my birth control? Would I have so willingly taken a hiatus from my life to make this new one, small and blank, a live round in my hands?

It is dizzying to imagine but somewhere, out there in all of the multiverses people talk of existing alongside our own, whirring like subway tracks alongside us, there is a Sofia whose future is a vast uncultivated landscape, rich and pathless, no milestones lingering. No pressure to marry or procreate or have a job, even. A Sofia able to discover the secret crevices of herself that require time and attention to notice. A Sofia with untold desires and wishes, a Sofia whose deep knowledge of herself keeps her suspended above the bullshit, lofty and knowing.

This Sofia dates with impunity, casually and needfully. This Sofia has a different walk, it is slower, leisurely. An unbothered gait, a confidence unmatched. Her community is wide, her loved ones many, and so the need for one person, one soulmate, is eliminated. *Soulmate.* She'd laugh at that word, this Sofia. She'd cackle at the notion that on such a limitless planet we might limit ourselves to the idea that one person is all we need.

I wonder if that Sofia ever thinks of me. I wonder if, late at night, she lies in bed and feels a tug of disembodied terror, my terror crossing time and space and the laws of physics to disturb her serene heart.

—*

Two days after my lunch with Dominique, on the heated tan leather seats of my Lexus, I watch the minutes tick by, waiting for the designated start time of what Emil was calling my *birthday surprise.* I feel shaky, and not ready for anything surprising. I had woken up that morning gasping for air as if I have been underwater, my lips salty. In the dream I couldn't breathe, and as I sat up the panic was stubborn, refusing to subside. Earlier in the year I imagined this birthday would feel like an arrival, I had envisioned it several times: my newborn prize clutched in my hands, a red-orange lip on my face, tired but invigorated. I thought it would feel like adulthood, but instead that morning I felt confused and blurred, unsure of my outline. Before I got ready to leave the house, a mandatory evacuation for Emil to get "everything" ready, I had leaned back onto the pillows and spread my legs to examine the stretch marks on my inner thighs. I noticed how tight they felt, as if the skin was fit to burst, as if I could have torn it off and something new would be there, someone new. My phone interrupted me as I tried to pull my stretch marks farther apart, to see if I could watch them split.

My mother again. I had watched it ring, waiting for it to end. There was no way that after fifteen years of silence she, a witness of Jehovah, was calling to wish me a happy birthday, so what could she want? My curiosity was piqued but not enough to pick up. The phone had emitted a dull beep, alerting me that a voicemail had been received, and as I sit in the car outside the house, I consider listening to it.

My mother was generally a sullen presence although sometimes she could sink deeper into moods; funks, my father would call them, before he left us for a new, uncomplicated family. *Your mother is feeling funky today,* he would say as a warning, as if she were a musician. During a good spell she would be at the Kingdom Hall daily, or out on corners in our neighborhood doing street witnessing, handing out the magazines. On a bad day she would ricochet around the apartment quoting scripture, everything was to be slammed—car doors and closets, the fridge, the drawers. My mother was never physical with us, but she didn't need to be—we were scared enough by her words, the threat of damnation, the intense assuredness that we would be tempted by Satan, even as we promised her we wouldn't, tears streaming down our little faces. I would come home to our silent apartment and the air would be heavy, dense, letting me know my mother was waiting for a reason to unleash all of her vitriol onto me, how I would never be divine, never truly be a good witness. All of her thoughts—how useless we were, how sinful, how much we burdened her, how God knew we were not fit for the kingdom of heaven—were poured out like water onto the flames of a fire that cannot catch, that has no chance of surviving. We were extinguished daily, until we were tall enough to push back. My childhood was spent tiptoeing around her, trying to make a snack after school without having all of Jehovah's teachings thrown at me like words of admonishment. Her rage was fueled by some notion of keeping us in line, making us behave, although it made us step away from her, not in line at all in the end but far, far out.

Devon and I tried to bond, but she made it hard. If the two of us were laughing over something stupid in the kitchen as we completed our chores, Eddie would step in as if sensing too much mirth, and begin reciting about the end times. It became easier to just avoid each other until bedtime, when our prayers were the only unmonitored conversations we could get away with.

In retrospect, I can intellectualize. I can see that Eddie was depressed, probably from a long line of depressed people, not that the elders in our community would have called it that. I try to feel sympathy for her, but I can't make it stick. Sympathy comes when I think of Devon, though. My younger brother, but somehow effortlessly cool. All his classmates liked him, and he was the one who knew before I ever did just how useless it was to try to find sense in Eddie's lessons, or a way out through the Bible.

Still, I left him.

He was self-assured, yes, but he was just a kid. Maybe he has found some peace and acceptance, maybe he'll forgive me and we can become close again. I sigh and redo the messy bun that has cemented my uncombed hair on top of my head, looking at bite-size portions of my face in the tiny flip-down mirror. My skin is drawn, the pregnancy glow is long gone. I used to like putting on a full face, relishing the time with my makeup, but this evening all I could muster was to wet a washcloth and vigorously scrub my face, moisturize as a treat. I should text Devon, like Dominique suggested. I should reach out: see how he's doing, see if Eddie has been calling him too. Later. After a drink.

Before Emil bounded me out of the house, boyish grin plastered across his face, I had put one of the hospital-issued ice packs carefully in my mesh underwear, and buttoned up a loose, clean Apiece Apart dress. The ice pack is not as needed as it was two weeks ago, but there is a comfort in the habit of it, the coolness of it on a warm spring evening. I had wandered around the small strip of boutiques on nearby Laurel Street, aimlessly window shopping. Back in my car I take a big breath and drive up to the house, where there are more cars than usual parked outside. Maybe this will be okay. Maybe this will be fun.

I pinch my cheeks a little too hard like I've seen them do in the movies, to get some color and wake myself up and remind myself that Emil has done a nice thing and I have to try to be grateful, I have to make an effort. This is what people do, I remind myself. I look down at my phone at the time: eight P.M. *This is what normal people do,* I repeat in my head over and over until I feel less like I am teetering on the edge of a precipice.

I head to the front door, the house dimmed before me like a sleeping face. I open the door and before I have even stepped into the room, I glimpse something. A shadow of a skirt or maybe a dress being pulled behind a cabinet and I confirm what this is at the exact same moment the room yells "*SURPRISE!*"

My friends, people from work, neighbors, and acquaintances are standing and smiling at me, drinks in hands, expectantly. I flinch as they yell because why would they yell when I have a sleeping newborn upstairs, but then I see the streamers, the banners, the balloons. The speakers softly playing Marvin Gaye. I do not like surprises, I enjoy knowing the next step of every plan, and this feels like an ambush, not at all the candlelit birthday gathering I had anticipated. Just as I am beginning to wonder why no one thought to stop Emil from such a tone-deaf idea, he approaches me. He is all smiles, a small, fresh yellow rose in hand, which he tucks behind my ear and as he does so he whispers a soft "Happy birthday, baby."

It is heartfelt and I am supposed to love this and so I brush his cheek with my fingertips and smile because my husband adores me and wants me to be surprised and happy on my birthday, I should be thankful and so I make myself thankful.

I will enjoy myself.

"What about the baby?" I question, trying to keep my voice light so as not to betray fear, like a lake of ice cracking beneath my feet. Emil makes a *woah* motion as if I am a horse ready to bolt.

"My mom is here; she's going to sit with her for a while. It'll be okay. It's your time to relax."

The tension has not left my shoulders as he rubs them playfully, handing me off to Dominique while he grabs a drink.

"Are we having fun yet?" Domi questions through a big faux teeth-gritted smile.

"Girl," I say, and she drops the faux, replacing it with a genuine grin.

"Girl!"

She laughs, gesturing in disbelief around the room at the friends and family in every inch of my living room, people sitting on the armrests of couches I had custom made for the space.

"Just think of all those birthday parties you didn't get to have, you're making up for lost time. Jehovah wills it!" She drops the goofy voice and rearranges her face to convey parental sternness. "They're here now, you might as well suck it up."

Domi knows birthdays were not something I saw much of, except for the few times her sweet, normal family took me out to some chain restaurant for a burger and a slice of cake. Before I can begrudgingly agree, Emil comes back with an icy drink to shove into my hand. He kisses my cheek and talks too loudly to Vanessa from my office, who I don't even like, who I don't even want in my house. She is probably itching to talk about the new author with all the buzz, the one I was assigned before I went on maternity leave and had to divvy up between assistants. He was recently on a talk show and made an audience member faint describing, in detail, a surgery he once read about performed without anesthetic. They had to cut to commercial five minutes into a prime-time show. The blogs are abuzz with him. Vanessa knows that my assistants who are holding down my desk can't handle it alone, not while I'm home with a newborn baby. She wants this author and she's the next in line for him.

The only reason she showed up is to see how weak I am, to gauge if it's time to pounce.

I sip my drink, wince. It's tequila and it's been too long since I had tequila but it seems to work instantaneously; all thoughts of Vanessa and her eyes on my office leave my head. I start to wind my waist to the definitely ironic "Thong Song," given the size of the underwear I actually have on, and allow Domi to drag me out onto the dance floor, which tonight is a rug we paid too much to have people look at, let alone dance on. I try to breathe out my neurosis, let Domi take my hands and hip-bump me, singing into my face.

I smile at her, the one person who has been my constant since we were children. I take another swig of my drink. It's not enough to taint my milk supply, but I can feel parts of myself unfolding, nourished again. I see Buffy wandering across the room with a stride as if this is her house, and I suppose it is. Most of her money paid for it, not ours. Emil's inheritance given early. This means she doesn't need to act like a guest and, apparently, she also doesn't need to watch the baby. She sidles up to Emil, whispers something a little too intimately in his ear, and he starts to pour her a drink. My brain begins to make a rapid-fire list of all of the ways a baby can die alone in a room. Suffocation, I think. Smothering. A blow to the head caused by something falling on her. I freeze, motionless. Dominique looks at me strangely.

"What is it, girl?" she jokes, corny twang in her voice, as if I am some kind of TV rescue dog. "Little Tommy stuck down the old well?"

It's the baby. She is howling. Everyone is oblivious, I seem to be the only one who can hear her.

"The baby . . ." I start, looking around for Emil, or his mom or literally anyone who could help me, but everyone is talking and laughing and drinking. The baby's cries continue and my nipples begin to leak through my dress, sensing they are desperately needed, two circles of milk blooming through the cotton.

"I can't hear anything but Sisqó, baby! Relax!" Dominique laughs, tossing her braids and spinning away from me to dance, leaving me alone and rooted to the spot.

No one can hear her, I think. Or if they can, none of them feel the responsibility I do. Even Emil doesn't care, he's attempting a white-limbed Roger Rabbit across the room. This is on me. This is my job.

I head toward the staircase, willing anyone to stop me. No one does. The crying gets louder, and I race upstairs, forgetting all about the creaky one-hundred-year-old floorboards because what does it matter now how much noise I make? My eyes adjust to the gloom and to my surprise, she is sound asleep. How is it possible that I so distinctly heard her and yet here she is, doing that gentle baby-snore she does? I could picture her in my mind's eye as I leaped up the stairs, mouth open in a tiny toothless O, hands grasping the darkness for me.

As I go to leave, to go back to the land of the living and get out of this dark room that just reminds me of sleep and how I cannot get it, I check my phone for the time. Ten P.M. Past my bedtime. And then, as if someone knocked it from my hands, the phone drops. I fumble to catch it before it hits the ground and fail. It smacks on the refinished hardwood floor face down with a satisfying *THWACK*. The baby erupts. I go to pick her up and abruptly stop myself.

Instead, I wait.

I wait to see if anyone else heard and remembered that I am

newly postpartum, my underwear is cold as ice, and my vagina still feels like the Indiana Jones boulder just smashed through. I wait to see if anyone else is coming but no one does, because it is me, just me, alone in this dark room listening to a scream that isn't mine, feeling a hot anger creep up my back like flames.

I bend over carefully to pick up the phone and notice that on the green call icon is a red 1. The voicemail my mother left earlier. I think briefly, doubtfully, of the happy birthday message I had wished for, and to the backing track of the baby's screams and the party downstairs, my heart pumping fury through my body so hard that I start to feel electric, I play my mother's voice.

"I know you don't want to hear it, but I've been thinking about that night . . . that last night at the apartment. There are things I need to tell you. I've been thinking of Matthew 7:27: *And the rain poured down and the floods came and the winds blew and struck against that house, and it caved in, and its collapse was great,*" she sermonizes, but I can't do any more, I am immediately regretting my decision. Even now, I feel catapulted back to a place I never want to go back to. I want to delete it but I hesitate, wanting evidence, proof of her madness, and so instead I swipe out of the voicemail altogether. I think of the night in the apartment, of the fire and the fury and how escape seemed not only possible but essential. I pick up the baby, my anger somewhat cooled by the sound of my mother's voice, a woman capable of more anger than I ever want to be. I am not Edwina.

As I sit on the edge of the bed, dumping out a breast into a screeching mouth, I stare out the windows that look out onto our neighborhood. It is dark, no twinkling lights, in fact you would think it was the country. We are so removed from the rest of the city that I feel like I am up high on a pedestal above it. I allow my gaze to drift as I stare into my own face in the glass, and for a second, I see another pair of eyes, blinking right at me. For a second, I think it is my mother. I squeeze my eyes shut and will reality back into the room. Back out the window there is nothing, no eyes, no lights, just me, holding a baby without a name.

5

The next morning Emil is packed and ready to leave, typing absently on his phone as I head down the stairs toward him. I have been steeling myself for this eventuality, watching him fold his clothes methodically, packing dress shirts and running shoes and books, all things that remind me his next few weeks, although for work, will allow for more free time than mine. He meets me and the baby, who is attached to my midsection, in the entryway, and pulls a large package loosely wrapped in pastel tissue paper out of his Porter-Yoshida Tanker duffel bag.

"Look. I know your party wasn't exactly what you wanted, I thought it would be fun, but I recognize maybe I wasn't picking up what you were putting down, so"—Emil shyly hands me the parcel—"happy birthday. It only just got delivered, I didn't have a chance to wrap it properly."

The understatement of the century, my internal monologue begins, before I snuff it out, banishing my knee-jerk thought to pay attention to the present in my hands. I haven't even thought about gifts, haven't even thought what I desire apart from sleep and quiet, and my fingers tear at the paper, betraying my eagerness. I feel soft wool, and I pull out of the package a beautiful coat, one I have been admiring and saving to my bookmarks so I could repeatedly add to cart, allowing it to lapse over and over. It is a fox of a coat, creamy white and chic. Six oversized buttons trace up the front, and a small collar can be fastened high and tight. Faux fur at the cuffs, feathering out, swanlike. It's Jackie O, it's Mia Farrow. It's embarrassingly expensive.

"Emil!" I gasp, eyes starstruck. "This is the coat!"

"It's the coat." He smiles. He is proud, trying not to grin as wide as he wants to. He looks happier than I am, and I realize how hard he has been trying and failing to please me since I birthed our child. I run my hand over the sleeves, the fabric giving way like white whipped mousse. I feel my heart swell.

"Wow, this is too much. It's stunning. Thank you! I can't believe it!" I drape it over my shoulders, over the bulky baby carrier and sleeping infant. I look in the full-length mirror for the first time in weeks, I take it all in. The mismatched socks, the bundle of baby at my middle making me seem ridiculously barrel-shaped, the ill-fitting sweatpants, stained at the crotch and thighs from the various "meals" I have shoved in my mouth, Tapatio reds and coffee browns, my eyes small and sunken from lack of sleep. My hair is its own story, a shriek of untamed frizz, begging to be combed. The coat has not, as I had anticipated, made me look chic. I instead look like an inpatient. I look unwell. I look like I have robbed this coat from someone who is actually put together, someone who likely knows what to do when a baby has acid reflux. I clasp my hand over my mouth in disgust.

"What? Don't you like it? We can exchange it for whatever you want!" Emil says, trying to gather back any semblance of my good mood like a flurry of colorful balloons released into a gust, the glimpse of my love for him threatening to disappear over the horizon.

"It's not the coat, baby. I love it. It's me. I look . . . unhinged."

I can't look away from the vagrant in the mirror, whose eyes are wide as if as shocked to see me.

"Why didn't you tell me I look like this? Did I look like this at the party?"

Emil takes my shoulders, turns me around to face him, holds my cheeks in his hands.

"You're beautiful."

I want to believe him.

"You're a liar. I look like I slept in someone's crawl space."

"No," Emil chuckles softly, "you look like a mother."

I don't know whether to be flattered or insulted beyond belief. I wish he had a gut and bad jeans and Merrell sneakers so I could tell him he looks like a dad, but he's perfect. Stomach taut beneath his freshly dry-cleaned APC shirt, the hair he grew out while I was pregnant hanging long and nineties in his face. I know he means well, and to double-check I scan his eyes for a hint of sarcasm. There is nothing, just my earnest Emil, who I feel like I could maybe knee very hard in the balls right now.

He pulls me in tight, a hug that loosens as he realizes the baby is on my body.

"Something has come between us," he whispers in my ear, an old joke from my pregnancy days. It seemed funnier then, now it feels like an astute observation. I wonder if he feels that too but before I can ascertain he kisses me on the forehead, turns to get his own coat and gather his bags.

Emil says his good-byes to me and the baby and leaves, almost leaping out the door into a waiting Uber as if thrilled to be free of us. I close the door after him, still wearing the coat. Emil may have dropped the ball with the party, I think, looking around to survey the remainder of the mess the cleaners and I have been left with—a rug that needs vacuuming, clean glasses that need returning to their shelves, furniture that needs to be rearranged—but he pays attention to the details. I run my hand over the coat's fresh wool, feel its silk lining against my bare forearms. It is now the most expensive item of clothing I own. I look down to check on the baby, her tiny mouth is turned to the side, lips pushed into an angelic pout. About an inch from her mouth, she has somehow managed to spit up and the beautiful wool is slowly soaking thick, curdled milk into its fibers. It has been sitting there a minute and I know that even if I dab it, even if I soak it in cold water, the stain is not going anywhere.

After patting at the milk stain forlornly and then feeding the baby, after setting her down in her crib and sitting with my birthday coat draped over the baby carrier I'm still wearing, I pace around the house. The late-morning rays are pouring through the windows, flooding the downstairs room like the brightness has been turned up, everything looks vivid. I feel a flicker of optimism. I am in a beautiful house with my newborn, I am married to a beautiful man who loves me. Isn't this it? Isn't this the dream?

Dominique's personalized text tone on my phone chimes through silent mode. I startle, and it takes me a minute to remember what this sound means. My brain runs through all of the things she could be texting.

Are you free? I'm bringing you food.

Hey how are you? Can I hold that baby?

Hey girl! Wondering how you're doing and if you have a sitter yet so we can go out!

I look down. Her actual, real-life text reads:

Ugh he still hasn't messaged me back. I can't come over this week btw, super busy, love youuuuu.

I lift my arm to throw my phone and the restraint I show in not smashing it to smithereens impresses me. The mood passes, and I sit contentedly with myself, like a person who has just finished a book they enjoyed that they must take a minute to contemplate before rejoining the world. I set my phone down next to me face down. I decide not to text Dominique back and then immediately change my mind and decide the opposite. I pick my phone up and calmly type:

All good! love YOU!

The house is silent around me and for a second, I miss Emil desperately, but I shake my head to free myself from that thought. It is too soon to miss him. I will be fine.

No worries.

All good.

II

Remember Sekesu, our island girl? She was heartbroken without William, but her belly grew in his stead. Sekesu decided to make her escape. There was nothing but shadows and grief left for her among the trees that had grown as she did, and Sekesu told herself she did this for her child, but really, if she looked inward, if she looked at where her mind went in the dead of night when her breath turned heavy, she would know that she hoped to find William and the sanctuary he gave her. She carried in her heart the hope that he had not died but that somewhere he was out there, free and waiting, and they would be together to raise their child.

She made it to the town, managed to lay low. She asked around for William, but all that people would tell her were the stories of the executions, shaking their heads over the floggings and hangings. The British had made a bloody example out of the entire uprising; no one was spared. The home she had found in William was lost and there was no time to mourn with a baby on the way.

It can be dangerous to let the pain of the past define you, but even more dangerous to ignore it.

She gave birth to a daughter, light like her father, hair like the sun, tight coils almost translucent with a brightness that reflected on the child's skin. Later on, the other children of the neighborhood would call her a duppy, her ancestry was whispered about. Unlucky, this hair color. And it is true that when she was born, something else came down from the village with her, a little of that ancient shadow from beneath the canopy had followed Sekesu, a permanent cloud she couldn't shake. To dispel the feeling of displacement and with the hopes of banishing it from her child's life also, she buried the baby's placenta at the root of a sapling, as her mountain people taught, to tie her to the land.

Despite this, the heartbreak from the loss of love and home would leave Sekesu (our first Caribbean girl) feeling untethered. Not even Sekesu and her herbs knew that within their lineage lay a haunting, a bewitching, an irreversible, inescapable shapeshifter—how could she? To know that she would need to know the truth, the beginnings of it all. Injustice is truth denied. What happens to injustice left to fester? Truth can be a bitter taste on the tongue, like nutmeg. Because what is truth, and do we always want it?

6

The baby wakes with a diaper that is seeping out of the sides, green foamy liquid goo that looks like something out of a science fiction movie. I change her onesie from the one with tiny ducks to the one with tiny bunnies. Boy onesies are always predators, foxes and bears and lions. Girl onesies are mice and ducklings and fruit, things to be eaten. I clean her thoroughly so she is fresh, scentless. Once I am done we head out of the house, desperate to do anything besides the mind-numbing routine that has become my cage. The house has begun to smell funny, not like diapers but like burning meat, or hair, some rancid leftover from the party. It is a cloying and undeniable odor; I cannot find the source. I fling the upstairs windows wide; safety isn't a worry in this neighborhood, I can air out the house, get the smell of drunk bodies out without fearing for my belongings. Except for a few pregnant waddles around the block and some exploratory wanderings with Emil, our new area mostly remains uncharted. I should get out there, be in the world for a minute.

On the way out I spot our mailman, Ruben. I don't know him well, just enough for him to know me by sight. It is nice to think that someone can see me and immediately know where I live, where I fit in. It is comforting. I wave at him as he heads up the path to our front door.

"Beautiful weather today!" he greets me.

"Isn't it?"

"They say it's going to rain."

"Do they?" I squint obediently up; it is blue blue blue. "There's not a cloud in the sky!"

"I know! But"—here Ruben pauses and I know what he is going to say before it comes out of his mouth—"we need it."

I smile and nod in agreement as I pass him and head out. It has become a common refrain in our state, a modern rain dance. A desperate plea to the skies to give us drought relief. I can't remember the last time I have seen rain. It isn't even the season yet but fires rage to the north, up there somewhere, but not anywhere we can see.

This morning I have used one of the authentic baby carriers—a vast swath of material for which I have watched several YouTube tutorials to learn how to secure the baby tightly. It was an optimistic late-stage addition to my gift registry, and even as I walk, I cradle the baby in my arms, uncertain I have done it right, not trusting the fabric to prevent my baby from falling. My mother had one photo of my grandmother, new to America, a new mother with a new baby strapped to her in a bandana that clearly came from back home. The fabric was red and plaid, the kind that is sold at Jamaican market stalls and airport vendors. I imagined my grandma picking it out when she knew she was pregnant, taking it out of one country and across another, wearing it with pride. My mother hardly ever mentioned Nana Catherine, and we knew better than to ask. The photo of her was tucked behind a passage of sun-faded scripture in a cheap gold frame. One afternoon while completing my chores I knocked the frame and the bottom edge came off, revealing the photo's corner peeking out. I was amazed to find it because its existence meant that my mother was not completely known to me, that she had secrets, there was more than just Jehovah. Maybe she missed her mother, maybe she spoke to her at night, whispering blasphemous secrets.

Nothing else Jamaican remained in our home, so maybe Nana Catherine had taken the bandana back to Jamaica when she returned to the island, or maybe my mother had it in her belongings somewhere, a relic, a cheap souvenir of something that was never hers. I double-check the knot on the generic baby wrap around my waist and wish my nana could have taught me how to tie it.

Headed down our leafy street, I receive a flurry of texts from my work colleague group chat. It is comprised of several women I see in the office of the PR firm, mostly white, mostly mothers. It has been a long time since I sat in my office and I imagine my plant wilted and dying, ignored by passersby, colleagues pilfering all my good pens, Vanessa making a beeline for the rock-star author making headlines. I imagine being forgotten, or of forgetting. I decide that I should at least try to get a little work done while Emil is gone, just to remind myself how.

The texts ask for pictures of the baby, which I dutifully send, and they gush and ask her name. I tell them we are still deciding and I get suggestions of entirely wrong names.

Madeleine? one co-worker offers.

Lydia! I always liked that name! says another, as if that should matter to me.

Lydia! someone agrees. Like Pride and Prejudice!

Lydia, I think. Like 1776.

Kitson comes from my young-blood primary assistant, Ruby,

typically hip and perfunctory. She follows up, Kit for short, and everyone agrees that it's good, this is what I should name my child.

I send a text far perkier than I feel: Omg thanku this is so cute! I'll run it by Emil whenever I finally speak to him, haha.

I shove my phone into my pocket, flick the switch to silent, try to put them out of my mind and immerse myself in the weather, the blooming trees, the blue skies. I hate phone-me. She is prone to reacting to texts with the heart reaction button as if she loves everything and everyone. She is compliant, she is overly apologetic, she is pandering. I keep her locked in my phone because I am embarrassed by her, I am scared of what her existence says about mine.

After a few turns into streets with no outlet, I discover the neighborhood playground. It's funny I have never noticed it before; it is one of the many buildings and businesses and parks that have sprung up fully formed since I had a child. They must have existed before but I was too busy with single-people things: cocktail bars, boutiques with silk shirts and overpriced candles, the best place to buy a good $11 matcha latte.

I hesitate. I haven't been inside a playground since I was small enough to use one, but then I remember I have a child, I have as much a reason to be there as any one of the moms who are dotted around the main play structure. I take a bench nearest the path so that should anyone object to my presence I can leave without too much effort. With the baby in her wrap, I can only do a sort of sit/lean perch I've perfected in my kitchen to facilitate eating, and I try it again here. I wonder if any of the other adults are judging me for suffocating my baby, the instructions on the wrap say not to sit but I so desperately want to rest. One of the moms, a light-skinned woman with hair in a Gucci wrap, is making her way toward me, and I stand out of nervousness. I worry that she is going to ask me to leave but I don't want to go back to the house, it feels like a prison these days and the fresh air is replenishing. The anger that seems to be taking root in my chest feels less persistent out here.

"How old?" the mom asks, smiling warmly.

"I'm th-thirty-four?" I stammer.

The mom laughs, hard. It's a kind laugh, endearing.

"No, no. The baby. How old is your baby?"

"Oh! Almost three weeks."

She is still laughing when I answer, and it's contagious. I can't help but chuckle too, she has one of those laughs that lightens and lifts.

"My goodness! I haven't laughed that hard in so long, thank you."

She wipes tears from her eyes, distractedly waves at another mom across the park.

"Three weeks! What are you doing out here?"

"I had to leave the house. To be honest I am going a little crazy in there, it feels like I've lost all sense of space and time."

I don't mean to share this with her but truth spills from my mouth. Her warmth opens something in me, she is the mother I want to be, I think. She is the mother I want.

"Oof, I remember that. And you're just at the beginning! It'll get worse before it gets better, that I can promise."

I must look crestfallen because she reaches out and pats my arm.

"I hope I'm not overstepping; you probably know that already, right? Don't you have girlfriends who have been through this?"

"No. I'm the first."

"Damn. That is rough. I think the only thing that got me through the first six months with Ethan and Oona were my girls."

Again, my face betrays me. She pivots quickly. "Okay, I am really not doing you any favors, am I? Can we start again? I'm Amina."

"Sofia."

"Hi, nice to meet you! Sorry, I'm talking too much. I'm just so thrilled to see another Black mom in this neighborhood! And what's little one's name?"

I cannot tell this seasoned parent that I haven't even done the first initial step of having a child and that my baby is nameless and that one day soon I will have to make a special, designated trip to City Hall to officially name her. I am coming up with an excuse when she explodes.

"Ethan! Eth! No! Absolutely do not ever eat the sand! You know this! If you're hungry I have your snack pack!" She turns back to me apologetically. "He's just a curious child. I hope. If this becomes a habit, I might just release him back into the wild."

I smile at her dumbly. I have nothing else to say but desperately want to fill the silence so she won't leave. Being with her makes the chaos feel normal, surmountable. Her child, a violently redheaded boy who I assume is Ethan, comes over breathless and sandy.

"Oh, I see, you *are* hungry."

Amina sits on the bench, swings a Chloe backpack around to her front, and pulls out a stainless-steel bento box with a space-themed lid. She flicks it open with one hand, baby-wipes the sand from Ethan's mouth with the other, and squirts some hand sanitizer into his palm before I have even managed to readjust my seating to avoid my healing stitches. Ethan eats his homemade fruit salad with gusto, eyeing me the whole time with a curious gaze.

"Don't stare, Ethan. And what do you say?"

"Thank you, Momma," Ethan garbles over a mouthful of pineapple.

"Do you want something else? Crackers?" Amina queries, but the child shakes his head and runs back to the play structure, sated.

"Wow," I gasp, "you make it look so easy."

"Oh, please! It gets easier, most definitely. It's still the hardest thing I have ever done, though." She glances sideways at me and repeats, gently, "It gets easier."

She scans the playground for her children, spots them, one, two, before rejoining my gaze.

"What about your husband? Sorry, partner. I shouldn't assume."

"Husband," I confirm. "He's . . . he's doing okay."

"Waste of space?" she suggests, smiling naughtily.

"No, no!" I insist. I want her to like him. "He's helpful. He changes diapers, he wants to do the bottle feeds . . . He's just away right now."

"Away where?" Amina asks, taking a bite of some kiwi.

"Away for work," I say, and she draws a breath through her teeth like a paper cut, "for three weeks."

"Oh my goodness! But you're only a couple weeks postpartum! You must be losing it." She double-takes the baby pressed against my body. Amina looks at me with something like pity, but kinder. I want her to embrace me, to hold me close and feed *me* sliced-up fruit.

"Yeah. It has been . . . well, it's not what I was expecting. Sometimes I do feel like I'm losing my mind," I admit, and bite my lip to keep from crying. No one has asked me about myself, no one has taken the time to figure out how I might be feeling since I was pregnant. If she says or does one more nice thing I know it'll make me cry.

"What did you expect?" Amina pushes softly.

"I don't know. I thought I would be better at this. Like I would know what I was doing, and feel confident and a natural and not . . . sad, or scared, or like I'm missing something," I list off, a little more strenuously than I intend. "I don't know. I thought I'd be better."

I look down at the bundle on my chest, this tiny nocturnal creature depending on me. I thought I was healed and ready to raise this child, but maybe I'm not. Maybe she'd be better off with someone like Amina.

"No one knows what they're doing. Anyone who says they do is lying. That little one there, all cozy in her wrap? She's breathing and living because of you! So, I'd say you're doing all right," Amina says. She sighs, unclicks the space bento box again, offers me the fruit. I burst into tears. She hands me a tiny, clean fork with an apple skewered onto it and I take it gratefully, the salt from my tears and the sweet mixing in my mouth.

Eating some fruit cut into small pieces helps more than I thought it would, and I begin to feel a little better. Maybe I was just hungry. Now I want to know more about Amina, figure out a way I can see her more, but before I can get a chance to ask her to adopt me, Amina looks at her phone, springs up, and calls to her children.

"Shit. Ethan! Oona! It's almost dance class time. We've got to hustle, kids!"

She turns to me.

"I am so sorry to leave you here like this. I completely lost track of time and my children are already late to everything as it is."

"It's okay, I'll be fine. Dance class sounds fun."

I try to be brave; I wipe my tearstained face on my shoulder, on my beautiful new coat. What's another little stain?

"I don't know if I would describe it as fun, more like forty-five insanely expensive minutes of sitting in a hallway pretending to have something in common with ballet moms. Which, FYI, is the worst type of mom," Amina deadpans, and I fall a little bit more in love with her.

As I ease myself up and off the bench, Amina is gathering her things and both children flank her, dragging her by the arms out of the park. I want to beg her to stay but I know this is not what an adult does, and so I wave and shout my good-bye at her back.

"Sofia!" she calls back to me, feet still stepping forward. "We're here after school most days, I'll be here if you need me!"

"Okay!" I yell back. "I'll see you around!"

My pocket vibrates. I slide my buzzing phone out to confirm what I already know. It is Eddie, with another voicemail. Three minutes this time. I cannot bring myself to listen to it, not now. I watch as Amina's SUV pulls away and disappears down the street. I realize it is too late to tell her I have no idea what time school ends, or that I am not sure I will make it through the weekend.

7

The first night alone is rough. The baby screams if I feed her, screams if I change her, screams if I rock her. She screams as I walk her back and forth in the upstairs hallway, bouncing and half singing. When she finally gets snatches of sleep, I try too, but each time I feel my lids close, she begins again. She is insatiable, until the morning when suddenly she stops as the sun rises. I am wired from the experience, and I decide to start the day, lack of sleep be damned. I bring her downstairs and place her in her portable bassinet, a collapsible thing that Emil calls the Taco. If it is a taco then she is the filling, crammed in and snug, somehow content despite her restless night. I pull the curtains open with a flourish, the very act of which feels wealthy, but I can't help thinking of *Sunset Boulevard,* of Norma Desmond, aging in her mansion. I welcome in the sunlight, which banishes the shadowed corners that seem to take over the house at night. With the baby snoozing in the Taco, I feel hopeful, like this new day is possible. The cleaners have already come and gone and everything is in its place. Rays stream in, pouring over the Italian coffee table, the Eames chair, the rug imported from Morocco.

Everything the light touches becomes ordinary, commonplace, as if it is normal for me to live in this neighborhood, as if I actually exist in the world of Bay Cliff. After I got out from under my mother's preaching, I would imagine myself in the future. Beautiful, young, married, wealthy, a mother. Any combination of those adjectives would do, I thought, and I repeated them like a prayer. I remembered what I had once read in a *Cosmo* in a dentist's office about manifestation—rather than focus on what you want, you are supposed to think about how you will feel when you get what you want.

I had imagined what happiness would feel like.

I can't tell if I got it right.

There is one corner of our large living room that somehow remains dark, shadowed. I pull the curtains farther back, tuck them into their hooks on either side of the bay windows, but the shadow remains. My ears ring as I look at it, hypnotized by a magnetic pull that feels as if it tugs at a string from my belly, as if I am a puppet. I take an involuntary step forward toward the absence of light. The unsteadiness in my feet is moving up through my legs, I am dizzy. I think of that dark day in New York when I wandered the city at dawn searching for a bridge high enough to see from. Something in me wants to get closer but my legs are Jell-O and the recollection of that time frightens me, I don't want to think of it. I tear my gaze away like ripping off a Band-Aid and bustle the baby out of her taco. I take her upstairs to get dressed so we can leave this house, shadows behind me, and breathe some air.

—*

I used to love being home alone in those final pregnancy days. It felt like a frozen tableau, a family life interrupted, this huge house filled with things, straight out of a magazine. And me, padding around like a trespasser, basking in the still and quiet like a warm tub, playing the role of wife. Now the silence that briefly comes between the baby's screams does not hold the same promise and instead it feels like trip wire surrounds me, and as if any moment could be ruined by her waking. I am on edge, constantly.

When the baby and I return from a walk around the block I set her down to sleep on our bed. I lie down next to her and try to settle myself, arms by my sides staring at the ceiling to find the still of sleep waiting for me, but against all odds I am wide awake. I find myself making mental notes of who I used to be, what I was like before this baby. I want to document, to sketch her outline before she dances away from me forever.

When I think of old Sofia, I think of days spent in the park with Emil, picnic blanket spread optimistically in the waning Bay Area evening, huddling close and sipping from tall cans. Wine tastings on the weekends, trips up to Sea Ranch for fireside romantic getaways. Working days decompressing in our old apartment kitchen, shoes off, eating noodles together and scrolling through house listings, planning. When the future was somewhere out there, waiting for us, and the past was long gone.

Arriving here in the future, it seems there's nothing to look forward to and nothing to lean back on. I want to always be the bride, never a wife, and pregnant and optimistic beats out postpartum and lost. I had a therapist once who told me I prioritize forward momentum over vulnerability, but I discarded that tidbit, letting it float to the surface and evaporate. What else was I expected to do, after surviving all of that? I had to keep going.

I give up on the idea of rest and decide to get some work done, I've been procrastinating long enough. I head to my office down the hall and sit at the desk, shuffling through memos and opening my laptop. At first it is like picking up a book written in a language I once knew but have now forgotten, but after twenty minutes or so I begin to find my stride. I know how to do this. It feels nice to find this work again, unchanged through my metamorphosis, waiting for me. I am reading emails from Ruby, who is currently taking the lead on my project for the time being until I get back in the office, whenever that might be. She just has to keep Vanessa the corporate climber off it. It's a novel, one of the new gothic horrors that resurfaced as a popular genre after a recent Mary Shelley biopic became an Oscar winner. Emil says he knew it was destined for an Academy Award. A film contract for this book is already on the table, offered to the buzzy author before it was even complete, so it will be an easy task to get it front and center. The only caveat is that the author is notoriously difficult and prone to gonzo tactics, in particular they favor graphically violent anecdotes, told like nursery rhymes. They are a prodigy from Yale and best friends with numerous celebrities, with an Instagram grid that spans the globe, pouting with a cigarette in Paris, in a macramé bikini in St. Barts; they are the literary Chloë Sevigny but with less charm. It feels good to jot down notes on placements for Ruby. I've been a publicist for years, starting at the bottom as an assistant in Manhattan, working diligently the way only an oldest daughter knows how, thanklessly and underpaid. I was ambitious then, hungry to carve out some space for me. I was building something, crafting a full life from scratch, I didn't know what I wanted to do, so instead I just took instruction. Turns out, having an emotionally abusive mother who expects more from you than one human can offer gives you excellent skills to be a publicist's assistant, and later a full publicist.

Now the notion of becoming director of publicity feels distant.

I had been close, a shoo-in, but now I'm on leave and all my accomplishments are fair game. The thing about Witnessing is you are only as good as the hours you just submitted, and work is no different. But maybe I could still have a shot, if I could just give our latest project some attention. I flick through the advance reader copy of the author's book and stop on a page. A description of a Black Miss Havisham, brokenhearted and traipsing through an overgrown rose garden, of screams heard into the night. I read three pages with ornate descriptions of the woman's broken heart, of the stinking gown she has not removed, of the baby she threw off a cliff to save it from a life like hers, before I realize my own baby is still asleep. I should be taking advantage of the quiet. Sleep when the baby is sleeping, work when the baby is sleeping, shower when the baby is sleeping. Take the fractured portions of time for your own, make lemonade out of lemons.

I get up from the mess of my desk and make my way to our en suite bathroom. I undress in front of the large floor-to-ceiling mirror next to the double-headed shower, but I do not look. The body I am in is not mine anymore. When it was mine, it was a good body.

It wasn't particularly noteworthy, I have never scaled mountains or skydived or trained until muscles bulged, but it was healthy. It moved when I told it to. It looked how I expected it to every day, predictable, solid. My clothing size never wavered; I had no need to endlessly try things on. I would look at something, decide if I liked it, buy it just like that off the rack. I knew my shape, knew its limits. Walks were spontaneous, I enjoyed hiking because it required very little from me in terms of preparation—water and SPF and decent shoes were all that I needed, and I enjoyed being outside by myself. Moving back to California meant hikes became easier, I was alone a lot with Emil throwing himself headfirst into work. But solitude was a childhood habit, and I could bask in it easily. I would frequently leave our office downtown and make the short drive out to the coast in my leased Lexus and trail run alongside the water until the sun sank. My companions would be the darkening sky and the clouds, almost touching the ocean, separated by a horizontal beam of setting sunlight like a door beckoning below the marine layer of fog.

A good body. A strong body. Breasts high, posture unbowed. There is a grounding to knowing the perimeters of your body. Knowing yourself inside and out, relying on it. I dream of my old body. Stomach soft and unlined, pre everything. Unsullied and fresh. The spread of my hips even, legs toned. Nails sculpted, painted, pedicured and manicured. Every inch of my skin moisturized right out of the shower. Hair combed and product applied, legs shaved, skin scrubbed.

Now I am a beast, a feral thing. Black Miss Havisham ain't got nothing on me. Leg hair unruly, bikini line blurred and uncharted. Hair that is matting, no time for curl creams and combs, no time for masks. Cold water splashed on my face occasionally. Lately, if I remember a serum or an oil, it is applied haphazardly, carelessly.

I step into our shower, feeling the water against my skin. The relief it brings is immediate and luxurious and I could stand in it all day, not moving, just feeling the heat from the water pounding, relaxing my shoulders and lower back, breasts heavy and swollen and leaking milk. I carefully wash between my legs, fearful of hurting myself. I wonder what it looks like down there, if it is different, a veteran, like it has seen some things.

Eventually, remembering what a gift the time is, I step out, not wanting to be shaken out of my reverie just yet by a baby's cry. I reach for my tub of moisturizer, try to recall the loving strokes I would give my body, before, when the time was unlimited. It is enjoyable, a muscle memory of sorts. A reminder of the small moments of self-love that set the day right, that make you feel like a cared-for human that someone loves, even if it is only you. As I finish up, I glance at the tub and realize it is not the moisturizer I thought it was, but curl cream. My entire body is coated in curl cream and I feel sticky to the touch. I am devastated, I do not understand how I have made such a stupid mistake. The only way to undo it is to get back into the shower, rinse off, and start again.

I get back in, hair product softening against my skin, I briefly think of the wonders it is doing for my leg hair, my pubic hair. *Nourishing and strengthening,* the tub says. *Encouraging hair growth.* Great. A baby cries down the hall from me and all of my muscles tense, all of my work is undone. I step out for the towel, rush to dry myself off, and dress once again in my dirty, worn sweatpants. I gather my wet hair up into a bun and head down the hallway. I am unchanged. Irredeemable. Stuck.

It takes me thirty minutes but I get the baby back down and return to the bathroom, which is still steamy from my shower. I think of my earlier trepidation with my postpartum body, those fragile parts of myself I am too scared to venture near, in case it should cause a vaginal avalanche. A vagalanche. I am so sick of tiptoeing around the once familiar geography of my own body, particularly the parts that I used to enjoy touching. It has been so long since I felt a certain kind of pleasure, so long that I can feel my curiosity rising. What would it feel like, I wonder, to touch myself?

I wash my hands thoroughly in the sink beneath the fogged-up mirror and then I insert a finger into myself, just to see, gritting my teeth in apprehension. It doesn't feel sexual; I conduct the investigation with a medical detachment, I want to see if I can feel the stitches and I can, a ridge of lines that my finger moves over, counting. It doesn't hurt when I touch them, which I am surprised by. They are also less prominent than I would have expected, dots and dashes, and I wonder if I can see them. I get out my hand mirror, perch on the edge of the tub, a bruised sky visible behind me through the picture window still smogged with steam. Like many people, I have inspected my own vagina before and I do not anticipate alarm, but when I look down at the glass I am taken aback by its new asymmetry. The shock of pubic hair frames my labia, thicker and wilder than it has ever been allowed to be. The opening of my vagina is slightly slack-jawed, a little pout of surprise. The stitches are not, as I had imagined, a neat row. They jut down the skin of my labia, down to the tender meat of my rear end. They are angled like the line of the letter Q, and that makes me think of the word *askew,* which they are. The stitches tug downward, and it gives the impression that my vagina has recently had a stroke. I am both disgusted and curious, and I watch my disembodied hand in the mirror, like it is someone else's, stroke the jagged line of stitches like a clitoris.

I flick the angle of the mirror up, at my face. From this angle, down low, my face is not dissimilar from my crotch. I am framed by the window behind me, and between that and the recessed lighting we installed into our heritage home, my messy hair is illuminated, strands escaping from the bun I had thrown it in. It has dried in a tangle and is flattened, and my eyes are the sunken eyes of a sleepless person. And my mouth. My lips are cracked and dry, and I try a pout, feeling the skin crinkle.

Flicking the mirror between the two scenes is like the reflection of a landscape in a lake, mirrored and rippling, making you wonder where one begins and the other ends. I turn the mirror back to my face and suddenly it is not the only face I can see, there is another, behind me, against the window, so dark it almost blends. A shadowed oval, but distinctly human. My heart freezes like a cornered animal as I try to make sense of what I am seeing, because I don't understand, because it isn't possible, because we are on the second floor.

The face has a hand, also shadowed, and it is pointing, finger hard against the pane, as if I am a bug beneath glass, waiting to be pinned. Fear opens like a trapdoor in my chest but before I can register, before I can say anything, the face is gone. I am breathing heavily but I am alone. I turn quickly, scan the room, and remember my extreme exhaustion. I am just tired. My heart beats loud in my chest and I lay my hand flat upon it. I have to allow myself to believe this narrative, because if I don't I have to gather my things, pack a bag and my baby, and leave this house, I have to acknowledge that I am terrified. I may never want to be alone in this house again. Or I can let this fear go, I can dismiss it, decide that I imagined the face, or dreamed it.

I pull my pants up and decide to be an adult.

I think of the old Sofia. Fear is inconvenient. Fear slows you down. I walk out of the bathroom and shut the door resolutely behind me. I do not look back.

III

Next we will learn about Sekesu's girl, Della, who we meet heavily pregnant, our duppy grown now. She covered her hair to go to market even though everyone knew what lay beneath her scarves. She was conspicuous in the village, hair like the sun, almost translucent, not so much yellow as it was the absence of black. The old women used to say that a birthmark was made by a pregnant woman touching her body and making a wish that did not come true, leaving an indelible mark on her child. What, then, had her mother wished for when creating Della?

While she worked in the field, her stomach jutting out making it impossible for her to bend down and harvest all she needed to, twenty-eight-year-old Della thought about the baby in her belly and prayed for it to be a boy. Fieldwork would be easier with a boy. Her mother's bush wisdom had been taught whether she wanted it or not, and so Della knew that when the gecko first crossed her path it was bad news. She first saw it when it was curled up in her house shoes, small and unassuming, striped with brown bands. She shook it out, lifted the slipper to kill the thing but it scuttled away, out of sight.

She immediately rushed to her mother's house to ask about the gecko and was told by her mother, who looked like she had expected this, that it was most certainly an omen. Her mother took her by the shoulders and told her she might just have a girl after all, husband be damned, and Della insisted this was voodoo, not to be taken seriously. Animals could no more predict the future than people, it was a load of nonsense. Della did not tell her husband what her mother had told her because he was a God-fearing man whose mind would have immediately gone to witchcraft. Della's obeah ancestry was never far from his mind.

Della had not gotten pregnant easily, which is the type of thing that angered men like her husband. To him, she was an expensive farm yield that had not come to fruition, and she did everything she could to appease him. He was a tough man born on a plantation to parents of the short-lived apprenticeship program after enslavement ended. That hard beginning had made him distrusting. He wanted what he wanted and he wanted it now, no patience for her foolishness and her monthly blood that stubbornly came right on schedule, paired with a wounded look and whispered apologies.

Della's mother had given her a steady course of herbs to bring about a child, but warned her it would be a long road. She had dutifully taken her medicine every morning and was rewarded for her diligence three years later. A precious, precarious gift that grew in her belly. When Della was growing up, she and her mother caused people to talk. Besides her yellow hair, rumors of witchcraft, of un-Christian ways were whispered all through town, she didn't want to give them something else to gossip about. A loneliness that wasn't easy to shake followed the both of them, and people could feel it, which might have been why Della struggled to find friends but eventually did, because she was kind and eager to please. She was lucky, the other mothers told her, to have any man at all, being so strange. And now she would have to work hard and show him that she was worthy, that he had made a wise choice. And she would show him by not resting, by cooking his meals right, by bearing as many of his children as she could. Boys, please Lord.

When Della walked down into the village from their house set back off the main dirt road, she would often see the little gecko, and although it looked much like other geckos, she could have picked it out of a bunch easily, weighed down as it was by the premonition she knew it carried. She felt it was waiting to be acknowledged and knew that if she acknowledged it, then what she feared would come to pass, so she never looked at it directly, purposefully keeping her distance.

Her daily uniform was a white cotton skirt with stitches unpicked and extra inches of material tacked in to accommodate her burgeoning stomach, and a bundle of harvest to sell in the village balanced on her head. One particular day, after spending time in the village chitchatting with the other women and arguing over prices in the markets, Della began to feel a tug below her stomach, an ache like her blood was about to come. It was time. Earlier than she had expected, but what could she do? She tried to hurry back up the hill away from the market-day crowds, for her house sat not far from her mother's, who also doubled as the local midwife, but halfway up she bent over in pain and knew there wasn't time. On the ground by her feet was the gecko, looking up and blinking, waiting for her to comprehend its message. Then it moved fast and snakelike into the trees. Della stumbled after it into a clearing lined with banana palm fronds like it was expecting her. The gecko was there, sat at the feet of a black figure only visible in her periphery, and Della would have been frightened had everything from that moment on not happened so fast—she felt a pressure down low, a pushing of pain that made her eyes dazed as if looking directly at the sun. Still standing, Della reached out her hand to the figure in desperation, wanting someone, anyone, to help her and tell her she was not alone. Her outstretched hand hit something hard and invisible, like the glass window of some fancy building up in Kingston, her on the outside and all that finery within.

Della didn't have time to wonder what the strange apparition was, because suddenly a scream pushed through the air as Della reached down and felt the spherical curve of a baby's head between her legs. Once the head was out it moved quick until it was out in the air, a pink and purple thing with a headful of black hair, still in her arms, eyes wide open and silent so that Della briefly thought the worst, but then the baby breathed in one big breath and screamed so loud and long that anyone who heard would know what had happened. Relief flooded her body and she allowed herself to lie down on the forest floor with the baby in her arms and wait for help, hair laid out around her like the white-yellow center of a flame. Della felt she was not alone. From her green bed that was now flecked with the evidence of labor, she looked up at the shadow and its gecko familiar, fear at her breast and a deep dis-ease settling like a thick blanket. Della's mother came bustling in through the trees as if she knew precisely where her daughter was. She seemed to pause at the shadow figure before she knelt down to silently check over the infant whose navel string was still attached.

"She's a big baby," the new grandmother said warily, knowing her daughter's hopes.

"'She'?" Della repeated, feeling disappointment creep in against her heart's wishes.

"Yes, Della. 'She.'" Her mother, like any mother, couldn't resist her one chance and added, "Me nah tell you?"

A man from the market who sold fruit entered the grove hurriedly, turning his head when he realized what he was looking at. He made his apologies and congratulations in the same breath and went to find Della's husband. Della and her baby sat in the clearing, her mother wiping Della's brow, rubbing her back. They both knew that once her husband arrived, he would make his disappointment known, so they tried to savor the quiet contentment for as long as they could. Della began the business of getting a breast out, offering it to the child who seemed to think twice before finally closing a tiny mouth around her nipple. The gecko blinked and scurried back into the brush, having done all it was there to do, but the shadow stayed.

Disappointment and sorrow left untreated can become heavy weights. Despite her beautiful baby, Della let herself sink.

8

There is a reason sleep deprivation is used as a torture method; you can lose yourself. I feel out of step with my movements, as if watching a TV show with subtitles that are a beat behind what is being said, and it feels worse inside the house because there are no other external factors, just me moving around as if trying to catch up. After a weekend of disjointed sleep, not to mention the strange hallucination in the mirror, I awake on Monday feeling uncomfortable. Being alone feels eerie. Sure, it was just a dream, it was just my imagination, but I have unsettled myself, like watching a horror movie when you know you're going to be home alone. To avoid being stuck with only my phone for company, which I have turned off in case Edwina calls again, I decide to go to the grocery store. It is a twenty-minute walk from my street and although I'd prefer to drive, the car feels dangerous and unwieldy, walking feels doable, with less moving parts. I change a diaper, repack the baby into the carrier, fill a backpack with diapers, wipes, a change of clothes, a pacifier, toys. Things I haven't even had use for yet but for some reason I pack anyway, as if perhaps I will be gone so long that the baby will grow big enough to need a bib or a teething ring.

I step out of the house onto our street. Bay Cliff has always been a neighborhood where the incredibly wealthy lived, the elite of the elite, back when this was just a port town, a town built by gold. Sawmill barons and oil tycoons, people who had struck it rich up in the mountains, come down to play at being gentlemen. Plaques sit proudly on the brickwork of some of them, announcing former homeowners of note. Before that, it was likely an indigenous homestead, because of its hill placement and good vantages, its proximity to the water, but there is nothing that tells of those people, you'd have to be told. Whose bones are my house built upon, I wonder, who died so that I could be here?

I knew kids who would make their parents drive all the way into this city to trick-or-treat in this neighborhood, famed for its full-size candy bars and elaborate décor, and it still feels surreal to think of myself as a resident now. Halloween was the only time these streets were welcoming to the children from my side of the water; if they had been caught loitering in the park, or at the lookout point above the city, the cops would have been called. I feel exposed without Emil around. His presence explains me, gives me the air of legitimacy. People smile when they see me holding his hand. Without him, even in my expensive coat, I feel like a vagrant.

As I move down other identical tree-lined streets just like mine, I begin to feel an almost forgotten bubble of optimism. The sun feels warm on my face and the air has that fresh spring scent before a heavy rain—everything is bulbous and blooming; I can almost taste the pollen. The baby, who was fussing as I fumbled with my keys, locking the front door behind me, has been soothed by my rhythmic steps. The pacifier that was lodged in her mouth moments before now drops, and it lands teat down on the earth. I have to squat to pick it up, not an easy move for me, and to my surprise it isn't painful but the memory of the trauma echoes. I can almost feel my vagina threaten to rip open again and I do a quick half-hearted Kegel. And then I do the thing I have seen all mothers do—I put the pacifier in my mouth, clean it by sucking. A sacrifice, a risking of my health for hers. I pop it back into the suction of her mouth and I should feel a step closer to authenticity but instead I feel like an actor going through the motions.

The grocery store is bustling with late-morning shoppers, people I have never seen before because I used to do my shopping in the evenings after work—MILFs in yoga pants speaking too loudly on their phones, distracted freelancers grazing at the salad bar, old people blocking whole aisles with carts. I guess I am one of them now: the new mother.

A dark-skinned woman with immaculate dreads and a septum piercing with a beautiful face so symmetrical it temporarily blinds me gives me a wide smile. For a millisecond I think she is flirting until I remember that I have a baby now. I am not an Eligible Mate anymore. I have been mated with; I am taken. I am a mother—sexless and useful, admirable. I smile back but she has moved on to the kombuchas.

I grab a basket, making a mental note to not buy much because I am walking home with the items, a prospect that is suddenly intimidating. The fridge is stocked and I have delivery services at my fingertips, but purchasing nonessential food items feels like the height of luxury.

Pausing in front of the wine selection I inwardly check with myself to see if that spikes any interest. It does not. I move on, selecting a dragon fruit purely on a whim. It is eleven dollars. My mother would laugh in my face if she could see the money I spend on utterly expendable items. My childhood kitchen was spartan, schooled on the lesson that material goods are unimportant, a distraction from our duties as members of the organization. During the week I was the cook, I mostly made things I could bake or pan-fry, the rhythms and nuances of recipes were never taught to me. But still, I could read. Flipping through the cookbooks at Domi's house, I would pore over photos of fresh vegetables, green salads with cherry tomatoes, grains topped with halloumi, pastas with truffle oil, decadent cheeses, citrusy dressings made from scratch. Now I can afford to buy my own dressings, vegan Caesars and creamy Italians and spices from countries I have never been to but could visit, if I wanted.

I pick up macadamia milk and consider its weight, put it back again. I buy strawberries and blackberries, green lettuce speckled with a fine mist. Romaine. Asparagus that snaps in two like a smattering of applause. Line-caught organic salmon, pink and raw. Some fancy unpasteurized cheeses because I can, because I am not pregnant anymore.

In front of the cut fruit and cold-pressed juices a short woman in her late sixties passes me. I can feel her eyes on my child and I can sense the imminent conversation she is about to start. The baby drops her pacifier again and begins to snuffle, a full-throated cry is not far away, but the woman takes her moment, carefully picking it up by the non-mouth side, and hands it back to me. Ignoring the question of how many people walk on this floor daily, I give it a quick suck and feel around for my baby's unseen mouth within the carrier, slot it in like a puzzle piece.

"How precious! How old?"

"Three weeks." I smile, trying to look legit.

"I have a grandson who is almost five. It goes so fast," the woman says, crinkling her crescent eyes up at me. I think of the past few weeks, slow like molasses, slow and sticky to the point of immobility. I feel like I am sleepwalking all the time, and I can't shake it, this half-time pacing, this note of dread in everything I do now that I am caring for the baby alone. I want things to move faster, I want to feel like I have some momentum. I do not say this to the woman. Instead, I turn my smile up brighter, nod.

The woman's hands are on the shelves in front of her, on the fresh glistening produce. We are reaching in synchronicity and laugh when we notice, our hands almost brushing each other. I gesture that she should go ahead, which softens this stranger even further and she pauses to smile as she reaches for deep purple plums, juicy in their punnets.

"Cherish this time. Take it from me—these are some of the most magical days of your life! You'll never feel more fulfilled!"

And with that she plucks the chosen fruit, plops it into a brown paper bag, and drifts off, back to her day. In response, an almost black plum drops onto the floor in her wake, it rolls toward me, all that supermarket filth. I pick it up and take a large bite before setting it back in its place.

IV

Remember Sekesu, our first Caribbean girl.

Remember Sekesu's daughter, Della.

This is Della's daughter, Agnes. Not much is known about Agnes, but we know the shadow followed her too. A girl wasn't what Agnes wanted. A girl is a target, a girl is a piece of fruit that, each day, ripens and ripens until someone takes a bite, often before it is ready. Agnes's fear would cause her to transmute into the type of mother who is never kind, who cannot be kind because you cannot be kind and vigilant at the same time. Agnes looked down at her child, even as she bled out the post-birth, cramps seizing her midsection in a pain comparable to the labor itself, and allowed a thought to come before she banished it to the beyond forever: She was a beautiful baby.

We know that Agnes would go on to have many more children, but throughout their childhoods the very sight of that first girl would inspire such a grip of grief at Agnes's breast that she had to swallow it down like a secret poison. The shadow that had followed the girl out of Agnes's body made her dizzy with fear. She tried to ignore it and, in turn, the child, pushing her away, keeping her far, making her a child who didn't seem to need much.

One day that child would need saving and would turn to her mother, the only person she believed strong enough to help her. By then it would be too late for a relationship, because all that would be left of Agnes would be the outline of a mother and a heart devoid of feeling, a woman only able to do one final act of parenting for her child. The seed that falls on the hard path will not grow deep roots. Agnes would push her even farther, out of harm's reach, out of the danger, out of her arms.

9

The next day, the cleaners arrive at the house as I prepare to leave it, baby in tow. An unfair demand of the American healthcare system is the requirement to drag your post-birth body and freshly oxygenated baby to pediatric appointments, but readying her in onesie and beanie, wrapping a blanket in tightly around her in the car seat, I feel hopeful that whatever the doctor tells me will bring me some relief. That I will relax with the knowledge that I am doing something right. That she is safe. Although I have tried to put my nighttime fears to bed, an incessant voice I can't place reminds me we're not alone. Not the standard voice of self-doubt, and a gut feeling isn't right either. I try to ignore it. I have my methods of keeping it at bay—by not looking into the shadows, by locking the doors and checking them multiple times throughout the night. It is a paranoia I am getting acquainted with. I can live with this if someone can just tell me I am on the right track.

When I get to the office, I am surprised by the detached nature of the pediatrician's receptionist, who scarcely looks up from her screen as she checks me in, asking for date of birth and clacking it into her computer. Not even the mention of the baby's birthday mere weeks earlier elicits any kind of softness from her, and I receive the same treatment when a nurse in pink scrubs ushers me into the examination room.

Pink nurse moves through the tasks of measuring the baby with a rote precision, handling her with a cool professionalism that could be mistaken for nonchalance. I look for an opening for some kind of connection, but pink nurse is monosyllabic to my questions and offers no kindness. She gives me the baby's exact measurements followed by the percentile she is in, already measured up against millions of other babies. Seventy-five percent for weight, sixty-five percent height, eighty-five percent for head circumference.

After the baby has concluded an impersonal appointment with a doctor we haven't seen before and we are waiting for the elevator, I text off these stats and a photo to the people who will care: Emil, his mom, Dominique, a couple of his aunts. Everyone but Emil sends back heart-eyes emojis; it feels like a gold star. Their approval delivers the shot of dopamine I've been missing. Emil says bet she gets her big head from me with that cross-eyed emoji with its tongue out. I stare down at my phone and feel disappointed, I'd wanted something, I don't know what, something more maybe? Pink nurse didn't even look at me twice.

Where is everyone? All those people at my baby shower who had touched my belly and pledged their time and attention, who promised they would be there. And in the hospital, when all those same people who had cooed over my baby brought copious stuffed toys and presents, cards and flowers and well-wishes. There wasn't enough space for all the plush purple bunnies, the fuzzy bears and ducklings brought by people who had evaporated, and I have no one but four heart-eyes emojis. And one crazy face.

We get home to an immaculate house, the cleaners have done their thing, everything has been polished and wiped down and put back in its proper place, hitting its mark. The stage is set. The baby has been sleeping decently enough, making it suddenly possible to get things done around the house, maybe I can take a real shower or eat a real meal but I am too scared to leave her. What if the baby monitor stops working? What if she gets free of the swaddle I have Velcro-ed her into, somehow suffocates? How would I tell Emil what I had done? What if the shadow in the living room that I have been keeping an eye on, that seems to be growing, is as threatening as it feels, what if something unspeakable happens? Instead, I sit next to her, a vigil, a sentinel. I am on WebMD the minute anything seems off. I Google things like *How to give a baby the Heimlich, How to get a baby to sleep through the night,* and scour Reddit for answers, taking notes. Nighttime is a different story, and she can't seem to sleep longer than thirty minutes at a time. Once again I turn to Reddit. Several posts on sleepless newborns cite darkness as a natural melatonin stimulant, and so I begin drawing the shades earlier, because studies say she should be sleeping eighteen to nineteen hours a day and if she's not doing those numbers then it's me, it's my fault, she won't hit her milestones.

At night the baby is fitful and demanding, it feels like Jekyll and Hyde. I cannot get my breast to her fast enough, gone are my worries about the pain of feeding, I shove raw flesh into her mouth, hurriedly, just trying to make the noise stop. She guzzles the milk as if she hasn't been fed for weeks, and as she does, I am overcome with a deep thirst I have never known, I cannot hydrate enough although I try sipping from a large plastic lidded cup gifted from the maternity ward.

In the darker times during the night, when I have managed to get her back to sleep but cannot do the same for myself, I trawl Instagram looking for something. I am not sure what it is, but I expect to find it in all of the mom blogs I feverishly followed after Emil and I decided to have the baby, excited to find community. I find one on the Explore page of Instagram, an undeniable family:

> *PHOTO ID: Clay, Emma, and baby Paxton sit on a brand-new CB2 sofa in Crema, everyone smiling wide except for baby Paxton, who looks doe-eyed and clean. Clay wears dark Levi's and a plaid shirt with enough top buttons undone to expose a silver dog tag. Emma wears what could be described as a boho top, lightly tasseled and embroidered, also dark Levi's and a wide-brimmed hat worn, inexplicably, inside. Baby Paxton is in a muted-tone onesie and a cream headband across her small bald head. Behind them, spelled in neon fluorescent tubing, is* This must be the place *in cursive.*
>
> Clay and I couldn't be happier to welcome baby Paxton earthside. Sure, labor wasn't fun but having her here has been better than words could describe. She is the sugar on top of a life I didn't think I'd ever get to have. Baby gurgles, sing-songing our way through an afternoon before nap time, she is a delight from the moment she opens her eyes to the moment she closes them. Thank you for choosing me to be your mommy, Pax. We love you!!! 🖤😄👶

When I was pregnant this sort of post made me rub my belly like it was a crystal ball, willing this future into existence. A manifestation: *I will be happy.* But in this pitch-black room, the white noise machine making me feel as if I am falling in deep space between the stars, these posts seem to merely underline how terrible I am at this. I continue to scroll, black screen lit with moms in cute outfits and children who match, homemade meals full of vegetables, Technicolor bowls of health, picture-perfect photos of kids in baths on sleds on beaches sandy and sun-dazed.

I do not sleep.

—*

On what my phone tells me is Friday, I realize Emil has been gone for a week. One week down, two to go. Birds chirp outside the kitchen windows, cartoonish warbles, and the world seems to continue on out there but in here, the baby has been crying since two A.M. She cries as if I have never given her anything in her life, a desolate howl of a cry. It should tug something maternal in me but instead I am angry, as if the baby has no self-control. During the early-morning hours I was sympathetic, understanding, running through her needs to figure out the problem, but now I want to shake the crib, rattle her around, I want to scream *What is wrong with you? What do you want?* I wonder what I am supposed to do here; there's no one to ask. The whole day passes with little respite from her demands. Where is that little nag of a nurse's voice now when it is needed? When I pick her up she squirms in frustration, I try to feed her a nipple and she purses her lips like she wants none of it. Her diaper is dry. I rock her, I shush her, I jostle her gently in my arms. The light outside is fading, I wonder what time it is, how much has passed with me like this in semidarkness? I am swimming in unfulfilled desires. I want to throw her in the bin. I want to run out of the front door and never come back. Almost in symphony, my phone begins to ring, Eddie coming through with cursed timing. The repetitive screaming is making my skin crawl, like a fork dragged across an empty plate, or a squeaky marker pressed against paper. My head swivels between the phone and the baby, uncertain of what needs to stop first. And because I know this is wrong, because I know this is not what a Good Mother would think or do, the guilt is suffocating. What do I want? A medal for not screaming at my baby? Not throwing her out the window?

Yes. I want a fucking medal. Someone to notice, someone to see.

I turn the phone off. A day has somehow elapsed without me really noticing, the natural light fading from the sky completely, as if the screaming was a wormhole to the end of the day. Finally the baby begins to settle as I pat her rhythmically. I am too scared to stop in case she wakes up, so I continue patting her in the near darkness, saying *shhh shhh shhh* even though there's no one to *shhh* except myself. When I can step away I lie on the bed, turning to my phone out of habit. The light from the screen scalds my eyes but it's comforting and I check Instagram and on the Explore page I find an array of peacefully sleeping babies. Captions that explain how well the child sleeps, partnerships with brands, I scroll and I scroll and find endless reminders of people who could do this better than I can. Through the screen it looks easy, effortless even.

> *PHOTO ID: a gorgeous child with eyes that look an AI-generated blue sits crisscross applesauce on a quilt that is clearly handmade. She is in a Pampers™ nighttime pull-up, logo visible, and smiles a dimpled smile at the camera. Blond curls frame her face.*
>
> Little Norah has never given us any trouble at night. When she was a newborn we had to wake her for feedings because she would sleep right through! But now she's 3 and we are night training her, and things are a little different. Sometimes she wakes at night because of a wet pull-up, which is why we're partnering with Pampers™ to bring you a special kind of diaper, one that absorbs moisture for up to 12 hours. And luckily for us, that's exactly how long Norah sleeps. We love you, Norah, and we love you, Pampers™!

—*

The second weekend without Emil is relentlessly sunny; on Saturday morning I open the kitchen blinds and then immediately close them again, my sleepless eyes feeling assaulted. It's too much, all this good weather. If it were rainy outside, I might have a chance, I might feel okay about bundling up indoors, waiting it all out, waiting for better, waiting for more. Instead, the sunshine makes me feel like I should be doing great because everyone else seems to be. How will I ever catch up to them, all those people sitting on picnic blankets in the park, babies cooing up at the sky, moms nonchalantly handpicking produce from the fruit and vegetable stalls outside the Korean markets, infants restful in their strollers? When will my life look like that, like ease and happiness and not monotonous work? I know I have it easy, I have it better than most new mothers, and the truth of this thought permeates my malaise. I think of Devon, wonder how he's doing. I pick up my phone to text him and feel a gnaw of guilt, one I have been denying for years now. I haven't been a good sister.

Eventually, when Devon came out east too, he called me all the time, tried to make plans to hang. It was an attempt to stay close to me but by then I had built something new, and the old parts of my wonky, broken family didn't fit. I wanted Devon to fit, he was the only relic of my past I wanted to keep close, but nothing he was doing meshed with my plans. He smoked too much, he didn't care what he looked like or what other people thought, he seemed like a person who had no goals, no dreams. I ignored his calls, I brushed him off, kept our sporadic meetings short. I would arrive at the station to meet him, dressed in a pristine preppy outfit, this Sofia had a job and an apartment she liked, she had a plan and a future and none of that involved getting dragged back into anything Eddie adjacent. When I dropped him back at the station I always felt immediate relief, like a crooked picture frame being straightened.

Devon took the hint eventually, found a place of his own in Atlanta, kept the texts to a minimum, and dialed back. Jokes, memes, check-ins on birthdays. Light, disposable, friendly. Sometimes I found myself missing our closeness, our hushed promises to each other during evening prayers back in the East Bay, the solidarity found in one another. Our imaginings of Nana Catherine, spurred on by the discovery of her photo, embellished over time until she was the most perfect, most patient grandmother, waiting for her grandchildren to come and find her. Pilgrimages in borrowed cars to Jamaican restaurants, Wu Tang and AZ and MF Doom and Grand Puba and Black Star played loudly the whole way, moments of rebellion, worldly things Eddie would have turned her nose up at, had she found out. Cutting the bonds with my old, dead family left me free to mold my new one. Like the beech tree in the yard, that old family was decaying. I couldn't help but wonder if he was lost to me, if I had been so cutthroat in my crafting of this world that I had lost the only person capable of understanding where I had come from. But we both escaped, didn't we? We made it out okay despite it all. That should be something to celebrate, that should be a victory lap, I reason. This logic doesn't sit quite right with me, and I don't have the energy to dissect it, so I set the phone down. Devon is thriving, he's happy, he isn't thinking about me and my life, that's for sure. I will spare him the reminder of our childhood, at least today.

I set the baby up in her taco so I can try to make coffee, she is snug and cozy but still squirming. I rock her, a little more forcefully than I should but she likes it, she hushes and closes her eyes. I continue rocking her with one foot as I extend my reach to try to measure out my half-caff into the coffeemaker. I wonder what to eat, stopping for a moment to turn my attention to the fridge, and somehow she senses this shift, opens her mouth to howl, eyes scrunched shut. She is expectant, she assumes that I know what to do here, that I will know how to soothe her. I leave the coffee, carry her out of her taco, and seat myself in a dining chair, latch her onto my nipple, anchored.

She is still screaming onto my breast as I try to express a little, hoping it will convince her that food is indeed what she wants. I realize too late that I have left the fridge door wide open, and even with my best stretch I could not shut it from where I now sit. It stays open as the baby's mouth closes around my areola, and from my chair I can see all of those well-meaning meals I pre-made when I was pregnant and thought to thaw out last night, breakfast burritos and bowls of rice and proteins and arduous sauces awaiting a healthy dose of fresh spinach, rice grain pastas and soups. Defrosting in the cold, my best-made plans going to waste. The door begins to beep, the room fills with the impatient, greedy sound as I feel myself float up out of my body.

I took a yoga class once with a teacher who outlined the process of astral projection, the power to leave your body and transcend, as we lay in savasana, corpse pose. I remember the steps: Let your body find a half-sleep state, focus on the mind rather than the body. Resist all urge to scratch or move. I ignore the pulling sensations on my nipples and I float higher, above the ceiling, out and over Bay Cliff. Time feels like water and I am a cork, bobbing away, away.

I find myself out of my house, cold and exposed somewhere up high. I feel a biting oceanic wind in my face, and my feet struggle to get a grip on the railing I am stood on. I know this scene. My right hand is above my head as I hold on to the support beams of the bridge, and all I have to do is let go, and I won't have to struggle to stay upright anymore. And then I feel the cold rush of water around me, moving faster than it appeared to from up there on the bridge. There is no sense of up or down, and I panic against the water that is filling my lungs and jerk my body as if out of sleep. I am back in my home, back with the sound of the fridge beeping insistently like an ECG monitor. I have a moment of panic as I realize I have been gone, but when I look down the baby has passed out, nipple rolled out of her mouth and eyes closed, brow furrowed like a caveman, mouth pursed and suckling still even in her sleep.

I would know that cursed night in New York anywhere, even if I have packed it away, even if I haven't thought about it for years. Sitting here in my kitchen I can feel the terror from that night, the desperation as I stood and wondered what exactly would be lost if I just jumped. I breathe out, eyes pricking with razor-sharp tears. I wonder how long I have sat like this; the minutes seem to have slipped by and the fridge is still beeping but the light inside has turned off, a sign that it has been longer than it feels. I transfer her carefully, slowly into the Taco, like a bomb defuser. I pause, doubled over, arm trapped beneath her tiny body. I pull it out inch by inch, slower than I want to be doing it. Success. She is asleep, my body and mind are mine again, however briefly this moment may last. I grip my arms in my hands, crossing my chest. The chill from the water under the bridge seems to have gotten to me, I could swear my shirt is slightly damp, I could swear that my ears are ringing with the pressure of being underwater. I am still shaking—this vision has scared me; I rub my arms for warmth.

I take stock of the room to center myself. High ceilings, natural light, my dream kitchen in my dream house. I am lucky, I think. I try to practice some gratitude, not for the first time. I shut the fridge to silence it, open it again and pull out a homemade breakfast burrito, black bean and peppers, thawed overnight from my freezer stash. It is still cold and I don't want to risk waking her with the sound of the microwave or the oven door opening and so I take a bite, savor what food tastes like. Good, well-seasoned food from a time before, when I had the luxury of taking hours to cook a meal. I am grateful for my past self; she possesses a fortitude and a telepathy that I no longer do. This gift of nourishment from the past is almost enough to move me to tears, I think to snap a photo of the half-eaten burrito held up in front of my sleeping infant, and I write the caption *Pre-partum me made postpartum me a meal. Thank you, past Sofia!* I have posted it before I even know what's happening, and I close the app feeling relieved.

A too-loud knock at the door chills my blood, and I freeze. The baby begins to howl as if she never stopped and I set the burrito down, torn between answering the door and tending to her. I head to the front door, open it a crack onto the bright blue day to see a man in a brown UPS uniform saying my house number like a question. I stare blankly, trying to think what could be happening, the baby's cries are loud behind me, the hard drive of my brain seems to be short-circuiting, and I cannot remember what is supposed to happen next. He repeats himself in a monotone, and when I finally nod, he pulls out a big bouquet from behind his back like a magician. I take it from him and he turns to leave, oblivious to the chaos he has unleashed in my world. I shut the door, walk back to the kitchen staring at these flowers that might as well be from outer space, they are so baffling. Who died? Why would anyone send me flowers? I remember that people send flowers for good news too, and this baby is good news. This is a Good Time. Congratulations flowers. Happy baby flowers. You Did It flowers. I lay them on the dining table, exchange the bouquet for the screaming infant, and the minute she is in my arms she is silent. I sit next to them, read the card. They are from Emil. Flowers instead of his presence, peonies instead of parenthood. I push them away with my elbow, out of reach, and then, still not satisfied, I extend my arm, push them all the way off the table out of sight, plummeting down to the tile floor, bruising the blooms and killing the sentiment.

10

My right breast has a clogged duct, something I discover from a late-night Google as I rock the baby, brightness on the screen turned all the way down. The breast is full and eerily spherical. It looks as if it would make a very satisfying sound in an empty gymnasium if you were to throw it up and spike it, like a volleyball. Blood vessels thread across the skin, and the slightest touch makes me wince in pain. I try to nurse the baby from it but it causes lightning rods to zigzag up through my right shoulder so I stop, and once she is down, I head to the living room, eyes glued to my phone, searching for a solution. I have a bag of frozen peas defrosting on the hot flesh of my breast before I read "cabbage leaves." Old folk medicine. Opening the fridge, I only find a plastic container full of washed romaine and wonder if it will do just as well. The internet says no. I flick open my shopping app and order two organic cabbages, request express delivery. I pay an embarrassing amount of money for things I should be growing in the empty planters in our backyard, and I pace by the front door, glancing outside as if "express" meant immediate.

Hours later, the cabbages arrive on my doorstep in the baby-blue dawn, silently dropped off on my front doorstep by a nameless someone who I tip, via the app, handsomely, gratefully. I throw them both in the freezer, I need them chilled and frosty for this DIY medicine, this witchcraft. The baby awakes while I wait, so I feed her from the left breast, change her, absent-mindedly rock her while I look at my phone, trying to distract myself from the pain. I Google *Jamaican plant medicine.* I read about bush remedies like aloe and breadfruit leaves and cerasee tea. Nothing I know anything about. I close Google and open Instagram.

It is a window to a life I have forgotten, friends who were at my party who drunkenly promised to visit, to bring soups and second-hand baby clothes and books I should read, as if reading was something I have the time or the bandwidth for. Friends who were posting photos of brunches I was not invited to, outfits I could not fathom wearing, hikes in far-flung places I don't recognize. I refuse to like these posts, out of spite, as if these people would know that I had withheld my internet love, as if they'd care. I stumble across an acquaintance's post, Lyla, a woman I only sort of know. We've had surface conversations at parties and she does something in fashion, one of those people who was always amused by the neighborhood I grew up in, thought it weird and out there, until it got a Blue Bottle Coffee and became a place *Vogue* did breathless profiles on, as if discovering a prehistoric Amazonian tribe.

Lyla is what Central Casting would call "ethnically ambiguous"—she could pass for Middle Eastern or Indonesian or even French, and she keeps herself vague that way, courting the ambiguity despite being pretty solidly Midwestern. Dominique and I used to laugh at her, all the things she borrowed from other cultures to wear and knew nothing about. Greek evil eye necklaces, bindis, henna, and

Ghanaian waist beads. And yet, as I look closer at this photo of Lyla at a farmer's market, Lennon sunglasses on and woven basket in an East African print on the crook of her arm, it dawns on me that I recognize her date. I pinch the screen, zoom in on Dominique's beaming face just behind Lyla's, flower tucked behind her ear, doing a coquettish pose for the camera. Betrayed, I close the app. I didn't even know they hung out outside of the occasional gathering or art exhibition, and yet here they are looking like best pals. Jealousy rears its head and I think back to middle school, when Domi began distancing herself from me. The shift was subtle. When we were alone it was business as usual, her family still invited me and Devon to dinner, I still met her after her weekend job, but at school I could tell she was nudging me away. And because it would have hurt more to let her push me out, I did us both a favor and became invisible again. It was painful but I knew she still loved me because she would tell me as much after her shift at the mall as we wandered around the Macy's home department. I forgave her, patiently waiting for her to return to me. And she was the one I called from the hospital ward in New York after everything, after the bridge.

I text Dominique like a cucked wife.

Hey how's your weekend going?

And I wait, venomously, for her reply. Lyla is my replacement? Lyla is the person she spends her free time with now, having daytime cocktails and flirting with twenty-five-year-olds? Dominique texts back, faster than I was expecting.

Hit up the farmers market then doing
Verve 💕 wish you were here!

My heart aches in my chest. Verve is our place. A cute hole-in-the-wall bar that is standing room only except for two stools crammed in near the bartender, seats we would always manage to fill. I imagine her there with Lyla, shoulders touching, the unseasonably humid air holding the promise of rain, bringing the men round like mosquitoes. I turn off my phone and head back to the kitchen, back to the freezer. I follow the internet instructions and place the stiff frozen cabbage leaf onto my breast.

—*

Emil texts.

Late nights on set, FaceTime soon?

I see the text seconds after it is sent, but I don't reply. I want him to know I am too busy for him, I want him to pity me. It is childish, I know, but I resolve to text him later. Let him worry. I hold the baby as I stare out the nursery window at the tree, which is missing a few more limbs than last time. The gardener is really fighting the rot. The expanse of sky pushes through where the branches used to be, the sheer vastness of it feels overwhelming, as if the house is capsizing.

Emil texts again.

I miss you.

I feel like I grew up in this marriage. I was so young, and so grateful. Grateful to have found someone safe and stable and reliable, someone who could be the pillars of my life, hold the ceiling up for me instead of myself, instead of me being the Atlas. But there's been a switch, I can't say when it happened, was it before the baby? Before the pregnancy? I feel trapped. Building a life around yourself means you can't get out. You're stuck.

Lately it seems that the work I do to maintain, to keep going, is imperceptible to him; the time I take to make sure he is thought of and his needs prioritized is not acknowledged. Whatever role his mother and her various staff members played, I am now playing. A subtle passing of the baton has occurred and I hadn't even noticed but now I am here, with all of this work that was, duh, so clearly mine. Work that would always have been done and never actually be called work. I was part of the furniture, neutered and utilitarian, sure, but you don't thank a chair, do you? If the chair were to begin to complain about always being sat on you'd say, but you're a chair? What more could a chair want if it was serving its purpose?

I break. I text Emil back a terse:

Sure.

And then, grudgingly and because it's true,

Miss you too.

—*

The shadowed corner is spreading. In fear of seeing faces that don't exist at the windows, I begin to keep the curtains and blinds in the house closed, not just in the early evening but all day. I resist the comparison of what happened in New York, this is different, I rationalize, I didn't see shadows then. I'm just worn out, and everything, the trick of light or lack thereof, can be chalked up to that.

The book on my desk is full of images of dark figures that have seeped into my subconscious. There's nothing here but fiction. Exhaustion sits between my eyes like a sinus infection, tiredness makes my head feel heavy, foggy. Nothing is helping, not the coffee every postpartum book advises me against, not the quick, tepid shower I take in an attempt to wash off my fatigue like a layer of dead skin, to hopefully emerge clean and reborn.

Night becomes day, day becomes night, week one is about to be week two and now Monday is back again. If only I could manage a little sleep, but it seems so unattainable. Is the crying getting worse? Is it colic? My nervous system jolts from every sound. I feel as if I am on a candid camera show; each time I lie down, silently, so as to not wake the baby co-sleeping in her bassinet on the bed, each time I close my eyes, she opens her mouth and screams. And when I stay awake the shadows of the trees outside shift and dance like a coven against the windows, backlit, their boughs like arms in the air, summoning. Often I get as far as drifting off, body and mind grateful for the respite, but then she bawls, a guttural scream that shakes me from whatever half-place I'm in and brings me back to this room, back to this needy mouth. I find I have her at my breast, nursing bra unhooked, before I even know what's going on. My body is doing the steps for me, knowing I'm incapable of catching up.

—*

Later, in my office I find the Smythson notebook front and center, although I don't recall putting it there. I want to open it, a forbidden tome, read aloud from the scripture within and find some spell, some alchemy that would change me. Change me into what, I'm not sure. A better mother? Maybe. But I'd prefer a tree, a cedar or a beech, waiting for a gap in the canopy to shoot up, be in the sun above it all. I'd stretch my branches out to the sun, take in the light, photosynthesize without even thinking about it. I'd let birds make their homes up top and deep in. I can't remember what I wrote, back before it all. I open the book, curious, and paw through notes scribbled in an inscrutable font, dancing loops through the lined pages. Notes on episiotomies, on breathing, on book recommendations, recipes for bone broths, simmering stews of marrow. And then, on a page I don't recall writing, in handwriting that is angular, wonky, unrecognizable, is written:

> And I will shew wonders in the heavens and in the earth, blood, and fire, and pillars of smoke. The sun shall be turned into darkness, and the moon into blood, before the great and the terrible day of the LORD come.

—*

Monday. I dream a lot. An online search tells me that short bursts of sleep mean you remember your dreams more vividly. And it's true. I remember even the small details—carved door handles and a skinned hare that is meant for dinner, going out in public with no shoes and knowing something is deeply wrong and yet when I look around everything is as it should be. I dream of vast palatial houses perched on cliff edges, locals warning me about soil erosion and seismic changes. Of Bible verses, of Matthew 7:27. *And it caved in, and its collapse was great.* Lizards, silent and unblinking, watching me from the ceiling above my bed. I dream one night of an egg, a small, black egg, hardened like a fossil. I've seen it somewhere before. It is precious, I know that. In the dream I hold it tight in my palm, the satisfying feeling of something that fits in those bones, that skin and muscle, like it is home, my fingers clasped around it with ease. When I wake the first thing I do, baby fretting beside me, is search the sheets for the egg. I am convinced it should be there. I peer beneath the bed frame as the baby begins to scream for me, and when I do not find it I am devastated and suddenly mourning, and as I put the baby's mouth to my breast I begin to cry, palms empty with an ache at the center of them.

The next night I wake and find myself standing still like a statue in the kitchen, a big vast space with a marble-topped island in the middle, and for a second I see water, rising water, cold enough to take my breath away, ankle and then knee high, a familiar sensation. A panic grips me and I cannot move, I think of water in my eyes and mouth and nose, pressing hard like a hand across my face, harder than you would imagine something so wet, so hard to hold, to be. The kitchen submerges, cups and plates and forks float around me in zero gravity as I suffocate.

I think to myself that this must be the end, and then I blink, with the deliberation you only have in a dream when you know you must wake, and all is as it was. The kitchen is clean and the zellige tiles reflect the recessed lighting like always, and the fridge is stocked with everything a family could need, everything is as it should be. The room is illuminated and the kitchen windows, the only windows in the house free of shades, are dark. I see my face reflected in the one above the sink, staring at myself as if I am a stranger, eyes out of focus, and then there are two of me. Except it's not two, it's someone else on the other side of the window, someone just in the shadows enough that I cannot see their face. They reach to me as if for help, hands up against the glass, mouth agape. I open my own mouth as if to speak. I step toward them against my better judgment.

The shadow steps back from the window, beckoning into the black, and then it is gone, and with it, whatever it was I was going to say.

Above me, the baby resumes her cries and I take the stairs two at a time to get to her, fear beating at my chest, something is wrong, something is so very wrong. When I get to the room she is fine, peaceful and cherubic, dressed in her onesie, swaddled and safe on the Coyuchi sheets she couldn't possibly appreciate. She is dry as a bone, but hungry. Always so hungry. I unbutton my shirt and lift her out, holding her like a life preserver.

And then as quickly as the dreams start, they stop. Shortly after that, as Emil's second week away slips by, any semblance of sleep stops altogether too. I am no longer even tired. The exhaustion has been replaced with a frantic feeling, like I have had too much coffee all the time, which I probably have. I often have the sensation of coming to, like the anesthesia is wearing off and I am awake on the table, bright lights in my eyes and feeling everything. The baby is safe and sleeping in our room, my room. I peer out the window for unseen intruders, cupping my hands against the glass, but the only thing I ever catch a glimpse of is my own eyes, my own skin shining back at me.

Sometimes I find myself thinking of prayers from childhood, prayers of protection that loop over and over in my head. All that Bible learning coming back fast, like words to a song I once memorized playing and replaying. My body aches. My hips feel misaligned and I briefly think about going to a chiropractor, finding some help. I drag out my yoga mat that hasn't been used since I was pregnant, when I would sit in goddess pose in my prenatal yoga class, full of anticipation. I try to do some hip openers. Somewhere in the back of my mind behind the soundtrack of prayers, beneath all the foreboding, is the pervasive notion that I must get my core tight, that this will help.

Instead, I find myself in the throes of a flashback, lying on my back with my knees bent and flopped open, I can distinctly remember the sensation of the baby's head between my legs, pushing beneath my pelvic bone. I remember that, with a mounting panic, I reached down and felt my vagina, felt a crowning head and stupidly asked the room what it was, what was happening. It didn't feel like this was happening to my body and yet the pain was mine for sure, a searing, impossible pain that seemed as if it would kill me, turn me inside out. Another body tearing its way through my own, head and mouth free and screaming, arms free that I felt against my thighs. My organs and bones had to move out of the way, make a path. Alien and impossible to stop. I remember Emil's hands bracing my feet, telling me to push, I remember begging him to push for me, that I couldn't do it. And then all at once the alien on my chest, covered in viscera and goo, looking down at this thing and feeling nothing, remembering nothing.

I put the mat away. I don't want these thoughts. My hips still ache but I move through it, willing it away. My vagina throbs with the heat of memory and I go to the bathroom to check my stitches and count through my ice packs obsessively, one, two, three, four, five. Five ice packs are not enough, what will I do when they are gone? Will I be healed? Will it be over?

—*

My phone is always ring ring ringing. I hear it in my sleep, I hear it as I walk through the house at night, making sure the curtains are closed. It rings again and I ignore it, swiping up before I can see who is calling. I know who it is, her dedication to sermons and scripture gave her a great basis for phone harassment but I am not in the mood to be preached to. I am busy, scrolling through Instagram looking for an Amina, one specific Amina, but there are so many. I squint at the phone trying to recognize her features on the tiny avatars. It's impossible. The phone rings again and before I can get rid of it, I see it is Emil calling, after more than a week of distracted-sounding texts, out of the blue. He is FaceTiming me, and I can't imagine anything worse than holding my phone up to my face, but this is what we do, this is the game I have to play. I dust the sleep out of my eyes, retie my hair to little effect. I try to smile, but the effort is staggering.

Emil is lit from the side by a midcentury lamp, and he looks undeniably good. He smiles his wonky grin and says, devastatingly, "Hey, babe."

"Hey!" I reply, mirroring his positivity, trying and failing to prop the corners of my mouth up like a circus tent. I shift in my seat on the couch, straightening my posture, holding the phone slightly above me at a more flattering angle.

"How was your day?"

Emil is on a perfectly made hotel bed, I can see the corner of a book turned down on the nightstand, the room is large and quiet. I zero in on his face, ignoring the jealousy that is already bubbling up my gut.

"The same." I smile. "How was yours?"

The minute I ask I know I do not care about the answer.

"Long. There's been a bunch of rewrites and it's slowing everything down, Max is pissed, everyone is pissed. We lost a whole day. I just finished dinner and got back to the room, I'm excited to not talk to anyone for a while . . . Wow, could you look any more bored?"

"I'm just tired, that's all."

This is a lie. The reality is that envy has cooled and hardened into a solid, immovable anger in my throat. I try to reframe it; he is working, this is how it goes. Why am I so mad?

"Where's Babygirl?" Emil continues.

"She's here." I flick the phone to the left of me, showing the baby, still in her taco bed. "She's sleeping."

"Hey, Babygirl," Emil says softly. It must be nice to look at her from a safe distance, I think, where nothing is required of you.

"Have you thought anymore about names? We gotta nail that down when I get back."

"Of course I've thought about it, Emil. I know she can't be Babygirl forever. I have more important things to worry about. I have to make sure we stay on schedule, that she's sleeping enough and hitting all the milestones, there's so much to do and I'm doing it solo right now, so maybe just give me a break."

There is more to come, I can sense it in my body. I know I must end this call because if I don't it will all pour out of me like a venomous sap.

"Okay! Jesus. I was just asking."

He is regretting this call, I see his eyes drifting, deciding what he will do next once he has ticked this task off his list.

"Okay."

". . ."

". . ."

"Wait. She's sleeping, shouldn't you try too? 'Sleep when the baby's sleeping'? You look a little . . ." Emil trails off, realizing he is about to step on a land mine.

"I can't sleep. I need melatonin or NyQuil or something but I can't because I'm breastfeeding."

I am spitting words now; I cannot keep a lid on the steady boil I am reaching, I have to wrap this up. I think of Amina, and my fingers itch to search for her again. She would understand, if I could just speak to her.

"Shit, babe, you gotta try. When was the last time you slept?" he persists, falling back on his strength, he always was a problem-solving person. He thinks he can fix me. He thinks this is something that will be tidied away.

I begin to wonder, truly wonder how long it has been since I slept more than a few hours. What does a good night's sleep look like? Reading in bed until your eyes can't focus on the words, then setting your book down, pulling up the covers, turning over without fear of a full-throated scream piercing the night? I cannot imagine the relief, although I try.

"Sofia?" Emil's voice interrupts.

"I'm thinking. A week? No. Only five days. Five days since I slept properly."

"Jesus. I don't understand why we can't just hire a nanny; you've got to rest."

Emil has shifted, body over the phone, hunched over like a coach bringing a team in for a huddle.

"Because I can do this! I'm not having someone else raise our child." Who could I possibly trust to keep her safe? And what would I do in the meantime? I picture myself napping as a stranger rocks my child. I've read all the books, I did my research, I didn't go into this blind. Everyone describes seeing their baby for the first time, the blinding flash of love that comes on, all heavenly choir and celestial light, and I waited for it in my hospital bed when they handed me the baby. I looked to Emil and he was crying, and it made me think I should cry too, but nothing came.

"Why don't you go out to my mom's? Let Marta make you soup and hold the baby?"

There is a *eureka!* tone to Emil's voice that grates. What a stupid idea.

"I am not doing that." The words are red-hot in my mouth, scalding my tongue.

"Why not?"

Emil wanders like a lamb in the conversation, completely oblivious to the fact he is in a slaughterhouse. There was a time, not too long ago, when I found this innocence charming, but I can see it clearly now. The naïveté that was once laced with sweetness, to which I would respond in the velvety softness of a mother explaining something to a child, was actually just plain old male incompetence. Nothing sexy about that, nothing sweet. I feel as if I am stating the obvious, as if we are living in two different worlds, side by side. The effect is igniting.

"You know why! I have more in common with Marta than I do your mom. I'm not going there."

My raised voice makes the baby stir, and I try to lower it, speaking through gritted teeth.

"You think Buffy is going to give me relief? I just end up making her endless cups of tea. She's rude. She treats me like a servant. I am too tired for that right now."

"Come on. She tries."

Again, Emil fails to perceive the danger, or how close I am to the edge.

"Does she? Last time she came over she told me I looked big for eight months and made me carry boxes to her car."

Emil smiles at this memory, and he tries to remove it from his face before I see it but it is too late. It is all too late.

"Is that funny to you?" I say, rage cooled but deathly sharp, iron in a forge.

"Babe, no, of course not. It was the way you said it! You just said it in a funny way."

"I'm glad it amuses you. Because if she tries that shit again, I will kill her."

The call goes quiet, and Emil is so still that I wonder if he is frozen. I didn't mean it, but I absolutely meant it. But I have to take it back. The rage that was metallic on my tongue now clanks back down within, sharpened for another day.

I smile. "Now *that* was a joke."

Emil laughs, uncertainly, as if he isn't sure, but I can see the cogs turning as he convinces himself. "You think you can survive that long without help?"

"Yes! Seriously, I'm fine," I say, shifting my voice into something so saccharine it makes me feel sick. I wonder if I am convincing him.

"Sofia. Come on. I know you don't want it, but you need help. My mom can help you. Let her."

I squirm, unwilling to admit out loud the truth of this statement. He is trying to help and I should accept it, I tell myself.

"I'm taking that as a yes. I'm texting Buff right now."

Emil texts while I am on the call, face close enough to the camera that I can see the sheen of his night cream on his poreless skin, five-o'clock shadow on his chin. When we are in bed he spoons me, rubbing his stubble on my shoulder, and I can almost feel it now looking at his magnified jawline.

"You're probably right. I need the help," I say, forcing a smile. He smiles back, relieved, cocking his head at me as if finally recognizing me. "It's been harder than I was expecting, I'm just tired and irritable. I'm sorry, baby."

"So, my mom can come?" Emil grins like a hopeful kid.

"Sure," I say, ignoring the tension at my jaw, "I can't wait."

11

After Emil's FaceTime ambush, my thoughts turn to my own family. Sixteen missed calls from my mother. I can't sidestep this problem any longer without giving up and buying a new phone, so I decide to make one morc phone call. All I have left of my old family are threads, loose threads of a larger woven tapestry, but maybe if I can grab a few, if I give them a pull, I can stitch them together and lie on them for a spell, make a hammock beneath me. I find a number for my brother and look at our last texts to each other. Stupid memes sent back and forth, nothing of substance. I click the call button, and as I wait for him to answer my heart pounds a warning. He answers.

"Who dis?" His voice is full with a smile, I can hear laughter in the background. It sounds like a party, music is playing loud and someone yells his name, singsong. I imagine him surrounded by friends, pulling sips from a beer bottle, paint from some job site beneath his fingernails, palm against his ear so he can hear.

"Devon?" As soon as I speak, I can hear desperation in my voice. I need to keep it at bay just a little while longer, at least until he understands what I need.

"Who is this?" he repeats, this time a little terser. The laughter and music fade as he moves away from it—I can almost see him, standing outside his apartment, broad back leaning against the wall, probably considering hanging up and heading back to whatever party I am pulling him from.

"It's me. It's your sister." There is a slightly too long pause, and I check the phone to see if we've been disconnected. "It's Sofia."

"*Big Star!* What's going on? From NYC to SF, they can't hold you! How you doing, Big Star in the big city? I've been meaning to reach out," Devon fires off, enthusiasm contagious. I smile, immediately feel at home. Why don't we keep in touch more? I allow myself to be softened by his use of my nickname, to believe that he really has been meaning to reach out. I just beat him to it, that's all.

"Not much, just living the dream on the West Coast. What's going on out east?" It's like talking to an old friend, an immediate rekindling.

"Oh damn! Well, it's hella cold here. Had a shower and took the dog out this morning, my dreads froze," Devon says, laughing.

"We gotta get ourselves back to the islands, Dev." I'm me again, Sofia of the past, just a kid, talking breeze with her little brother, making him laugh that bark-laugh of his.

"You remember that one spot, Islands 2?" Devon asks, as if we haven't had this exact conversation a thousand times.

I know where it is going and lean in, relishing the familiarity of it all.

"Oh my god, yes. The worst service ever."

"They told you to shut up! Remember?" He spits the words out through his laughter. The noise of the party returns and I imagine Devon leaning in the doorframe, making everyone laugh along with him. We had gone to a Jamaican restaurant together without telling

Eddie when we were teens and he had recently passed his driver's test, one of the last trips we took together before I left. We drove his friend's '94 Nissan Sentra all the way down the peninsula, an hour and a half from where we lived, just to try a restaurant famed for its curry goat. Any lover of Jamaican restaurants knows that the worse the attitude of the people who work there, the better the food. Islands 2 had staff members who acted like you had broken into their house, walked into their bedroom in the dead of night, and demanded they cook for you, but the curry goat was like nothing on the planet. The few fond childhood memories I have took place in the car ride there, listening to bootleg CDs off a portable CD player plugged into the tape deck, cracking jokes at each other's expense, then sharing a meal in near silence, both of us knowing the reverence of the moment.

"They told *you* to shut up! With your booming-ass voice saying there were too many bones. What was wrong with you? Almost got us banned for life." I bask in the comfort of the tale.

"'Lak yuh bloodclaat mout!'" Devon loudly does his best patois impression of the waitress, and I am jealous. We grew up in the same house with the same woman who wouldn't be caught dead speaking patois but somehow, he can pass as a real Jamaican. He bursts out laughing, and I can hear the party in the background join in. You can't hear Devon laugh and not laugh too; he does it with his head thrown back, big mouth open. Maybe he has Jamaican friends. Maybe he has found a way to be part of the community. Maybe they celebrate holidays together, rice and peas instead of roasts and boiled potatoes. Envy makes the hair on my arms stand up. We have always been so different—fitting in was never important to him and as a result he has made himself a nest of friends and chosen family that he doesn't have to pretend in front of.

"That's it!" I smile at an image of him at the restaurant ducking curses and making his apologies between laughter. We'd had to tip more than we could afford that day, dollar bills shoved into the plastic jar by the register, staff side-eyeing us as we did so. We waited months before we dared to return.

"And that one time Eddie heard me say it to you?" Devon continues, voice still smiling although we are close to touching a live wire. "She said, 'Where did you learn all that bloodfire talk?'"

I remember. She had said "bloodfire," but it came out with an accented lilt, unmistakenly Jamaican, despite herself. Devon and I had glanced at each other in shock, Eddie had caught it, and we had been swiftly punished, kneeling on uncooked rice and reading scripture while she reminded us of what it meant to be a good Witness. A good Witness is devout, a good Witness lives in the Truth, a good Witness has no time for the temporary distractions of earth, when the spiritual is what needs feeding. I don't want to think about this time, or how, immediately after my escape, I sprinkled out a handful of rice in my Bronx apartment and knelt, hoping to feel redemption.

"I never knew Eddie could speak patois, did you?" I ask, shoving discomfort aside.

"I'm blessed to not know much about that woman." Devon sighs, satisfied at the conclusion of this story. Eddie is fiction to him, a distant memory that can be chewed over and spat out, undigested. A cozy quiet settles between us, and I don't want to be the one to break it.

"So come on, Big Star, to what do I owe the pleasure of this call?" he says, mimicking formality. "How are you?"

"Yeah, I'm good. Great," I lie, chickening out. I need to get to the point. "I just . . . I needed to talk to you."

"Congrats on the baby by the way, what's his name?" He sidetracks.

"Her. It's a girl. Your niece," I correct, trying not to bristle. I know next to nothing about his life, I reason, why would he know anything about mine?

"Wow! That's crazy. Congratulations, seriously. You gotta send me some photos or something." In my mind's eye I see him glance back at the party through his open apartment door, desperate to get off the phone. We have gotten through the pleasantries, had a moment of sibling bonding, he feels we are done here, I think.

"Thank you," I parrot, because the wall I have built between my internal and external is strong, and I cannot remember how to answer anything honestly.

"So, what did you want to ask me? I don't want to be rude but I have my people round; I don't wanna be a bad host." *His people,* I think. I am not included in that round-up. I am the distant sister, only thought of when I pop onto his Instagram feed. I am Islands 2, I am West Coast, relegated to the past.

"What?" I say, dazed, trying to hold tight to my reason for calling him.

"You said you needed to ask me something?" he prompts, his patience waning as I knew it would. He is his mother's son, after all.

"I don't think I have a question or anything like that. I just . . . I needed to speak to family." The word tumbles out of my mouth, mealy and useless. *Family.* As if that's what we were, and not simply two people trying to escape. We are war buddies, we are vets, we are survivors. There was no space for that woolly warm familial love, I must have imagined it.

"Oh," Devon murmurs, understanding.

"Yeah."

"Emil out of town?" he asks, and I feel the insinuation. Oh, *now* you need me. Oh, *now* I am family.

"He is, but . . ." I feel defensive, but I have to lay it bare now or he might shut the door in my face. I take a breath, spit it out. "I never told him about any of that, and he never asked. He wouldn't get it. I needed to speak to you because Mom's been calling me and I wondered if she's been calling you too."

The silence on the other end of the line is like an empty room, dark and flat where sound gets trapped. The playful warmth between us evaporates into nothing. I am sure Devon has his phone in the palm of his hand, away from his head, on speakerphone now as he paces up and down the hall.

"Please don't hang up. I need to talk to someone who gets it."

"Sofia." Devon finally answers, saying my name sternly like a father. "You know I haven't spoken to her in years. She doesn't even have this number. And please don't give it to her, I can't have that bullshit back in my life."

He pauses, and then asks the question I think he has been wondering since he answered the phone. "Is she still in The Truth?"

"I don't know. I haven't actually spoken to her."

"I thought you said she's been calling you?" Interest spikes in his voice, against his better judgment I am pulling him back into a mess he has always wanted out of.

"She has but like, I haven't picked up. I can't. I'm trying to figure out what she wants, Dev. It's driving me kind of crazy."

"Heard," Devon replies, the word is punctuation. "Well . . . I don't know, maybe you should answer, see what she's saying. Anyway, I'm in the middle of something right now and I really don't want to know about Eddie, so . . ."

"Please! Please don't hang up!"

"Are you okay? You sound . . . not okay." Devon's concern causes my eyes to sting. Panic flutters behind my ribs, birdlike.

"Yes. No. There was something else I wanted to ask about, but it's going to sound crazy. Can you just . . . can you just hear me out? For two minutes?" I urge him with my mind to agree, and he sighs with resignation.

"Okay. Go on."

"Did you ever . . . do you ever see things?" The words escape my mouth like a swarm of flies.

"What are you talking about? What things?" His tone is wary.

"I'm just so tired. I'm not crazy, okay?" Which is something only crazy people say.

"Okay. What . . . things . . . are you seeing?"

"There's something in my house. I see it at night sometimes," I finally admit, relieved to have it out. The rest pours from me, an uncontrollable flood. "I can't explain it, but it's watching me, like a ghost or something. I know how this sounds but . . . you remember that night with Mom, right? Before I left?"

"I remember when you left, yeah," Devon replies softly.

"That night with Eddie, right before it all . . . I think it started then, I think it's always been there, and I just wanted to know if you had ever felt that? Like you're being watched? Like Eddie is still around?"

Devon is quiet again, the party in his apartment can be distantly heard. I try to picture his face, what his face would look like now. A beard maybe? Does he still have the long dreads he had in his Facebook profile pic from years ago, before he deleted it, or did he cut them short? I think back to his face that night with Eddie, as all of her years of madness came to one, undeniable head. We had locked eyes, as Eddie screamed and ranted about our grandmother, with the resolute look of two people who know they must escape by any means necessary.

"Devon?" I whisper into his ear.

"Look, like I said, I'm in the middle of something. It was good to talk to you, Sofia. I have to go." Whatever door that was briefly opened between the two of us slams shut, leaving me in the cold.

"Wait! Please don't leave me!" I beg, tears streaming down my face, nose snotty. I wipe my face with the back of the sleeve of my hoodie, which is cashmere, which cost hundreds of dollars, but who cares.

"Me leave *you*?" He scoffs, almost laughing. "What the fuck is wrong with you? I am so sick of you pretending like you were abandoned, not the one doing the abandoning. Calling me up begging me not to leave, telling me about shit you're seeing. You sound like Mom with Nana Catherine, cutting everyone out and then crying victim."

His words hit me like a dagger, as he means them to. They have the heavy weight of words left unsaid for years, rusted and old.

"I-I-I'm nothing like Mom," I stammer.

Devon explodes at the exact second I realize this phone call, the whole situation between us, has been a ticking time bomb.

"I know where you stay at these days. Hobnobbing up in Bay Cliff, making sure you wear what they wear, eat what they eat. Yeah, I remember you in school, Big Star, you think I didn't notice how you studied those people? All quiet, trying to fit in? How is that any different from Eddie? You're doing the same shit. Damn, you doing field service yourself. How many hours are you putting in, huh? To *maybe* someday be accepted. You gotta stop playing yourself."

"I'm nothing like Mom," I repeat, less convincingly. My grip on my phone is tight, my palms sweaty. Devon is unstoppable now, whatever cork he had put in place has come loose, and a tide of years of resentment spills out toward me.

"Yeah, keep telling yourself that. You've never once called me out of the blue in years, and now here you are bringing your drama to me, always with some notion of churning up the past? You and Mom can stay back there, trying to find the answers to your own fucking riddles while I am out here building a future. I have a life too, you know, in the here and fucking now. I got a job and bills to pay, shit that I'm saving for. I'm seeing someone! Hell, I even go to therapy. I'm working through my shit. If you stopped to think about anyone but yourself for two seconds maybe you'd already fucking know."

Three beeps signal to me that this phone call is ended. I've burned a lifeline, perhaps my only one. I had been drowning in that apartment with our mother, and I had to save myself, leap off a sinking ship. I wanted Devon to understand, I had thought he knew that it was every man for himself, but he thinks I left him there to sink. The panic that has been thrusting itself against the inside of my ribs pushes through the bones like jail bars and floods my system. I look around me, trying to get my bearings, but the lights are harsh and bright above my head. Walking room by room through the house I turn them all off, one by one by one by one.

—*

If people hear you haven't slept, they imagine waking up too early, sun in your eyes, alarm chirping like a morning bird. They think, *I know that feeling. I've been tired before,* they believe.

They don't know.

The tiredness first hits your eyes, heavy and fluttering hard against a wave of exhaustion. Then after a day or two, it hits your stomach and food is difficult or even pointless to consume. Days three and four begin to affect your balance, sentence construction, you have headaches that go nowhere, that resist all pain medication.

Life becomes very flat: a nighttime desert devoid of dunes. No rest for the wicked. Things you would have looked at with abject horror become nothing, boring, like a plain soft slice of white bread to be turned over in your hand. You seethe, quietly. Routines and the commonplace decompose at double time, like a meal abandoned in the heat. It is quiet until it is loud, and you realize you have been thinking what arteries you might sever if you plunged your fist through a window, whether the cold air would feel good against that hot skin and blood or if it would make it hurt worse but at least make you feel awake.

You can Google how much sleep you need to stay alive. You can read about all those people in Guantánamo Bay in the Frequent Flyer Program, and all of the people the CIA tortured. You can see how a person can buckle and break beneath the weight of exhaustion. Five hours can feel like too little sleep, but you can make it work. What about two? What about one? What if that one hour was diced up into segments, what if when you feel the desperate pull of sleep a scream of terror was heard and you weren't sure if it were real or imagined?

Sometimes, after a few days of no sleep, you will find yourself crying. Tears will be streaming down your face before you have thought to question them, hydration leaking from your body, which tbh explains the headaches.

For the most part you can pretend to be fine on four days of little sleep. It's day five that gets you. It's day five that's the line, five five five, look alive. When I was five I shucked and jived. Day five that's the day. That's the day the outer part collapses and the inner part takes over, hands on the wheel veering off into the night.

Once day five happens it's all over. Day five is where the magic happens.

12

Just as threatened, in a cloud of Baccarat Rouge, Buffy comes over. I am still reeling from my call with Devon when she knocks on the front door like she's the authorities, forgoing the doorbell. Buffy is the kind of woman who wears a silk neckerchief and stockings that she buys from an honest-to-God haberdasher. When she first met me, I think she was shocked that I was Black, I don't think she was expecting it. I was the first of Emil's girlfriends she ever met so it made sense, because if she'd met any of the others, she would have noticed a pattern. I had never really thought about it, this United Colors of Benetton array of exes of his. We'd met in one of the most diverse cities in the world, so it wasn't that odd, but Buffy's reaction to me (a constant look of assessment that morphed into barely concealed shock whenever I said something she thought was smart: *You're so articulate*) reminded me of Emil's whiteness, and what it meant in certain spaces. It meant we didn't fit. It meant we didn't make sense. We were aliens from different planets, not Venus and Mars, one of the other less romantic ones, but Neptune and Mercury, Jupiter and one of its moons.

Buffy enters my home and already I feel like the perfunctory tidy I did right before she came in was not enough. I think about vacuuming but she's here and it's too late for any second-guessing, besides my exhaustion has gone beyond my bones. I am tired down to my marrow. Buffy is all I have right now, I wince at the realization. She's here, and she disapproves.

"Hello, darling. Does my granddaughter have a name yet?" Buffy demands, trying to keep her tone light, but her comment is heavy. I have mismatched socks, and my sweatshirt is stained in some dubious infant substance. Poop? Milk? She removes her coat (an immaculate Eileen Fisher) and hands it to me, lightening my load in exchange by taking the blinking child.

"Hi, Buffy. No, no, we're still working on that," I stammer. I am used to her abruptness that borders on rudeness disguised as comedy, but today this shakes me. "We're close, though."

"I should hope so! Now what have you done with sweet girl's swaddle? Didn't they teach you how in the hospital? In my day, we took a class in school. My girlfriends and I knew how to swaddle a baby by the time we were twelve!"

She sweeps by me, seats herself at the large dusky blue sofa, lays my baby down, and starts to fuss at the blanket I have inexpertly wrapped her with. "Why don't you make some tea, and when you come back, I'll show you the proper way to swaddle. Then you can tell me all about the birth, now that it's just us girls."

I take a breath, look at the tiny child in her arms, and turn to hang up her coat. The shadow corner beckons, but I ignore it. My hands shake and I stretch my fingers open and closed to steady them. I chew over the birth in my mind—the pain that was like an inescapable explosion, like an ice cream headache, a cold but all-encompassing pain that took all the air out of my lungs. The attempts, like a ship at sea, to get on top of each wave, surf it, only to find myself drowning, reaching out for Emil's hand, the bed frame, anything, before finally screaming for an epidural. The misplaced shot, my inability to sit still while the hunk of an anesthesiologist tried to thread the biggest needle Emil had ever seen in between my vertebrae. The way I vomited, not neatly and primly into the provided bowl, but in dribbles down my own chest, and when the nurses tried to clean me up I pushed their hands away, I couldn't take another thing, I couldn't take another person touching me so that my baby was born and placed skin to skin on my breasts that were sticky and sour from my own stomach bile. And later, the maternity ward nurse who kept calling me *Mommy,* which confused me because no one had ever called me that, I was nobody's mommy. I was me; my name was written in marker on a whiteboard along with the date and time of birth, and the room number. But the nurse hadn't even looked at it. I wasn't Sofia, not anymore. I was *Mommy.* Anyone's mommy. The baby's, this strange nurse's, it didn't matter. What else could possibly have defined me more than the small child in the room?

I wonder what part of the story Buffy wants to hear, although I know the answer. She wants an abbreviated tale about the wonders of the female body, maybe even a confiding whisper about her son, and what an attentive husband he was. And that is what I shall give her. She will coo and say how different it was from her day, that Emil's father stood in the waiting room watching the baseball with other prospective dads, smoking and drinking and talking loud over the sounds of wives in various rooms. That the nurses brought around whiskey when the babies were born like underpaid waitresses while the men clinked glasses together in congratulations. I will let her tell me how lucky I am, I will let her tell me about the "husband stitch" she insisted the doctor gave her, how even when she was at her most vulnerable, she still was thinking of someone else's desires above her own. I will dig my fingernails into my palm to stop from slapping her. I will restrain myself.

"She has your nose!" Buffy calls in at me from the living room. I freeze in my position in the kitchen, getting ready to express some milk. I can hear her slurping her tea, even without turning around I can picture her with her feet up, thinking she is helping by holding a sleeping baby.

"You're right, she does," I say brightly, it has been a long time since I had a conversation with someone and I sound phony, like a talk show host, but Buffy hasn't noticed. She says nothing in reply, so I continue, "When I was younger I used to want to have a nose job. I'm so glad I didn't!"

Buffy is quiet, no agreement there, and I turn to see her through the doorway, frowning at my infant's nose. She sighs, boops it.

"Well, at least you saved yourself a lot of money!" she jokes. "You might need it for someone else in a few years!"

I grit my jaw and feel my back molars clash together and I hold them there, trying to shove the scream that is threatening to erupt back down my throat. I file this slight away to tell Emil, when he calls to ask how it went. I heave my Medela breast pump onto the counter in its sad little bag and begin to assemble the pump. Bottle, filter, nozzle, tube. Everything clicks together easily like I am an assassin in every single hit man movie, hidden away somewhere quietly constructing my weapon with a practiced ease. I attach it to my breast, switch it on, and wait for the tugging sensation.

Rrr-row, rrr-row, rrr-row. The machine whirs loudly, a mechanical sucking sound. I allow myself to get lost in it, zone out, but the usual white noise is interrupted and I hear a voice. It is talking, a squeaky falsetto tone. I turn to see if Buffy has heard too but she is on the sofa, scrolling through her Facebook page, probably resisting asking me to change the temperature on the Nest to a balmy eighty-five.

Kill-rrr, kill-rrr, kill-rrr.

I look around for the faces I have been seeing around the house, are they whispering sweet nothings to me? No, there's nothing. It must be the tinnitus I've been experiencing: the phantom baby screams I hear overlapping and overlapping and overlapping in my head in a collage of noise. I shake my head, willing my ears to readjust, but nothing changes.

Kill-rrr, kill-rrr, kill-rrr.

Killer? What did that mean, killer? Am I the killer?

"Sofia, this house is absolutely freezing. What do you keep it on? Turn it up, please, we don't want this baby to catch a cold," Buffy calls from the other room, oblivious to the fact that I could be doing anything else with my time.

"It's already pretty high, Buffy. Couldn't we cover her with a blanket?" I say distractedly, trying to tune out the pump for a minute. I pause for Buffy's response but there is nothing, just silence. She is waiting for me to come around to her way of thinking.

I know there is no way through this, and so I say, "I'll turn it up."

"That's the way, good girl."

I flick open my phone with my one free hand and stab at the screen to crank up the temperature on our thermostat app. *Good girl.* As if I am a dog or a child and not the wife of her only son, the mother of her only grandchild. I switch over to the other breast and I realize the pump hasn't stopped talking.

Kill-rrr, kill-rrr, kill-rrr.

It's not an accusation, but a command. It is asking something of me.

Kill her.

Kill her.

I rip the pump off my breast, secure the cap on the milk I have expressed, pack the whole thing away. I feel like something has snapped, something is gone and will not come back.

"Sofia?" Buffy enters the room, holding the baby in one arm with confidence. The palm of her free hand is firm on the counter next to me like a flag planted, as if she is saying that this too is hers. A shiver runs down my spine. *Someone walked over your grave,* Dominique would say, a phrase that both thrilled and scared me. I tear my mind from thoughts of the dead and turn toward Buffy, whose face is expectant in a way only older white women can be.

"Sofia," she repeats, as if I am a petulant teenager, "this house really is too cold for a newborn. You should be wrapping her in more layers."

I look down at the child in her arms, who is wearing a beanie and a onesie and is wrapped tightly in a swaddle. The snapped part of me feels jagged, sharp. I cannot hold on to this charade of normalcy for much longer.

"I turned the heat up already," I say, tight-lipped smile holding me together like tape. "It feels warm to me."

"Well, you probably have a higher base temperature, because of your ancestry."

I pause, smile faltering. "My ancestry? I'm from California, like you."

"You know what I mean, darker people are from closer to the equator, you keep the heat better," Buffy replies, as if this is logical, factual. Although, I think, wouldn't equatorial blood make me more susceptible to the cold, not less?

As if reading my mind, Buffy continues, explaining as if this is all very fascinating.

"Some things are genetic, like diabetes and high blood pressure. African Americans are predisposed to those things, aren't they? I imagine Black skin keeps the heat better too." She says this breezily, looking into my face with a neutral smile. I am supposed to absorb this, I am supposed to take her word for it. It would be easier if I did.

"I haven't heard that," I say tersely.

"I have some wonderful books you should read on it, all sorts of interesting facts about people from third world countries. Their genetic makeup is entirely different," she continues, turning from me to the baby, fussing with her beanie.

What books? I wonder. *The Origin of Species*? *Mein Kampf*? I long to text Emil this exchange but I can already predict his response. He will say she is from a different generation; he will say she means well. He will say she loves me, that she doesn't know many Black people.

Kill her.

I need to get out of this house.

Buffy has family who came off the *Mayflower.* The name of the boat is etched in U.S. history—it sounds fresh and dainty and beautiful, like her. She says it to show her allegiance to this country, her ties to the land. *The first settlers,* she says, omitting so much. Omitting what she wants to say, which is: *unlike you.* I'm reminded of all those eighties horror movies I watched as a kid, where the plot twist was always the haunted house being built on top of an Indian burial ground, but no one ever asked why the bodies were there in the first place, or who did the killing.

"Can you stay with the baby an hour or two longer?" I ask, ignoring the alarm in my chest at leaving my child with this clueless woman.

Kill her.

"Of course! You go off and get some fresh air." Buffy smiles odiously. "Maybe it'll cool you down!"

I imitate a polite laugh and head out of the room to text Dominique a time and a place. I grab my new coat, threading my arms through the sleeves as I slip out of the front door.

—*

In the months before I left for New York, which was also the year before Devon left home, Eddie had become suspicious and pressing. Despite her dedication to her faith, she had begun doing out-of-character, superstitious things—salt on the threshold, a spoonful of nutmeg in her tea before bed. She had begun talking about her mother, my Nana Catherine, who had long ago returned to Jamaica. We had never been, never even talked about the possibility of visiting. According to Edwina, we were African Americans and Witnesses, that was our identity. I didn't dare bring up the irony of the "African" part, which seemed strange to acknowledge if she wouldn't pay attention to the in-between point that brought our family here. If anyone asked, I would say my family was originally from Jamaica but what did I know about it? Nothing. All I had from my honeymoon visit was a rasta-colored beaded necklace and a large conch shell that was an unnatural shade of pink.

The first thing we hung on the walls of our house, freshly painted in Farrow & Ball Wimborne White, was a map of Jamaica that Emil bought, a reminder of where my people come from. I wanted to know something about it, anything at all. Emil surprised me with a honeymoon there, spending thousands of dollars and two delayed flights to arrive in Sangster International Airport, sweating from the heat that caused sweat to drip down my backside, down my legs. Baptismal. I loved it. I felt a part of a place that I felt was a part of me, despite my mother's best attempts. It was drenching me, welcoming. After all, the country's motto was *Out of Many, One People.* I belonged.

The Jamaican countryside flew by at breakneck speed. Moss grew on telephone wires, vines crawling up the poles to join it. Gray concrete homes flickered past, unfinished with metal rebar stabbing the sky like an unusual fern, empty rooms of unrealized potential. Cars passed us on one-lane roads, no one slowing down, honking horns in thanks. Ficus trees reached high, and clown-red hibiscus was everywhere, vines draped on trees like necklaces, in some places thick, more like toupees. It was a hair-raising car ride through the mountains, and then on through a village full of market stalls and young men leaning out of old Toyotas to talk to girls, dogs panting at the side of the road and laughter leaking into our cracked taxi window, and then we arrived at the gates of the hotel. There were people selling trinkets and bottled water on one side, and on the other, pristine pools and grounds that went right up to the ocean, to a private beach dotted with wooden loungers, each that came with its own butler.

After the busy scene we had driven through I was surprised there weren't more locals swimming in the water. Only a few pale tourists walked the shore, and the others sat around the pool bar, dressed in Gucci and Ralph Lauren. Before I could ask Emil if he noticed, a tall, lithe man in the hotel's uniform whites came to take our drink order. When he came back with two mojitos I asked him if everyone can swim here, and he had looked at me blankly, and I had the feeling he thought I was stupid. Yes, everyone can swim here, anyone in the hotel is welcome. No sharks, no jellyfish. The water is clean.

"I mean like, people who live locally," I clarified.

He had smiled as if understanding.

"No, no, no one from outside is allowed here, this part is just for you." My heart sank. He thought he knew me, what I wanted.

Emil bought the framed map, dated 1900, sixty-two years before Jamaican independence, for our first anniversary. For the first anniversary the Victorian custom was to give paper, he was proud of the idea, but whenever I look at it, I think of that trip. I think of the sterile hotel, I think of the waiters who smiled at us and whose names we never even asked. The shadows that fell long as the sun dipped, the tourists chasing the last of the rays. When I look at the names of the parishes, of Clarendon and St. Mary and Portland and Trelawny, I wonder where my family hailed from and feel the grief of not belonging.

—*

Eddie had never wanted us, that much was clear. She married my father because that is what you do. She had children because that is what you do. Her entire life had been dictated by the things she felt she was supposed to do. And once we were born, we were a chore; we were also earthly temptations, and she resisted us well. We were sinners destined for Gehenna and eternal damnation, berated with our failures for redemption.

Nothing I could do was right, nothing I did could impress her. I didn't know struggle; I didn't know pain. Her verbal abuse was rampant, she was sharp-tongued with words and quick, she knew just what to say to devastate me. Even after I left she echoed. It took me years to leave her voice behind.

Devon understood that our mother was an unfillable hole, that trying to make her love him would be like pouring bucket after bucket into an ancient well, and so he didn't. He treated her like a lamp, or a chair that didn't interest him. We talked of rebellion and escape in our snatched time together, but there was something duplicitous in this—the rest of the time I was a good Witness, well on my way to Pioneer status. In the dark I pledged myself to escape, but in the light I had to continue on the tightrope. Devon was never two-faced, when he looked at our mother, it was how you might look at traffic before you cross the street: a temperature read, a look for the gaps in cars so you can slip through unscathed.

That final year in the apartment was like living with a madwoman. Something had slipped for Eddie, that much was clear, but we couldn't work out what. She spent every waking moment out on the corners doing her field service, and in a voice thick with emotion she would plead until there were tears in her eyes for sinners to come into the truth. The elders at the Kingdom Hall stopped allowing her to go door to door because she got so many complaints, and other members of the organization began to shun her. Shunning was common then at our Kingdom Hall: a literal turning of the back whenever she walked into the room. She covered mirrors like she couldn't stand to face herself. When she decided that the vanity of hair was worldly, she cut her own short and, without the help of her reflection, she nicked her scalp. Without hair she looked smaller, cuspate like a pulled tooth, roots exposed and jagged. Our apartment was sad, our mother was sad, there was so little joy within those walls that we tried to spend as little time as possible there, me in the library or at Dominique's house, Devon in the park or walking the streets with his boys or playing basketball till it was dark out.

One evening we came home, streetlights outside the apartment window illuminating telephone cables like lines sliced against the night sky, and the kitchen was on fire. My mother was throwing handfuls of my grandmother's letters from an old battered suitcase onto an out-of-control flame in the trash can, screaming curses in a patois we had never heard her speak. Devon and I quickly put it out, but not before the ceiling was irrevocably charred, a black halo circling above the three of us. I had a realization that would have raised the hairs on my arms had I not burned them off—my father had left, and now I had no mother. Perhaps I hadn't for a long time, but that night clarity came to me. I was on my own, down there in the dark. No amount of prayer or divine intervention could change that.

So many stories were lost to us that night as my mother burned the only links I had to my remaining family. Had I known that my grandmother's voice echoed in that apartment through her letters, I might have been able to find her, I might have been able to make contact. The only thing I salvaged from that night was a half-burned envelope addressed to *Edwina* with a return addressee scarcely legible: *Catherine Hamil.*

Leaving isn't cheap. It requires planning. And although I had been sure that I wouldn't be under Eddie's thumb forever, I wasn't as prepared as I thought. Finding our father wasn't an option. When he left my mother he also left the Witnesses, and with it, all notions of parental responsibilities. He sent my brother and me generic birthday cards, signed with a hand we didn't recognize but assumed was his new wife's, and inside each was tucked a hundred-dollar bill. Devon spent his, hoarding his sneakers and clothing and other treasures at his friends' houses so that Eddie wouldn't discover them. But I saved mine.

—*

Buffy ushers me out of the house; I catch a glimpse of Susan in her yard, she is watching, always watching. The baby stays in my mother-in-law's arms, swaddled too tight per her instructions, which surprisingly soothes her. I am annoyed that Buffy knew something I didn't. Nestled in the muslin fabric the baby is calm for the first time all day. I have been given full permission to go and meet my little friend, have a lunch, hell, even a glass of wine! I could gulp down a glass right now, I am so thirsty.

Outside the house my hands feel embarrassingly empty, but the freedom I craved is impossible to grab with two arms and I feel aimless. I stand stupidly in the driveway, purse slung over my shoulder, as if I have forgotten something. A buzz in my hand reminds me of where I am and what I'm about, stock-still on the walkway of our house, and as I look down at my phone my heart leaps at the thought of Emil getting his timing right, and then swiftly plummets as I see another missed call from Eddie. I ignore it, shoving the phone down in the pocket of my long-coveted coat. I plug my earbuds in and choose a random classical mix, to calm me. I think back to Devon, to his words. The clear lines he drew from my mother to me, can everyone see them? Am I doomed to repeat some echo of Eddie with my baby? I feel less and less like the Sofia I am supposed to be every day. She is capable, knowing, together. She is nothing like my mother.

—*

For a few months out there on the East Coast I was a ghost. I worked long hours, getting home smelling of kitchen grease to watch endless movies, making up for lost time. Hiding out in my room in a dirty apartment shared with strangers was a far cry from the fantasies I had when I was cooped up in my childhood bedroom, daydreaming about freedom.

I would text Domi only shiny happy lies of life in New York and all the things we'd talked about doing there. We had promised each other that when we finally left the Bay Area that was where we'd go—as far as we possibly could without a passport. But then I left and she got into a West Coast college and had a reason she couldn't join me, so I remained alone. For six months I existed on kitchen scraps and chicken wings from the bodega I lived above that let me run a small tab. I was wasting away and found a type of sick pleasure in it, like it was punishment. I felt light, like I could slip through the cracks of this world, out into the atmosphere. I still prayed. It reminded me of Devon. I wanted to call him, but I didn't want anyone talking me into going back. And I still thought about the end of days.

There is some comfort to be found in your world ending. I had always imagined breathing a sigh of relief when it finally happened, as all of the sheep who had rejected the message of Jehovah were slaughtered. No more trying to be good enough, no more balancing act. I would be ash or I would be saved, no more in between, and it wouldn't be my mom deciding but Jehovah himself, and his 144,000-strong army of faithful. In the Bronx I felt both free and adrift, and I fluctuated between the joy of finding myself accountable to no one and the dizzying feeling that no one, absolutely no one, could save me. It was that seasick feeling that eventually drove me to the bridge.

—*

Susan waves wildly from across the street and despite the fact that I do not want to be lectured further by another old white woman about how parenting was different when she was a new mother, nor do I want to be interrogated about the baby's name, I find my legs betraying me, moving me swiftly toward her. I remove my headphones, Maria Callas's soprano loud in my hand as I shove them into a pocket. She looks at me, expectantly. I look back, wondering what I have forgotten.

"The baby?"

"What?" I reply, bewildered.

"Where is the baby, darling? I normally see you walk her around in that little carrier thing. In my day we had these big unwieldy carriages, the one my children used was the same one my mother used with me, if you can imagine! Back in the dark ages!" She twinkles, amused at her own joke. She looks at me, awaiting a response.

"Oh," I answer distractedly. "Yes. The baby is with my mother-in-law."

"Her *grandmother*!" Susan corrects, gleefully. She so enjoys having people all squared away with their little labels. I bet she has a label maker. I bet she has a pantry full of labeled jars. Dried pastas and grains, homemade jams.

"I suppose so, I've never really thought of her like that."

"'When a baby is born, so is a grandmother!'" she half sings.

"What?" I say again, feeling completely out of my depth, head swimming.

"A quote I have cross-stitched on a pillow, I'll have to show you some time! Perhaps I should get one for your mother-in-law. The new grandma! What's her name?"

"Buffy."

I feel pleased to have been able to remember this. The sky above me feels as if it is moving too fast. I feel as if I will keel over.

"Buffy. How darling. Well, I won't keep you. It's just that, well, Michelle Mulaney in 333 said that she saw your lights on late at night. Now, there are no rules against this, of course! I'm not here to scold you! We were just concerned and I wondered if you were having trouble sleeping so I brought you this . . ." Susan reaches in her woven basket, because of course she has a woven basket, and hands me a bottle of melatonin. "It's perfectly safe for breastfeeding."

The sun feels impossibly hot on my forehead and I remember that I forgot to put on sunscreen and that cancer runs on my dad's side of the family. I am probably multiplying malignant cells just standing here in the light, I am probably developing some nasty tumor as we speak, why else is my breast pump making murderous demands of me? It must be a tumor because if it isn't then I am going completely mad. Off my rocker. The ground is shifting beneath my feet, a boat capsizing, so I solidify my stance, touch my hand to my temple. I take the bottle, thanking Susan, making my excuses. She seems completely unaware of this sudden twist in the world's axis, and I am out of there, desperate to recalibrate. My brain feels on the brink of simmering, my skull is a slow cooker, my goose is cooked.

13

Moving through the city alone feels strange, as if I've missed something. I keep checking my pockets and purse for something forgotten until I realize it is the baby I am missing, and I resent that I feel lost without her already. Her absence leaves me feeling buoyant, as if I might float away never to be seen again. When I left the house Buffy was singing to the baby, her reed-thin voice crackling like an old record, something old and culturally Caucasian: "*Daisy, Daisy / give me your answer do.*" I only caught that line but it snagged somewhere in my brain and I can't shake it. As I step from the taxi the next line slots into my brain mechanically: "*I'm half-crazy / over the love of you.*"

I quicken my pace, sweating beneath my coat. I move through the park, past people picnicking on red gingham blankets, hot sun beating down, unseasonably warm and no one seems to care, no one, that it's too early in the year to be this warm, that somewhere off in Death Valley the mercury in the thermostats is already cresting into the nineties and all of this is wrong, a kite flies overhead like a hawk following me even as I scurry like a field mouse to the center of it all through the ornate tunnels that yawn like a giant maw toward the park's main concourse where a brass band is playing the national anthem, children are laughing running around waist height and I need to be still, the blood in my veins feels molten, fevered, nuclear. The kite is still moving above me, the wind knocking it this way and that like a blade twisting. If I could just sink my body into the fountain I could cool off, calm down, make some space in my brain for a clear thought. By the time I reach it and remove my coat, slip off my shoes, sit on the stone edge, Dominique is already beside me, purse in hand and sweaty.

"Sofia? Hey, what are you doing? Are you okay?" She tries to wash the panic off her face but it's too late, I've seen it. Domi tries to recover. "I know it's hot, babe, but it's not hot enough to climb into that. I can count at least four cigarette butts."

My foot hovers above the surface of the murky water, deliberating a second before pulling back. I pull my knees up, lean my head on them.

"It's hot."

"It's fucking hot. Where's the baby?"

"'*Where's the baby?*' I am so sick of people asking me that. Where's the fucking baby as if I am the sole responsible party. She has a dad, you know."

"Jesus, okay. I just meant I thought you were bringing her. Isn't Emil out of town for another few weeks?"

"I'm sorry, I'm tired. He is, he'll be back in a week or so." I sigh. "His mother is helping out. I use the term loosely."

Dominique smirks, sits down next to me, and tracks a cute skateboarder who rides by shirtlessly. She raises her water flask to her mouth, pauses, and asks, "What's her name again? Bitsy? Muffy?"

"Buffy."

"*Buffy?*" Dominique chokes, passing me the flask. "I knew it was something pretentious as hell, but Buffy? Lord, the audacity!"

"They say it's a nickname for Beatrice, but how?"

"*How?*" says Dominique in perfect synchronicity. She cracks up, and for a second, I feel as if the clouds are parting and the past is visible. Back when Dominique and I were the type of best friends who could kill a lazy afternoon in the park making fun of people without a second thought. My phone buzzes, the brief reverie shattered: my mother. I glance down at the screen pulled from my purse, but it is just a text reminder of an upcoming OB-GYN appointment. I put my hand over my heart to settle it; these calls from my mother are getting to me, I feel panicked at the thought of them.

"Is everything all right, babe?" Domi inquires gingerly. "You seem like you're not okay."

I would like to tell my best friend everything. The lack of sleep, the loneliness, the things I have been seeing. I would like to tell her about my conversation with Devon, let her comfort me, tell me he was wrong. I want to confide in her like I used to, to have her take me in her arms and make this stop, make me stop. I think about Lyla, her gorgeous, easy friend. Drinks in a bar is what Domi wants. Casual fun, people with no stress, no problems. I want to give her ease. She is smiling at me gently, a hand hovering lightly over my back but not actually connecting with my skin. Something about this infuriates me and all my desire to share goes away.

"I'm fine." I smile falsely. "It's just . . . new baby stuff. You wouldn't get it."

Domi falters and removes her hand from its hover behind me. I cut too deep, I think, but she seems to take it in her stride.

"Okay, if you're sure," she says. "I hope you know I'm always here for you, though. You're not alone."

You're wrong, I think. I am alone, and you're not here.

"Sofia, what's really going on?" Domi pushes on, straightforwardly.

I make an innocent face, wide-eyed and baffled.

"Woman. I've known you for too long for you to play this 'I'm fine' game with me. Tell me." Domi prods me with a finger and a confession comes out like a burst balloon.

"I called Devon," I admit, feeling an immediate relief.

"And?"

"I told him . . ." I contemplate telling her what I've been seeing, the hallucinations, the faces at the windows, but I am not my mother, this isn't the Bronx, I want to hang on to whatever semblance of sanity is at my disposal, she doesn't have to fix me again. "I told him I've been having a hard time and he kind of went off on me."

"What?" Domi says in disbelief. "What do you mean?"

"He kind of implied . . ." I say. "He said I only check for him when I need someone."

Domi takes a beat to ponder this, as if she feels the same way, I haven't asked her anything about her life lately besides what she volunteers.

"Hmm," Domi muses, a little later than I'd like, seemingly confirming my fears.

"'Hmm' what?"

"Nothing!" she says too loudly. "But when *was* the last time you spoke to him?"

I think back. I know when he got his new job, I for sure sent a *congrats!* text. When he was active on his Instagram page it was easier, I would just double-tap on his photo, sisterly love in digital form. Could it be that we haven't spoken since he called to tell me he couldn't make it to my wedding? Am I punishing him somehow for not wanting to come back to this side of the country? I know how hard he worked to get free of Eddie, I know why he doesn't want to be in her orbit, am I really holding this against him? I let my head fall into my hands, fingers gripping my hair a little too tight.

"Hey." Domi takes my fingers in hers, untwines them from my kinks. "Look. Sure, maybe you should reach out to him more often, but right now you are a new mom with a lot on your plate. I don't think we need to pile it on. Like I said, I'm here for you, babe."

"Are you?" I ask, feeling a distinct desire to blow something up.

"What's that supposed to mean?" Domi asks, defensively crossing her arms across her chest.

"Verve, Lyla? Just off making new best friends, people who don't have kids to care for and can just do what the fuck ever all day?" I can hear that I sound like a teen, but I can't help it. I want her attention, I want her to fight with me, anything. Domi surprises me and instead of yelling, she smiles, tilting her head to the side, that signature Domi move.

"Oh, because I went for a drink with Lyla that means I'm abandoning you?" Domi laughs.

"It's not funny!" I pout, unable to shake this childish mood.

"Come on now. We've been friends for way too long for me to leave you for someone who went to Barcelona for a long weekend *once* and now exclusively calls it *Barthelona.* I love you, girl."

I laugh despite myself, feeling a warmth that has been missing for the past week and a half. Domi pulls me in for a hug I don't want but I allow for my head to rest on her shoulder, for her to rock me slowly side to side. I try to remember the shadows but out here in the sunshine, in her arms, I can't remember what they looked like, or why I was so scared.

"You just need some headspace, more you time. Maybe make a

salon appointment, buy something pretty? You deserve it. You need to take care of yourself too!"

Maybe she's right, I think. Domi pulls me up from our fountain seat toward our favorite coffee spot. She talks lightly of her work, her apartment renovations, a far-off travel destination she's been researching. She holds my hand, fingers interlaced while in line for a coffee, orders a cappuccino in a faux Lyla voice to make me laugh, Italian twang on the third syllable. We drink the coffees in a parklet, sat on tall stools opposite each other, legs intertwined, close enough to lean on.

After Domi kisses my cheek, hugs me too tight, and heads off down Haight Street, I stand for a minute outside Amoeba Records, savoring the equilibrium she gave me. Legs stable now, I call an Uber and head home to Buffy and the baby. The OB-GYN appointment reminder jogged something in me, I try to recall what it is I am supposed to be doing for postpartum care. They told me something at the hospital, they gave me a printout, called it homework. Kegels were important. Whenever I remember, I try to do some Kegel clenches. I have some vague notions of a tighter pussy, a better core. I think of Buffy's husband stitch and involuntarily clench my Kegels. It seems insane to be thinking about the tightness of my vagina or the bounce-back of my abs when I feel like I just steadied myself and I'm vaguely aware that I am clinging to reality with a white-knuckle grip. I pull out my phone and delete Instagram. Done. Well, not Instagram exactly, but the icon. I have made it harder for me to click and see all of the eyes as I fall. Because I am falling. Despite the reprieve of Domi's company, a voice from within tells me I am free-falling into a place I have not been for years, and

I am scared and also, perversely, hungry with anticipation to get there, where it is dark. I don't remember my way around but I also know that once I arrive, the fear will subside and I will find the calm. Because right in the things you are dreading the most, right in your deepest fears lies a tranquility, an ease. Once I land there all forward momentum ceases; there will be nothing else, nowhere to go.

I get back to the house. Buffy walks me through, the child in her arms, talking about all the ways she would improve the space. She has a painter we would love, she has a molding expert from Italy, she could even get us a deal. She talks about the history of the neighborhood, speaks of my existence here like it is a privilege I should feel. I drift in her wake, trying to listen, feeling like a background extra in my own life. With Buffy around, I feel like I don't exist, my edges blurred. She is so certain, so resolute, she moves through the world with a self-assuredness that makes me seem clueless by contrast. I follow her around our house, picking up and putting down things she has pointed at, trying to understand. Anyone who touched me would go right through me. Eventually she hands me the baby and I feed her. She eats greedily, and I have the irrational fear that she will suck me dry, I will be a husk and nothing more, and then Buffy can discard my skin and take my place. As I tuck my breast back into my maternity bra, Buffy stands up and insists I get a little more freedom. I am promptly pushed out the door again like a wet nurse. I have done my duty and now I am to be relieved, off to do whatever a wet nurse does when she isn't feeding someone. I am supposed to be grateful for the free time, I am supposed to re-enter society as if I am the exact same person I ever was but my thoughts are running a mile a minute. Buffy gives me my freedom as if I can pick up where I left off, back to the old Sofia. What am I supposed to do? Where am I supposed to go? I would rather be lying in bed, in the dark, still and quiet, waiting for her to return to me, so we could reunite like Peter Pan and his shadow. Old Sofia had purpose; she knew where she was going. Ever since that Sofia left treatment she had a clear plan and knew what to do to build a life, to be a person. I miss the comfort that meeting Emil brought. Maybe if he was here, I would come back to myself.

I blame the sleep; I feel compromised by my lack of it. I cannot eat, and a feeling of weightlessness has become the norm. I glance at my nails and think of Domi's advice, settling on the idea of a manicure, because I always enjoyed a manicure. I sense a rising fear at the thought of leaving my baby alone any longer but I tuck it away and from the front lawn of our house I call an Uber to my favorite salon.

I find myself childless, staring forlornly at the rows and rows of nail polish. What color best imparts a feeling of maturity and responsibility? I fire off a text to Buffy, let her know where I am and how long I will be, although I know it is not needed.

"What color do you want?" says the technician designated to my nails, less a question than a statement.

"I don't know . . . I can't decide."

I gesture at all the choices, as if it means anything, as if hundreds of people do not stand in front of the same panel of colors and make a decision. The woman, black hair swept up high on her head in a messy bun, pink T-shirt with gemstones spelling out *G L A M*, sighs, gestures for me to stick out my hands and I show her both, arms outstretched like a zombie. She takes my hands in hers, gently, peering at the nail beds and cuticles. She strokes a thumbnail with her index finger and all at once throws my hands back at me, barks like an oracle, "Blue."

She turns to the panel of colors, plucks a fifties shade of baby blue, and shakes it decisively in her hand, paints one of my nails, and waits for me to inspect. I need to telegraph a message and I do not know what blue says about me, isn't blue for sadness? Something about saints and martyrs shimmers in the back of my brain. Still, I can't help but feel grateful that someone else is taking charge, that someone else seems to know exactly what I need, and so I nod over-enthusiastically, say, "Perfect!"

I pay before I sit down, anticipating the drying but still-wet nails that I will have in less than forty-five minutes. In the chair my fingers itch for my phone, I want to post a photo on my deleted Instagram, title it "mom time," but one hand is soaking in the warm water meant to soften my cuticles for trimming, and the other is being carefully filed and shaped and anyway I'm not supposed to be on Instagram. My breasts are inflating with milk, ticking time bombs, grenades at my chest, reminding me of how little time I have left. What is Buffy doing with my child, is the baby crying? Does she look up into Buffy's face and wonder who that is, are her eyes searching for me? What untold damage am I doing to her already? I place the thoughts out of my head and firmly barricade a door against them, focusing instead on a poster behind the nail technician's head. It is a softly rendered picture of pink rose petals falling, some a pink so light it is almost translucent, meant to give the impression of downward movement. A creamy white woman's face is upturned in the center, eyes closed, eyebrows perfectly arched. Her skin is flawless, poreless. She looks rested, her face holds a faint trace of a smile, and in her hand is a product that she holds close to her neck like a lover. She is content, washed with petals. The name of the product is inscribed in cursive, and although I know this poster is supposed to make me feel relaxed, supposed to sell me the product that will make me younger or plumper or happier or something, it fills me with a desire so deep and so thirsty that it turns into a crackling jealousy, a desert surface cracking beneath heat.

The nail technician is painting my right hand, smooth, determined strokes. The blue looks good, she was right. I try to settle into it, imagining what kind of person would choose this color, what kind of person the nail technician saw me as. My heart beats faster. The panic comes on like scattering pigeons, all flutter of wings and frantic motion.

I picture my baby screaming in the crib, mouth widening, my mother-in-law on the couch downstairs, immersed in her tea and Sudoku, firing off demands to Marta via texts typed out solely with her pointer fingers. A shadow person inside the house standing over my baby, ominous, translucent. Reaching down to touch her. The taste of ocean is in my throat again, memories from my dreams but come to visit in my waking hours. I can almost hear the mounting screams in my ears and even though a tiny logical voice in my mind tries to soothe me like I am a skittish horse, the panic builds until I am standing, nail technician looking up at me quizzically, and I move before they can stop me, I have my purse and my beautiful nail beds and one hand painted a forlorn, smudging blue as I hurry outside into the street to call another Uber to take me back home.

Out on the street, the sound of the nail technician in the doorway urging me back to my seat in my ears, I cough and cough and cough and do not stop until a burst of salty bile spills from my mouth and onto the pavement, undeterred by the blue-nailed hand trying to stop it and the blue is the blue of Mary Magdalene, an ancient blue, the blue of bereft mothers, a baptismal blue. The blues of the Adriatic Sea, water against foreign shores, far from home.

—*

Right after we first bought the house in Bay Cliff we made plans to visit, but I was running late from work to meet Emil and Buffy there, to get the keys and walk through the palace. Almost at the end of my second trimester and moving slower than usual, I had taken a cab that had gotten lost in the neighborhood. I didn't know where I was going either, so the driver and I both craned our necks out the window in the brisk winter air, going five miles per hour, trying to discern where home was. Eventually we pulled up, I bundled out, relooped my scarf around my neck. Emil's Audi and his mother's Mercedes were parked just out front, and I hustled up the walkway to the front door, ready to make my apologies for being so tardy. The front door was locked, they must have locked it behind themselves, forgetting about me by accident. I knocked and knocked, but no one came. It was getting colder, and the sun had already dipped low, casting a moody blue over the building. I stepped into the flowerbed and peered through the glass; hands cupped over my eyes. From this angle I was able to see them both, at the farthest end of the house, arm in arm and laughing at something private, something I would never get to hear.

Finally, I called Emil and he let me in, rubbing my shoulders to warm me, apologizing for not hearing the door. I walked into the empty house, footsteps echoing, and smiled a big smile at my mother-in-law, who made eye contact with my stomach before she did with me. I wanted to ask them what was so funny, I wanted them to tell me the joke line by line, but instead I just grinned like an idiot, explaining away the pinpricks of sadness in the inner corners of my eyes as a reaction to the cold.

The memory comes to mind as I walk up to the front door, ignoring the path and heading straight across the lawn because there is no time to waste. I imagine Buffy moving about in the living room, holding the baby like she's hers. Singing unknown songs to her, passing on plastic surgeons' phone numbers. I want to walk right in and snatch the baby, tell Buffy she doesn't have any claim to her, keep her far, far away from our child. She doesn't know anything about babies because she didn't actually raise Emil; she had a fleet of nannies to do the labor for her. A night nurse in the dark, a day nurse so that tennis could still be played, martinis could still be sipped. My keys fumble at the lock, I can never remember which is which. I imagine her dropping my baby, or not supporting her neck so that her head rolls back like a kid in a horror film, and I burst through the front door, but despite everything the house is calm and bright. No baby cries, no shadows lurk. Through the entryway I can see Buffy's feet on the couch, up on the cushions with her outside shoes on. I enter the room breathlessly, staring at her feet, fear immediately transmuted back to annoyance like a shapeshifter.

"That wasn't long at all!" Buffy starts, one foot moved down on the floor but the other still decisively tethered to my couch cushions. I am livid.

"Your salon is so much faster than mine, my goodness!"

"I didn't stay, I was worried about the baby."

"You didn't . . . didn't stay?" Buffy is sitting up now, eyes searching for my hands to verify the nonsense I am spouting.

"Where's the baby?" I state, an inquisition.

"She's sleeping! Where else would she be? What do you mean you didn't stay, didn't you want your nails done?"

"I couldn't relax, I needed to leave. I need to be home, she needs me. I need to watch her."

"Needs you? We had plenty of help when Emil was born. Perhaps you should consider hiring someone, there are all of these apps nowadays, it's very simple. You just have to be able to step away, allow time to get back to your old self."

I resist the urge to laugh. Back to my old self? Who was she?

"I just wanted to be home, okay?" I snarl, taking off my coat and heading toward the stairs. "I don't plan on having my child raised by a bunch of strangers. You can go."

"Sofia, I just want to help," Buffy says, earnestly. "You don't have to be alone, you know. It's perfectly fine to just say you need help."

Help? I think, and the word is tempting. She's right, I don't have to be alone. But I want to, don't I? It's what I know, it's how I thrive. Besides, it's too late for her to suddenly decide to be kind to me. Her presence is making me even more exhausted; I want her gone.

"I don't want any help from you," I reply without turning around, final like the grave, and that is the end of it. I hear Buffy mutter something behind me, gathering her things. I've done it, she's leaving. I shut myself in the baby's room and sit in the corner, vigilant and waiting, watching her sleep.

V

Remember where we started.

Sekesu, our first Caribbean girl.

Sekesu's daughter, Della.

Della's daughter, Agnes.

Then Agnes's daughter, Catherine, who was the first to leave the island. She was pregnant the very first time she was on a plane, looking down out of a tiny window at the greens and impossible blues of her island, being relegated to her past even as she soared, improbably, into the air.

Her grandmother was the one who taught her about the importance of grounding, slipping off her shoes to walk foot-to-earth, river silt squelching to make way for her toes. Her grandmother never cared about dirt or mess or if Catherine's clothes were marked in soil the way her mother did. Once, when Catherine was a child, her mother had slapped her, hard, for an unclean skirt. It wasn't filthy, just a little mud, enough to trigger her mother's temper, which didn't take much. Her mother was always worried about what Catherine's stepfather would think, but he never seemed to care about much except if they knew their scripture. It was a skirt Catherine had made herself and she had it packed somewhere beneath her on the plane, an old bedsheet that had been her parents' cut into triangles and stitched by hand, the small running stitch Catherine prided herself on because were you to look at the seams, it would be almost imperceptible.

Catherine's mother was a gnarled woman, not old but aged by anger and child-rearing, wizened like a walnut and just as tough. She was still raising babies well into her forties, sometimes back-to-back breastfeeding, it made her hard. But her grandmother was soft. Not soft like weak but unflustered, understanding, infinitely patient.

Catherine's grandmother loved their island, often taking her grandchildren to swim in the river beneath the bridge, standing in waist-high brown-green waters, smiling up at the sky, telling Catherine and her siblings about Mami Wata, the stories of Anansi, obeah and its power, things her own mother had taught her. A healer and gifted with plant medicine, she taught them about sinkle bible, how to cut it lengthways and press it to a burn, how the bitter taste of it lingered on your fingers for hours after. It was hard to believe that this woman bore any relation to the one who had birthed Catherine, because in Catherine's home her mother was strict, she was Bible-taught by a stepfather with little patience for softness, and in Catherine's home a woman's duty was to bear a child, to be quiet and serving. Nature was not invited into her home, it was to be shut out by the shades, brushed out with brooms.

Catherine's grandma taught her and her siblings what to eat and what not to eat out in the wild. Taught them how to shimmy up a palm tree, even the girls, even in skirts, to reach the freshest of still-green coconuts. Taught them how to slice the top off one with a machete bigger than their little arms, to get to the jelly inside, which they ate with their hands. Nutty, clear jelly that cooled them on hot days. She showed them a tree, big and tall above their child-heads, and then pointed to the ground where their mother's navel string was buried alongside those of her ancestors the day she was born, and the children marveled at this tree that was also part of them, and they were also part of it. All of the best things that Catherine knew about her island she learned from her grandmother, that tiny, bony woman with hard hands and light skin like cracked tan leather, hair white like sea foam, and a smile that left her mouth and traveled up to her eyes.

Near the end of her life, when the children asked her if she remembered, remembered how to heal a man like her mother had taught her, how to make it so the sun shone through the rainy seasons' clouds, how to be as strong as the wind and the moon, she would look sad and say she had forgotten. She would hold her bony bare hands up against the backdrop of the old cotton tree, examining them like the winter's branches, brown and gnarled, grandma's hands.

Catherine's childhood was cut short the day her grandmother died. For the funeral she wore what her mother had laid out for her to wear and sang the hymns she knew her grandmother would have kissed her teeth at. She waited until after the service and then she took off running, took off her shoes and her stockings and ran behind the smattering of houses that made up her mountain village and into the forest to find the tree, her grandmother's tree, and only then did she let herself cry. She cried for her loss, cried for the end of all the goodness and wildness she would ever be allowed, cried that the earth beneath her outstretched open hands held a part of her grand-

mother she could never access. Catherine's stepfather always said she had country feet, and she felt it as she slipped off her church shoes and felt her soles touch the dirt. Foot palm to tree, foot palm to tree, up and up and up. And if you climb high enough, if you dare risk your neck and the bottoms of your feet, you can have it all. The vantage, your pick of the fruit, the quiet that is rarely afforded to a girl with eleven siblings, so many precious things. Before she left the tree, she plucked a small jet-black pebble from the dirt at its roots and pocketed it, a tiny keepsake.

After her grandmother's death, the urge to run never left Catherine. In her haste to leave her mother's house, she ran into the arms of the first man who said he loved her. And he did love her, at first. Catherine mistook his lust for passion, his ferocity for dedication, his jealousy for a single-minded ardor. It wasn't until she was married, until she had taken the few things she owned and joined them with the few things he owned, that she realized he was a monster. A brute. Vicious with his temper, he had broken her collarbone during their first year of marriage, and her ribs followed shortly after.

Catherine crept around their small house, anticipating his every need before he had thought to think it. Sheets were straightened, meals were made, drinks were poured, all in absolute silence. Her mother had taught her well. She now understood a little more of her mother and the anger Catherine knew was loneliness, because she too was lonely in her new marital home. Eventually her husband would want what he wanted and would take it and in those moments she would feel even more desolate, but if she remained very still, if she pretended that the ceiling wasn't the ceiling at all but a painting, if she let the swirls behind her eyelids become patterns, she could see things that felt like premonitions: of a mother and a child, disappearing from all they had known and escaping their life to find another, which promised the freedom, safety, and joy Catherine had always wanted.

And sometimes, when she would feel her husband's heavy presence upon her chest in their dark nighttime bedroom, a shadow would come to her, whispering, showing her possibilities. She listened to the whisperings of the shadow figure as her eyes saw through premonitions like a crystal ball. The vision of how her torment under this man would end, and she knew it would have to end with her leaving her island. Catherine had tightened her eyes and willed the future to come into the present.

On Pan Am flight 76, with a ticket that had cost much more than her family and their church combined could afford, high up in the sky above the Caribbean Sea, Catherine opened the patent leather purse that had been her mother's and found the jet-black pebble, unremarkable in her palm. She held it tight and looked out at all of that water, the ocean an unironed tablecloth beneath her, and her island now reduced to a lurid green.

When she made it to America it was colder than she expected. At night, in the tiny room of a family friend's home that was made out of two shower curtains at right angles to each other, on an old mattress under older blankets, Catherine would dream vivid dreams. They would always be about her grandmother. She was a tree in these dreams, tall and thick but always bare. The wind would pick up and it would blow her branches so that it seemed like she was shaking her head once more at Catherine's forgotten knowledge. What becomes of those familial ties when they are cut? Can you find your way back, or are you lost forever? In America, Catherine often felt like she was gasping, a lack of oxygen that she knew would only be solved by go-

ing back home. But still Catherine didn't go back, and she wouldn't return to St. Ann's Bay for twenty years, until she knew for certain that her husband was dead, but by then the navel string that attached her to Jamaica was a dry rind, and there were no more ties to hold on to.

14

I wake up, which makes me think I was asleep. It feels difficult to believe since my eyelids are as heavy as storefront shutters. I don't know what day it is. My mouth is dry and chalky tasting, like I have a mouth full of ash. My T-shirt is soaked from my breast milk, but my breasts remain solid and still full. My head hurts, I explore my scalp with my fingers, searching. I find the tender part and it only takes me a second to remember that I had sustained this injury the evening before, when I punched myself as hard as I could in the head to keep myself awake, stop myself from screaming. I cringe as I remember last night, after I ran Buffy from the house.

I had stayed awake for as long as I could because staying awake is better than severed sleep. Maybe I was asleep and I dreamed the whole thing? I have memories of walking the hallway to the stairs to the living room and the whole entire time, a noise followed me from within the walls, or maybe behind them. I remember the sound of drums, distant but familiar. As I sit in my half-awake-ness trying to cling to the remnants of what must be a dream, it vaporizes. Despite the sleep I must have had, I am still so tired my exhaustion feels flu-like. My muscles ache and I am sluggish; the snatched moments of rest only served to highlight a deficit.

The baby is asleep next to me in her bassinet. I try to decide if I should risk relieving my aching breasts by feeding her, but she dozes so soundly it feels criminal to wake her. I should lie back down, try to sleep more, but it feels pointless. It'll take me forty-five minutes to relax and it'll take her forty-six minutes to wake up. I yank myself up, using whatever shred of abs I have left under the loose sack of skin my stomach has become. It is neither fat nor thin, it is just skin, an empty house abandoned. She could probably fit back in there, I think. I could probably tuck her back up and seal her in.

The next morning, during the second week, eight days till Emil comes home, I find myself propped in bed, sun pushing its way around the blackout shades we bought specifically for the baby, with big, heavy, wet boobs. I smell like a dairy. I order nipple pads off the internet, off a site I swore I would never use, unwilling to line the pockets of another heinous, petty billionaire, but here I am, seized by agoraphobia, ordering tiny little things to be brought to my door like offerings.

I develop an affinity with dairy cows. I will no longer buy cow's milk, I decide; I find it upsetting. All that liquid gold meant for a baby's mouth and here we are, adding it to coffee and cereal like it is ours. I consider becoming a vegan but cheese seems to exist in a different category for me, it is one of a few things I can eat that doesn't make me sick, that I can shove in my face and feel nourished.

I undress the baby, I clean the baby, I redress the baby, I feed the baby, I rock the baby. The pump is always out on the kitchen counter but I am afraid of it. I feel certain it will talk to me whether I want it to or not, and I'm not sure what I'd prefer. If I can build up enough of a bank of milk, I think, perhaps I can apologize to Buffy and she could come by for more than two hours. Perhaps I could go out, take an exercise class, go for a walk, eat a leisurely lunch, spend a day like so many of the women in my neighborhood, in luxurious solitude, indulging in things that do not feel like an indulgence if you do them often enough. Fifteen-dollar lattes with hearts in the foam, croissants freshly baked and filled with unpronounceable pastes, a new white shirt in alabaster, preshrunk and preworn. Quebecois cheese aged for seven years at $44.99 a pound, hyperoxygenated water for $24.99. A Dries Van Noten brown-belted satin twill skirt. A bone hair clip, a mug made by a local ceramicist, coffee from Nicaragua, and leather sandals from Greece. A biodegradable phone case, the phone itself unbiodegradable. A $22 martini with imported olives, an uneaten heirloom tomato salad for $30. A secondhand copy of a first edition, money dropped like it is nothing, tiny purchases barely making a dent in the bank account. Perhaps I would meet myself again, up there at the register.

As a child I was fascinated with wealth, sneaking peeks at magazines in the grocery store while my mom shopped, staring at the popular girls in my class in all of their Abercrombie, and I would listen to them talk till I knew the prices, knew where to buy them. Devon was right—I studied the way they spoke, always hoping to fit in, to be the good girl. I was studying so that one day, when it was my turn, I would know what to get. I would know what to do. Although my mother didn't come from money and didn't care for material things, we shared a desire to belong. I looked at these shiny new objects calling out to me, each one a platform, a step away from my stale family.

For Edwina it was a life of service that called out, a life of loving an invisible god instead of the flesh-and-blood children desperate for even a drop of affection. I turned to the items that could bring me some kind of joy, even if it was fleeting, even if the next dopamine hit would need to be bigger, more expensive. For a moment I could become someone else, shed the trappings of a life on the poverty line and transcend, caterpillar into butterfly. Like the ugly duckling into a beautiful swan, soft white coat donned, above it all.

—*

As we cross into the final week mark, I realize I do not miss Emil and I feel bad about it. His nightly check-ins have fallen off, which is my own fault; I have declined his calls with a swiftness, the ringing of my phone makes me jump, I assume it is my mother. I have used the baby as my excuse countless times. And for his part Emil does not protest, probably relieved to not have to listen to my seething silence, my quiet sobs, my obvious reluctance to speak to him. This way he can live in his fantasy work bubble, showing people photos of the baby, or that one shot of me looking giddy in my hospital-to-home outfit, a duck-egg-blue cashmere loungewear set with a choirboy collar, hair combed and off my face, which glows like they say it should. Hormones glittering beneath the surface. The outfit I had bought in a last-minute frenzy—preppier than my usual style, it made me look like I was from a time of words like *hysteria* and *transorbital lobotomies*, too prissy and buttoned-up but it was what I thought a mother would wear. That photo is a testimony to the last time I remember smiling big and wide—I'm perched at the edge of the hospital bed, baby in my arms improbably small. A happy photo, one I can imagine mounted and framed. Emil can live in this photo if he doesn't want to hear my voice, hear my emptiness. He can live with his beautiful, clean, well-dressed wife and his frozen, silent baby forever.

Here in real life the screaming is so constant I hear it ringing out even when she's eating and her mouth is too full to manage more than a satisfied whimper. It is a high, high whine that refuses to cease, even when I cover my ears, even when I hit my head with the flats of my palms over and over in the night as she sleeps. I change sloppy diaper after sloppy diaper, losing count at twelve, dutifully washing my hands afterward so that at the end of each day my palms are dry and devoid of oil. I have a thought, somewhere in the recesses of my mind, to get out of the house, see a tree, witness a flower, but the day escapes me through the endless wheel of care on which I am stuck. I feed her I burp her I clean her I dress her I nap her I pick at my teeth noncommittally with floss, I change my industrial-size pad, which is no longer needed but which I still switch out because it feels like self-care, I try and fail to remember what self-care meant to me, before.

In the afternoon I find myself standing out on the front porch and staring, unable to imagine leaving. I cannot envision stepping down into the street, the fresh air would rip into me, tearing my limbs apart. I belong to the dark now, to the four walls of my grand house. But I like to look out the window, I like to watch my neighbor bring his trash cans to his driveway, over there, across the street. I like to see all of these funny people doing these funny things like they matter, like they care. From the threshold I take a big breath of the outside air that is almost too fresh to my lungs, like I am an avid smoker taking a break climbing Mount Everest, too crisp too clear, I may die if my lungs expand too much. A little is fine, I just can't breathe too deep. I imagine myself asking my neighbors for help, how stupid I would sound. A woman with my means; I should have nannies and housekeepers. When I open my mouth to scream at them, to get their attention, nothing comes out. I remember that it is not *help* we should yell, but *fire. I'm on fire*, I want to yell, *pull me out.*

Eventually, when the sun dips back down and I have let go of any notion that I might get dressed, I stand in front of the refrigerator chiseling a hunk of cheese with a spoon, because all the knives are in the dishwasher. I am not hungry but know I should be. My only constant is my incredible thirst. I clutch the jumbo hospital-brand Big Gulp and fill it with icy cold water, ready to sip as I wander around the house, socked feet padding silently, doing a lunge every now and then when I remember. The silence comes easy. Stepping carefully around my house so as not to wake my baby feels like muscle memory from childhood when I was expected to be good and silent. Heel toe, heel toe, heel toe, one foot in front of the other. Carefully along the high wire. Don't look down.

Maybe getting back in shape would make me feel more like myself, maybe I could starve myself out of this funk. Maybe calorie counting and run tracking would feel familiar, I've done it enough times that it should. I could get one of those Thule running strollers, I could be one of those moms who bounce back, back from this lonely pit, catapult myself into the light and sun where my brain is rested and my body holds no more surprises for me. Emil could come back and be stunned, reach for my slender waist, my toned stomach, thighs that are at once strong and vulnerable. There might be a redemption in that, I think. If I had something to focus on maybe the shadows would stop, maybe the noise would become quiet.

I turn the cheese I am eating over in its package and read the calories. So many. I calculate how much of my daily allowance I have just eaten up and how much remains. Too much math, I can't be bothered. The thing saving me from myself is math, I think. I can barely tell the time these days. I'm not starting an epic calculus experiment with the end goal of weighing less. I take another bite of the cheese, close the fridge, and almost on cue the screaming commences. The cheese sours in my stomach.

—*

I remember Genesis. *In the beginning.* I think often of Eve, and her first sin. Eve was stuck in the quagmire, never to be redeemed. I too feel like I am in a swamp, stuck in cartoonish quicksand. Each day is spent adapting to it, and if I am ever able to disentangle myself and walk among the rest of the world, I am supposed to describe the swamp as a piece of cake, a walk in the park. No one must ever know about the swamp. Even after being disfellowshipped, here I am in the dead of night, splitting myself between the light and the dark, the sun and the moon. Can I undo what was done to me, and Devon? Tell me if I'm warm, tell me if I'm close. Help me understand.

—*

And then out to the street with people passing you, on their way to jobs and dates and places you'll never ever know about because all you know are the paper cuts from the pamphlets, the cold against your legs even in your wool tights beneath the heavy skirt, heel toe heel toe one foot in front of the other hair pulled back face exposed dragging the cart behind you full of literature, which is what you all call it as if it is Twain or Brontë or Baldwin, but there are things to be learned and that's what you tell yourself, that's why you drag it out here in the cold to stand on the street trying to catch people's eyes, trying to say with your own please believe me, it's coming, the end is right around the corner and I want you to know I need you to know because if I save you then I save me too, smile smile smile, dot dot dot dash dash dash dot dot dot, but you are a drab streak of gray in a world of whizzing color, you see Alanis Morissette's video for "Thank You" on MTV at Domi's house and you recognize yourself in it the whole world moving and you are naked and stock-still, stuck down, sinking sinking sinking and no one to pull you out and that feeling is something that follows you to the end of the earth even later when you escape even later when you think you're free every other step feels sticky, like it's got you again. At the wick of you, that is all there is.

—*

I decide that what I need, what I truly need right now, is to see someone who understands. I find my hidden Instagram icon and search anew for Amina. Still nothing. Frantically, I go to LinkedIn and find her after a few minutes. I should have looked here first. She is the executive director of a nonprofit, of course. Her headshot is kind, hair wrapped, eyes crinkled. I screenshot and zoom in on her profile picture, her face as warm and open as I remember it. I stroke the screen, imagining her feeding me apple slices, hugging my head against her breast.

With her LinkedIn avatar solidified, finding her through the dozens of Aminas on Facebook becomes easier. Her Facebook page is boring in a comforting way. Halloween photos of children dressed up, long-winded captions, and bountiful hashtags. I Google her, I find her office number. I call, get the voicemail, leave a message. I message her on Facebook, I follow her on LinkedIn. I find a dot org email address. I send an email. I describe, in detail, the shadows in my house. She'll want to know, I think, so she can help. I tell her about my mother's calls, I ask her to explain them. I ask her to come over. I send my address; I send my phone number. I snap a photo of myself, so that she knows who I am. I attach it. I send it.

An hour passes before I remember that she could be in the park. I think of Amina, imagining her on that same park bench as if she had never left but is frozen in tableau waiting for me to return and reanimate her. I prepare to leave the house, feeling a thrill of blossoming friendship.

The last time I felt such a thrill was with Dominique. She was the only kid in school who did not see my family's status as Witnesses as a deterrent. Domi's home life was a fantasy—her mom, Sabine, was an ex–ballet dancer, fun and light and prone to pirouettes in the kitchen with two small girls. We would watch her favorite movie, *The Red Shoes*, over and over during the holidays, which of course my family didn't celebrate. My favorite part was the ending, when Vicky's red shoes dance her out of the theater, out to the train tracks, and the ballet impresario Boris Lermontov tells the waiting audience, "Victoria Page will not dance *The Red Shoes* tonight, or any other night." The drama of it all. The red shoes had made Victoria's decision for her, finite and bloody. Domi was an only child, and her parents loved her and each other with such an unambiguous clarity that it shocked me. I didn't know that families like that existed and they seemed like good people, even if they were destined for eternal fire and brimstone. I was immediately one of them, absorbed so completely that whenever I could escape my own sad family, a place would be laid at the table for me. I would have followed them to the ends of the earth. You could call it loyalty, but really it was desperation—desperation to be liked, to be loved, to be seen. When Dominique's mom died of cancer our senior year of high school I mourned Sabine like my own mother, I held Domi like a sister, sobbing for a life that wasn't mine.

My park friend Amina feels like a drug, and one huff might get me through the evening and this sense that I am drowning. Dominique doesn't understand what it means to be a mother, I need someone who knows. I need to share the unspeakable with her, the things that have been going on in this house. Maybe she will have answers, maybe she will rush to the house with a crucifix and a vial of holy water, cast out the demons, celestial light surrounding her like a halo. Maybe afterward when the house is clean again she will find a family remedy for me, make it on the stovetop, a brew thick with herbs and stinking but I will drink it and she will tuck me into bed and kiss my forehead. I feel high already on optimism alone. My grip is slipping and soon I will be free-falling, but if I can just see Amina, if I can touch the edge of her dress and heal myself, even temporarily, I will be new again.

I check the time, the large clock above the stove reads two thirty P.M. I vaguely remember leaving school at this time, it sounds right. Fuck it, I think. I change the baby and strap her on, throw my birthday coat over my shoulders, slip into my sneakers.

I am striding out the door, baby at my chest, so thrilled to have a goal, so thrilled to find some common ground, that I nearly bump head-on with Ruben. His mailbag is slung over his shoulder and two letters and a flat-looking parcel are in his arms, clearly destined for my door.

"Oh! Ruben! Hi!" I say breathlessly, trying to look normal.

"Hi there. How's the little one?"

He smiles at me, unperturbed by our haphazard collision.

"Good. Good. Nice day today."

"The rain is coming, though!"

"Well," I say, reaching for the cliché as I stride by him, "we need it."

"We sure do!" he replies, and waves me off. It is humid and the rain feels close.

I panic at the park when I don't immediately see her, until I notice some violently red hair bobbing along the monkey bars. I wave stupidly at the child, who seems utterly oblivious, and I look around for his mother. I see a man, stern-looking, tall and bald, attending to what can only be Ethan's sister, a redheaded girl with snot barnacled around her nostrils.

"Hi, excuse me, hi." I step intrusively toward him, rapidly thinking of a way to make what I am about to say sound ordinary. "Is this your child? I mean, are you Amina's husband?"

The man frowns at me, puzzled, and answers slowly, "Yes?"

"I'm Sofia. I'm a friend of your wife's. I mean, kind of. We are kind of new friends."

"Oh, hi?" The man softens slightly, trying to place me. "Have we met?"

"No. No, but I wondered if Amina was here? I needed to talk to her but I don't have her number. I emailed her but it's kind of urgent."

"She's not, I pick the kids up on Monday."

It is Monday today. This is good information to have.

"Oh, right. Okay . . ." I feel awkward, like this was a mistake. My fingers stretch and release frantically, I can feel the cold mania seeping through my joints and I don't know how long I can hide my metamorphosis from him, I have to be quick.

"How did you say you know Amina?"

He is suspicious, I can tell. I can feel my hair escaping from its loosely wound tie, I know that the collection of clothes I am wearing do not make an outfit, that my gray-ringed eyes betray any touch of normalcy I might attempt. I put my hands on my hips anyway, authoritatively and for effect, like I am just a mom in a playground speaking to a parent.

"From here. From the park. She was really nice to me the other day, gave me some advice about being a new mom."

Here I touch my baby tucked in safe and warm against my body, beanie hat with matching booties on her tiny frame. This works as if it were a magic button and the tension in the man's brow eases.

"Oh wow! Congratulations!" His face is kinder when he is smiling, his two front teeth are slightly crooked, which is endearing, and I imagine him and Amina on the sofa together after the kids are in bed, her socked feet in his lap, him absent-mindedly rubbing them while they talk and drink wine.

"That is a tiny baby! How's it going?"

"Great!" I lie, knowing that I could sour this sudden goodwill with an admission of the truth.

"I miss the newborn phase so much. You were this little once," he says, looking down at his daughter still fussing with her Velcro shoes, trying to get the straps to align perfectly. She looks up at him nonplussed, still incredibly congested. "You were! Six pounds, three ounces. It's a magical time, treasure it!"

I've changed my mind. I do not like this man. I could hurt this man. I have to keep this moving, connect the dots to Amina, before the mask slips and I show a side of me best kept in the house.

"Do you think I could give you my number? To pass on to your wife?"

"Sure. Here." He passes me his phone, open to the notes app. "Put your number in."

I pound it in frantically, give him what I hope is a good smile, a trustworthy smile. Almost in response the rain begins, lightly at first, but then so heavy that he gathers his children under his coat like a mother hen, ushering them to their parked car. I wave a goodbye at his back, covering the baby's head with my folded arm, and dash back toward our street. I kick myself the whole way—I should have taken her number because now the ball is in her court and I am back to waiting, waiting for a prophet.

15

On the walk home the name of Amina's place of work comes to me like a bolt of lightning. I find the address for office hours. I scribble it down on a scrap of paper from my purse and fold it three times, sliding it into the pocket of my Acne canvas overalls and do a one-eighty, headed to the part of town her office is in. I once saw a woman wearing these exact overalls as she crossed Grant Street toward Maiden Lane. She looked so effortless, she was alone but had this amused look on her face, as if she was thinking of a secret joke and playing it over in her head. She was a bubble of happiness drifting through the city, and I couldn't tear my gaze from her. I had pulled out my phone immediately and looked at the Net-a-Porter website, found them in my size, and ordered them feeling an immediate satisfaction.

Amina's workplace isn't too far, twenty minutes, I can walk, the rain poured for only a few seconds and now it is light enough to feel refreshing. The baby is still attached to me, head protected beneath the baby carrier's rainproof hood, and I have plenty of time to consider what I am doing. I should have left her with someone, but there is only Buffy and I don't want to call her. Besides, the baby is asleep. Who knows how much time I have before she wakes and begins her demands, a literal time bomb. Maybe Amina will be moved by the baby, sit me down and shush me when I apologize for calling so much. Or maybe she will sit me down on her lap and stroke my hair. The building is turn-of-the-century, ornate and solid, and a plaque indicates that it was once an almshouse opened in 1866 to house all of those desperate gold-rush-seeking souls, the ones who couldn't strike it rich. The ones who couldn't face going back to where they came from and saying they had failed. I imagine them arriving here, the scarred and forever changed hillsides receding behind them, stinking of dynamite and earth, to land at this place and finally admit defeat.

The building is bustling with interns and staff, people who look like they know where they are going and why. I turn to the building directory that is inlaid on beautiful old wood, probably mahogany, maybe oak, definitely the type of wood that needs to be imported here now. I try to calculate the cost of paneling a large hall like this as I scan the list of names but stop when I find an *Adjoa-Doyle, A.* in gold inlay near the bottom of the directory. Room 304, third floor. I repeat it like a spell as I climb the stone steps up and up and up, 304, third floor, 304, third floor, 304, third floor.

By the time I reach Amina's floor I am out of breath, sweat glazes my forehead, sticking the baby hairs down with it. I do not look presentable. I try to iron out my overalls with my hands, I readjust the diaper bag on my shoulder. I would feel freer if I didn't have the baby, here, strapped to my chest. *And ain't that the fucking truth,* I think. But the baby *is* the explanation, the baby is my pass. Amina will understand, I soothe myself, and the drunken heat of worry dissipates. Her door has a frosted-glass window that looks like it would feel good to touch, but I don't, I resist, I act normal. I feel underdressed in this building full of stylish twenty-somethings, but I don't need to worry—I am invisible to them, like high school all over again. An apparition in a hallway, nothing to see here.

I open the door unceremoniously, catching it on the lock on the first try so that I have to twist the handle again noisily. The rattle causes Amina, who is seated in a swivel chair facing away from me, to turn. I smile at her and try to ignore the clear *what the fuck* she mutters under her breath as she stands. She is wearing an immaculate suit, royal blue, Sergio Hudson and a printed Gucci headscarf I don't recognize, it must be vintage, probably cost a fortune or maybe it's a family heirloom, maybe she has a glamorous mother to hand down beautiful, precious silks and pearls of wisdom.

"Amina," I say, breathlessly. Now that I am in front of her I am at a loss, what was it I needed? What was it I wanted to say? I grin at her, too wide, and I can tell by her face I am menacing, I am not warm. I am an animal baring its teeth as a warning, and she holds tight to the back of her swivel chair, keeping it between us.

"Hi . . . It's Sofia, right?" Amina's voice immediately soothes me, the hairs on my arms rise in response and I feel the overwhelming urge to hug her. She is appalled, dark eyes wide, but I can see she's holding it together, for me. She makes eye contact with the baby in the carrier, softens. I'm touched by her concern. "I got your messages, I'm glad you felt you could reach out, but . . . Is there someone I can call for you? I can tell by your emails that you're having a hard time. I think I remember that your husband is out of town, but is there someone else, your mom, a therapist?"

I take a step toward her and this stops her as she tries to be the good Samaritan. It spooks her. Stupid, stupid, stupid. I have to slow down. She inches toward the phone, abandoning this approach.

"Can you step back, please?" Amina says shakily. "You have got to stop calling me. And emailing. I don't think I am the person you need right now."

"But you are! Look, I'm sorry, I know you're busy. I think the last voicemail I left you before you blocked my number . . . I think I didn't express myself properly. I felt it was important to explain in person," I stammer, getting closer still.

Amina edges away from me toward a phone on her large desk. Without taking her eyes from me she lifts the receiver, and with a heavily diamond-laden ring finger she stabs the number 6 on the phone, waits a beat, and hangs up. Some invisible cavalry has been summoned, and I know I am on borrowed time, I have to get to the point, if only I can remember it.

"Look, I understand, life is tough." Amina shifts her tone but still sounds fatigued, a mom on the edge trying to get her kid down at bedtime. "But it's tough for all of us. I'm a working mom, I know I look like I'm all put together but I struggle too."

I step toward her, ignoring my hurt at the way she steps back again, her back almost to the wall.

"I'm not going to hurt you," I think to clarify, gesturing at the baby on my chest as if in explanation, laughing to indicate how silly this all is. The laugh is hoarse, like gravel. "I just wanted to see you. I wanted to tell you I think we could be friends."

"Friends?" Amina repeats, confused, eyes on the door behind me. "I don't think it's friends you need, I think you need someone else. A doctor or something."

"I've seen doctors before, a long time ago," I confess eagerly. "It doesn't cure anything."

Amina noticeably relaxes as the office door finally opens and two men in cheap security uniforms come in. The power balance shifts and Amina stands up straighter, folds her arms. The security guards are wearing white shirts that are almost transparent, you can see their undershirts, which makes me pity them, and the pits are yellowed where they have sweated through because the heat is stifling outside. They get closer and I can smell them near to me and it activates some lingering morning sickness, I want to gag. I look around at them, disgusted.

"This woman can't be here. She shouldn't even be on site. Can you remove her, please?" She speaks over my head, as if I am a child.

"I just want to talk," I beg, as the two men try to move me out of the room. I stand my ground.

"I don't want to talk to you, I don't even know you!" Amina shouts, emboldened and furious. "I have enough friends, please stop fucking contacting me!"

"I don't want to be alone! I think you could help me!" I am feeling hysterical, the heat of the day starts to wear on me, my coat feels too much for this sun-warmed day, these old turn-of-the-century buildings never did work out air conditioning.

"I don't fucking *know* you! Get the fuck out!" Amina snaps, whatever was left of her patience is long gone.

The baby strapped to my chest begins screaming and this seems to snap Amina out of her anger, and for a brief moment she looks tender. I know she didn't mean it. I'll call her later and tell her as much. The two security guards finally guide me out of the room doing all they can to avoid the conjoined baby, and even though Amina yelled, even though she made it clear she doesn't want me, I saw a glimmer of remorse and now all I want to do is get back to her, to reason with her, to make her understand that I just don't want to be alone.

Before they escort me and the baby, who has been settled slightly by my movement, out of the building, the security guards take my photo and add it to a list of people not permitted on the premises. I try not to think too much on the ethics of being borderline arrested while wearing your newborn. There isn't time to dwell, and besides, the security guards are not police, that much is clear. They are older and already sweating from escorting me out, wide around the middle in a way that tells me I could outrun them, even in my current state, and making a call to CPS is something that would involve paperwork and overtime and who wants that? I feel certain they won't make any further calls, and no one will follow up. I feel sure, as if I have been here before, done this before. And as I predicted, in their tiny prefab office, instead of phone calls I watch them pin up my mug shot on a board full of other delinquents, the smell of their overworked bodies is dizzying in such a small place. When I leave their office dusk is approaching. I stop to feed the baby on a park bench on the way back home. The clouds threaten to open up again so I cut the feed short and run as fast as I can with a baby carrier on, my coat off and draped over the baby's head. I hold her tight against me like she is still in utero, and we are one. The rain chases me back to Sea Cliff, back home. My feet strike an uneven beat on the pavement beneath me, my breath ragged, and I feel something slip away, out of reach, as I get closer to some unseen conclusion.

—*

I get home and hang my damp coat up, rote, going through the motions. The minute I get inside the door, the rain stops, having done its work of getting me back into this cursed house. The last of the afternoon's sun pierces the gloom and catches the cut glass in the front door, casting askew rainbows across the entryway. I see the coat in this light and it is filthy, it looks like an animal pelt from the pioneer days, as if I have traversed a country in it, as if I have discovered uncharted territories in it, as if it was my skin, my fur that I have shed. The baby has made a mess of the neckline, spit-up-and-drool encrusted. I intended to spot-clean it, I thought it could be salvaged but now it is a flag, stabbed into the ground, marking a madman's land. I can scarcely recall how much I wanted it, at the beginning, agonizing over the price. I thought it would say something about me, how far I've come. It says something all right, but not anything I want said aloud. Not anything I can bear to hear.

—*

I take advantage of the silence; the rain has cleared the atmosphere and the sky is darkening. It is almost a reasonable bedtime, and I finally decide that one of Susan's melatonin would be okay, just one 5 mg, I was so chaste during my pregnancy that 5 mg will probably knock me sideways, and besides, I need to sleep, I need to rest my body for when Amina calls and comes over and so I take it. For a moment as I slip into the sheets I wish were clean, I think that I may get what I'm searching for. Just a little pocket of sleep, just a moment. I am drifting off when the baby's shrill shriek startles me awake again. I feel the hair follicles on my head take a step toward gray, I feel the collagen draining from my face like hot candle wax. I try to settle her. I bring her to my breast, I let her nurse and then set her down again but she is restless still and cranky. I change a messy diaper, I reswaddle but she will not quiet and I am so tired I am rocking her from a lying-down position, my brain is fighting against the melatonin my eyelids flickering shut and being forced open. My brain stretched like taffy across time and space. It feels like it could snap. I don't know when, but I know it will happen.

I am half asleep and half awake.

As I wait for unconsciousness to flood me, I hear a chorus of distant screams, not close enough to be the baby's—it sounds like a hellish choir of coyotes; the screams are genuine and feral and in ghastly harmony and I close my eyes tight against the possibility that real harm is coming.

—*

The baby is tugging on my nipple, drinking deep and grunting. The pain of the past few weeks is gone, my breasts are no longer engorged, the nipples are tough now. The curtains move with the breeze of the overhead fan and I am hunched, my spine in a lowercase *c* position because I do not have the energy to sit up straight, when I see something in the mirror. I am at once terrified and relieved. My worst suspicions confirmed.

Something shifts wild like an animal in the shadowed corner and I turn so fast the baby pulls off my nipple and it's painful and I remember that I have to make sure her mouth is off correctly or my nipples will elongate over time and I will be left with nipples that resemble pool cues. The baby has her eyes closed, mouth open and searching. I shove my boob back into her mouth, I say, "Hello?" Before me, I see: black shadow standing on black legs, thin and brittle, torched matchsticks collapsing. I get no answer. It doesn't move. I squeeze my eyes tight shut and when I open them it is gone, the room is loud with my heartbeat.

It is sudden, this reveal, but in some ways, I realize it has been happening for a long time, making its way inside. It has been watching and now it is here. All this time I thought I had imagined it, begun to see things in my delirious sleep-deprived state. And now that I think about it, it wasn't like an animal at all. It was more like a person.

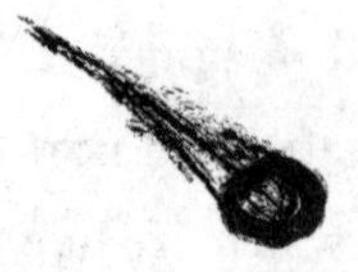

The phone trills in my trembling hand, I am stood with my back against the bedroom door, barricading the baby and me in. Emil's voicemail message starts. I hang up and call back. He answers on the second ring.

"Hey . . . it's late, what time is it there? Is everything okay?"

Emil's voice is sleepy, I woke him. I imagine the hotel room, dark and safe.

"I don't know . . . I don't know. I think someone was just here," I say, trying to control the tears, keeping my voice even and low so I don't wake the baby, who sleeps, unfazed.

"What do you mean someone was just here? Who?"

His words are thick, as if he's trying to figure out if he is asleep or not.

"I don't know who, someone. I saw them in our bedroom. I don't know where they came from but I definitely saw something. Someone. I am so scared, Emil; what should I do?"

"Okay, shit, shit," Emil says. I can almost see him sitting upright, eyes bright and awake now. "Are you okay? Is the baby okay? Have you called the cops?"

"We're okay, she's okay. I don't know if I should call the cops, I thought about it, but . . . what if they think I'm the intruder? You hear things like that happening all the time."

"That is not going to happen, Sofia! Call them. I don't feel good about this. Maybe I should send my dad round."

I can hear him pacing, trying to figure out the solution. I feel the flicker of a smile in the corners of my mouth, he is worried about me! He will come home to me and this will all be forgotten, forgiven.

"Okay, hang up the phone, I'm going to call 911. This is fucking insane."

"No! Please don't do that. It's okay, I'm okay," I say, unsure why I am the one trying to soothe him. I wait for him to tell me he is on his way. I hold the phone against my shoulder, crack my knuckles of my left hand against my right.

This has always been our dynamic, I realize as I hold the too-hot cell phone to my ear. When I tell the story of our first meeting we stick to the romantic details—the rain, sharing the overpriced fashion magazine as an umbrella (*with Grace Jones on the cover!*), the subway station's overhead fluorescent lights illuminating my face as I repeated my name for him over the din of the trains. But really there is more to the story, more to see if you could only zoom out. I've had the information all along, I've always known who he was I just chose to ignore it. On his phone constantly with endless work calls that had him mouthing apologies to me, the girl who was trying to fall in love with him. Stepping out of whatever bar we were in to do crisis management in some other place, for someone else.

Missing the woman in front of him, missing what was going on in front of his face.

The pause continues, he doesn't volunteer his return. I want to scream at him to come home but really, I know it would be more than an inconvenience, it would be a career ruiner, and so I try to smile, reassure myself, but the corners of my mouth where the smile is begin to quiver. Don't cry.

"I just . . . I just need you to talk to me for a second, okay?"

"Have you locked all the doors and windows? What did they look like?" Emil says, full superhero mode.

"I don't know. I didn't really see them. It was dark."

"Did they say anything to you?"

"No. I was putting the baby down and I turned and they were there and then they were gone."

". . ."

"What? Why are you making that face?" I demand. I can feel my crisis waning in his mind as I talk.

"What face? You can't see my face. I'm not making any face."

"I know you and I can hear it in your voice, you don't believe me."

I am trying not to whine but I can't help it, I want him to pay attention.

"I mean . . . you haven't been sleeping," Emil ventures. "Do you think it's possible you imagined it?"

Fuck you.

"Emil! I didn't imagine an intruder! I saw something, I know I did. And it's not the first time, either." I talk in a loud whisper, trying to sound compelling. I want him to believe me, I want to believe me.

"'Something' . . ." Emil repeats, skeptically.

"Some*one.* Someone in the house," I clarify. I am outraged. I snap, my anger pushing me over the edge of an invisible line. "Shouldn't you be on a plane over here? Shouldn't you come home?"

There is a pause on the end of the phone, and I can feel Emil trying to figure out his next move.

"Do you want me to come home?" he asks, finally. "Say the word and I'll get on a plane, baby. That's the deal, remember? If you need me just say."

"Okay. I need you."

My voice is steely and challenging. I can feel where this is going already, and a sadness descends into my body like hypothermia. This is not a problem worth his time.

"Okay, that settles it, then," he says firmly, although the next sentence is out of his mouth too quickly for it to feel like an organic thought. "Shit, I'll have to leave after shooting tomorrow, though. Tomorrow's a really crucial day. If I miss it, it sets the whole thing back."

My next line comes to me and I surrender to it, as if I am an actor on a stage under a sole, blue spotlight. I know my part.

"No. No, don't leave. We are fine. We'll be fine. You're probably right, I'm probably just tired."

"Are you sure?" Emil is relieved, though he tries to hide it.

"Yes, I'm sure. I'll even call the cops, okay?" I concede, reading my lines off an invisible script. I slide down the door till I am sitting on the floor, defeated. The room around me is pitch-black, I open my eyes wide against it, ready to catch any sudden movement.

"That would make me feel better. Can you call me back when they get there?"

Emil is already returning to the hotel bed, I can hear it creak and his voice change as he reclines on what's sure to be a king-size mattress, settling back in for a full night's sleep despite this interruption.

"Sure."

"I think we should invest in those security cameras we talked about. I'd feel a lot better if I could log on and check everything out, you know?"

Somehow, we have returned to Emil's docket of things he wants. He is clever like that, and if he hadn't gotten into the industry, he would have made an excellent politician. He knows just how to find a way back to his own agenda.

"Spy on me, you mean."

I am playing at putting up a fight, but my head is rested on the door behind me, and I long for bed. My fear has receded. I blame the excitement of the day and not enough sleep. I should be resting; I shouldn't be going out there.

"No, I don't mean. I want to check on the safety of my family," Emil says.

"Sure, I guess so. You're right."

I pull myself up to standing, wincing at the effort.

"Well then, that settles it. I'm making an appointment with a security company for tomorrow. And tonight, what do you want to do? You want to get a hotel room?"

"No, she's finally asleep, I don't want to wake her. We'll be fine. The doors are locked, everything seems okay now, I'm going to call the cops and head to bed too," I say, convincingly, because maybe I am a great actress after all. Then hurriedly, in a Sofia tone I despise, needy and desperate, I add against my will, "I'm sorry I woke you."

"Always wake me for stuff like this, baby. I'm always here for you, you know that. I just wish I could be *there.*"

He's proud of himself, I can tell. A good husband, a good dad. He feels like he handled this well, and will likely roll over and pass out without much effort. Hatred for the man I married bubbles up out of my throat like backwash, and the worst thing is I am beginning to enjoy the taste.

"You could be."

The words fly out of my mouth before I can stop myself, as if someone else is speaking them.

"Don't do that. You know I can't, I already said I can't. I love you; I'll be home in less than a week. It's not that long."

Not for you, I think. I was drawn to what I thought of as Emil's natural glamour; it didn't take me long to realize Emil is just like everyone else, desperate to please, desperate to sit out in the bright lights, desperate. Emil has always been nurturing—he is good with strangers, particularly with children and animals. He squats down, gets on their level. He is goofy. Attentive when it suits him. But his head is on a swivel stick and if it's not pointed at you, then it is hard to remind him you exist. Emil is a good boy from a good family, and really, when you strip away the discreet stick-and-poke tattoos, the shirts from boutiques in Paris, the casual hair that takes him more than a casual amount of time to perfect, really that's all he is. He isn't charming and heroic and spontaneous, he's pretending too. We are all pretending.

—*

The cops come and stand at my door, red and blue lights flashing against the house, making more of a scene than is appropriate for this private street. We are too new and I am too Black for cops to be stood outside our door and so I usher them in and they earnestly wipe their feet and go room to room. I hold a sleeping baby in my arms and trail after them, although in my heart I know they will not find anything.

I even call Emil back, whose voice is once again weighed down with sleep, hand the phone to an officer, who seems to be relieved to be talking to the man of the house. I can't help but notice a glance he gives me as he listens to my husband, a glance that is wary and pitying. I have the urgent need to know what was said, but before I can speak to Emil, the officer hangs up, hands me back the phone.

"Sounds like your husband is going to follow up with a security company. Good idea too, in this neighborhood," the officer clips, his partner's hand is already on the door handle. They want out of this domestic scene; they probably have more important places to go, although I would do anything to make them stay, I don't want to be alone with my thoughts, let alone a presence I may or may not have imagined. All this time I have been trying to ignore it but maybe I need to look hard. I want to tell them that I am losing it, but instead I nod dumbly.

"I'm sorry for the trouble," I apologize, trying for a winning smile but seeing a glimpse of myself in the hallway mirror. I am no longer a woman who could smile her way out of anything.

"No problem. Have a nice night."

—*

The next day Emil still insists on security cameras, something we have been planning to pull the trigger on since we moved in. The system he chooses is simple and I probably could have installed it myself, but Emil has signed up to have a technician come to the house. He doesn't trust me with it. SafeSec, the security company, sends a courtesy text. Your technician is 30 minutes out. I put a bag of frozen peas on each eye, I wash my face, comb my hair. I think of the word *presentable.*

The minute I hear the truck pull into the driveway I begin opening the blinds, try to make myself seem like a nice, normal mom in a nice, normal home. I watch a man hoist his jeans up as they walk to the front door, bridging the gap of pink flesh between denim and ill-fitting company hoodie. I open the door to him, a protective hand on top of the baby, tucked away in the BabyBjörn.

"Hi! SafeSec?" I chirp, immediately flinching at this shiny, ultra-femme version of myself I have chosen to present him with.

"Yep. Mikey."

Mikey taps his badge that has been pinned crooked to his hoodie but that states both his name and the company.

"You requested full installation?"

"I did. Well, my husband did." I again cringe at my heteronormative role. Little wife home with the baby, clueless and subservient, high voice cracking with the need to please. "Where shall we start?"

"Your husband I think it was? He requested a full service. I have everything I need." He pats the side of his big canvas bag like the flank of a horse. "You show me where I can set down my bag, my tools and stuff, and I'll get to work, ma'am."

Mikey follows me in through the foyer, he hasn't removed his dusty work boots, I notice disinterestedly. He clomps behind me to the kitchen and the back door, and as I show him the points of entry, the blind spot in the backyard, I agonize over his choice of the word. *Ma'am.* In an ordinary world, before I gave birth to the needy creature hanging from my chest, a man like this would have faltered in his steps in front of me. I was put together, a carefully studied portrait of a young, hip, cosmopolitan woman—mini dresses and little jackets, distressed expensive jeans paired with a tight tank, no bra, breasts way up firm and high. *Ma'am* doesn't compute. *Ma'am* doesn't gel with who I think of myself as.

I pour Mikey a glass of water, plopping ice cubes in to make it feel less like basic tap. My reflection calls again to me from the kitchen window. I am pale, my eyes are sunken. I have tried to change out of my pajamas but clearly forgot what I was doing halfway through because I am still wearing the top, warm and soft against my body. I am a mess. I am absolutely a ma'am.

When Mikey is done, I thank him, tip him well. I walk up to each camera I come across, throw up a peace sign, just in case Emil is already logged in and watching. I want him to see that I am okay, that I am doing it, the thing we agreed upon. Manning the helm, keeping things on an even keel. It is jarring to know my every move is being recorded, but I think of the intruder, and of irrefutable proof that I am not crazy. This is real, he will see. The house feels placid, bare, and I start to wonder if it was all a bad dream.

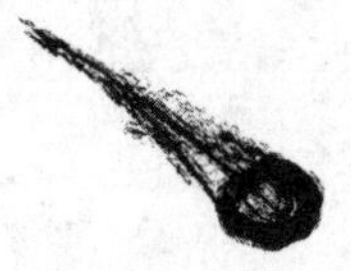

Sleep is thin. A cold, still ocean, light from a distant sun filtering above. My phone calling my name from somewhere: It's my mother again. I let it ring out. It is late, the baby is asleep upstairs, and I pace pace pace as I listen to her most recent voicemail. Her voice is still hushed as I remember it, and the way she says my name is the same, the *f* sound prominent. She begins a new sentence, but it is too much, I can't listen to her. I hang up, delete, play the next one. Same sentence, same stern "Sofia." I delete. I delete. I delete.

—*

Dominique texts me a meme. A photo of a maternity ward in Iowa that had set up ten pumpkins, one for each stage of vaginal dilation prebirth. Their vaginal mouths stretch in horror, and pumpkin number ten has the look of a ghoul. It is meant to be amusing and so I reply, *haha* and do three half-hearted Kegels. It feels like trying to resuscitate a heart. What was it they taught us in the CPR class? Do it to the tune of "Stayin' Alive" by the Bee Gees. I can do the *ah ah ah ah,* but the *stayin' alive* part feels unfathomable. I imagine a giant pumpkin between my legs, silent scream mouth aimed at the floor, seeing some unseeable thing, terrible, coming straight for us.

—*

My sleep is so light that I can feel myself in it, I find a word for this feeling online. *Depersonalization.* And when I wake it is like it snowed but didn't settle—pointless and cold. How long have I slept? The glow of my phone dims, it must be after ten P.M., it's doing that soft light thing that it does when it's trying to get me ready for sleep. Despite the thrum of exhaustion being ever present, a heaviness behind my lids, I know if I lie down nothing but fear would come to me. I hear a sound, flick the light on, daring something to happen, but I haven't seen anything since the police came round. Outside the windows there is nothing, not even in the dark.

My voicemail is empty, my mother hasn't called again, and despite my better judgment I find myself missing her presence that even just through the phone was starting to feel routine. I will her to phone me, staring at the screen, scrolling through endless posts on mom blogs, panicked, unanswered questions on Reddit from mothers trying their best to find footing, but she doesn't call. No one calls.

Amina's face that day in her office comes to me often; the look of pity, of regret maybe? If I just had another chance to talk to her she would understand. I try to find Amina's Facebook again but she must have blocked me, no results under her name appear. I find the corresponding avatar on Instagram, which somehow I still have access to, but the last post is from two years ago so she clearly doesn't check it much. I scroll and I scroll and I scroll. I watch her life in reverse: the frame full of the kids and husband who dote on her, a move from Chicago to the Bay, a lavish expensive wedding all smiles and bouquets, and before that it is the two of them as a couple before kids, drunken waifs laughing too hard in a bar. I go back even further to a MySpace-like photo from 2009, taken from above, Amina pouting in a bandage dress. I zoom in on her face, try to understand the happiness in this picture, I try to discern the difference between this happiness and the one I witnessed in the park, and as I do I unwittingly double-tap, a heart filling the screen. I unheart it but it's too late, she will see this. And I don't care. Let her know that I miss her and that I need her and that I am waiting.

And very very soon the sun will be coming up, I will make coffee and try to slap some life into my face.

I read on a mommy blog that babies die of SIDS for various mysterious reasons but that one common cause seems to be heat—they were too warm. I change the thermostat to sixty-eight and I pace and find all of her onesies and cut off the sleeves with kitchen scissors, which takes a minute because they aren't sharp enough and I have to do a hacking motion to really get a purchase with the blades and then I turn the thermostat to sixty-five and then sixty-six because maybe that's too cold. I do this on my phone on the app, the dial I rotate with my finger on the screen makes a satisfying clicking sound, click-click-click up to sixty-eight, click-click-click-click-click down to sixty-three.

—*

My hands look like claws in the dark.

—*

The smell of decay that I first noticed the day Emil left has returned and is overwhelming, like burning, rancid meat. I try breathing only through my mouth because I can't risk opening a window and letting a cold breeze chill the baby. I have to keep the temperature just right. I get up and silently stalk the house, I need to find the source of it, it smells like death and earth and something else, burning hair maybe. I sniff maniacally. I pull shirts out of drawers I lift toilet seats and sniff open the fridge and sniff I cannot figure it out but it's in here. I will the baby to stay asleep, turn up the white noise to mask my nocturnal stirrings. I'm so tired that at one point I find myself backed against the wall, a knife clenched in two hands like the huntsman in *Snow White*. I don't know how I got here; I am ready I am primed for combat but who am I fighting? It scares me, this glitch in the matrix, this is not how I should be behaving when I am safe in my house. I put the knife back and make the coffee early, I am shaking before I even take a sip. I can't tell Emil; I can't tell anyone. They'll think I'm broken.

I get really into deleting texts. I delete at an alarming rate with little discrimination—the work chat goes, all those seemingly innocent remarks that mask the question *When are you coming back to the office?* I delete all those friends cooing over baby photos. I delete the texts reminding me of upcoming appointments, I want my inbox clear I don't want to see a name I don't want to hear a question I want to be left alone and finally I hover over Emil's name, considering it. I look at his last text—This hotel room is so empty without you—and I think what it might be like to be in a quiet empty room alone, no agenda no nothing but my thoughts and desires only and

I am filled with a rising urge to scream that is only sated when I swipe on the text chat and delete, blotting him out. Inbox empty.

I go to my home office, I take the manuscript and curl up with it on the Eames chair in the corner. I flick through the pages, stopping on a line that jumps out at me as if typed in bold:

> *I looked at the stars, and considered how awful it would be for a man to turn his face up to them as he froze to death, and see no help or pity in all the glittering multitude.*

I jam it into an empty drawer, close the door tightly behind me.

At some point, at around dawn, my mind drifts and I begin to think of clouds, nebulous and whirling. I wonder if it's cold up there in the sky, if you can feel the water droplets as you move through the cloud, about how the sky looks when you're in a plane above it all, flat and white, almost solid. I can feel my body relaxing, the grip on my phone loosening, and even unconscious I am so grateful for the oblivion to come when suddenly she is screaming crisp and shrill and it is like being shaken awake by the train conductor when you are about to miss your stop I am gathering my things I am trying to remember where I am and what I was doing and I'm up on my feet before I am fully awake, charging into the bedroom to her bassinet, like Victoria Page, incapable of control, simply following my feet. I swaddle the baby tightly. It looks like a straitjacket. And then I blink and, like I am watching a badly edited student movie, two slices of film spliced together, the scene is different. The baby's arm is out of the swaddle now, she has worked it out and her hand is free, pressed to her mouth and sucking, comforted.

I feel the presence of something, and I turn and can almost make out the shape of this thing, of this shadow. A person for sure, low to the ground and hiding, features indistinguishable. The presence stands from a crouching position, spine unfurling loud like snapping firewood, or the hands of my mother as she cracked her knuckles hard in her own palm. Again, and before I can be afraid, a jump cut and I am back in my bed, the blinds drawn against the sunlight, the taste of nutmeg in my mouth.

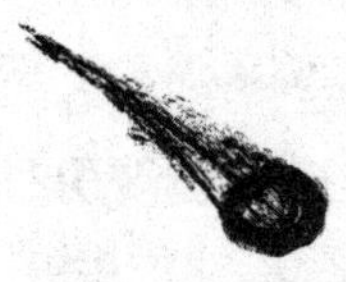

My keys go missing. And not just my keys, other things too, but the keys make it difficult to leave the house so that, even in the moments when the baby is passive in the carrier and the sun is shining tantalizingly out of the window, I cannot join the world. I find the keys in various places, in the freezer like some mad cliché, in the trash. On the pillow next to me. When I discover them I suspect the shadow. I look around desperately, certain I will catch her this time. It. I should say it, because I don't know for sure it is a woman. I know it is here with me, sometimes in the dead of night I can hear the rasp of its breath, although every time I turn my head it jumps out of view like a spider evading the glass being placed on top of it, a trickster. The wood beams in the kitchen that run along the ceiling look like a person bracing themself up there, and when I turn off the light I feel it, suspended above me and waiting to pounce.

My toothbrush is something else that frequently disappears, and often I brush my teeth with a finger and paste like an ill-equipped camper, sometimes three or four times a day because I can never remember when I did it last. I begin to hide things from the shadow person, I tuck little tokens of my former life around. Lipsticks. Condoms. Things I no longer need. Into backpacks and unused winter coats and the diaper pail. I do this while the baby sleeps, secreting around like a madwoman. I know this is silly, hiding things from someone I have never seen, not properly. Somewhere in my skull is the sense that I must lean into the madness that approaches like a great tidal wave from out at sea, sent by underwater seismic currents.

The baby goes down in her taco bed, night-light on. I check the closets and corners for intruders, shut the door, and storm around in Emil's wrap party sweatshirt from some movie set, *Trailblazer* streaked across my chest in flame-tipped font. I head down the stairs, creeping, as I have started to do, down the far side of each step and avoiding the middle where I know it is creakiest. I head into the TV room to turn on the local news, see if there's anything more about high levels of mercury in the tap water, a story I read on Instagram while I was worried the baby was going to get osmosis poisoning in the bathtub.

I sit there, the news turning to static, and my mind begins to drift. Instead of fighting it I let it take me, hoping for sleep, even here upright in this room. I am in a forest, the ground is littered with unfamiliar leaves, so covered that my eyes can't focus and I have to look up to the blue sky, bluer than I have seen it, to center my vision. The sky is streaked with evidence of planes like stripped vertebrae against the blue of the sky. I look down to find a woman, screaming in pain. I want to help her, I reach my hand out but instead there is a lizard, staring at me, unblinking. Striped body telling me something. The woman is just behind it, mouthing words at me that look like: *Listen. Listen. Listen.*

I come to, the news still on, the house quiet. My body is cold with an interstellar chill, like I've been outside and have only just come in. I notice something next to me, someone sitting on the far end of the couch. They are barely moving, they do not turn to look at me and I freeze, unsure of what to do next. I have never seen the shadow this close, and it is detail-less, a void. No teeth, no mouth. Quiet, black, unmoving except for the heaviness of breath, which is raspy, more like the sound of someone snoring gently on the other side of a wall.

"Hello?" I murmur, still frozen. When I get no response I repeat, "Hello?" but louder, more demanding, a petulant stomp of the foot, tired of being ignored. The shadow person turns and then is at once there and not there and I am alone, suddenly standing in the TV room in a big empty house, talking to the walls.

—*

The walls are alive with shadows. In the dark, it looks like things crawling, spidered hands skittering up, necks snapping, bones reaching ever upward. My notebook lies beside the bed, and when I glance at the open page in the gloom it reads:

LET US IN.

But in the morning, there is no notebook, there are no words. Reality is blurring, things are coming undone.

—*

Sixteen, my mother's apartment. My dad was long gone and I would practice my field service. An elder suggested I rehearse it, even though it was meant to be off the cuff, feel natural, there was no way I'd meet my quota at that speed. They had to see you, the elder continued, even before they open the door, they have to know you're out there. Through the frosted sliced pie windows of a front door, they had to see you and know that salvation was close. I stood in front of the mirror that was screwed to the bathroom wall above the sink, chipped and spattered with toothpaste flecks, and smile. I would spread the grin wide, show all of my teeth, let the smile move up round my nose as it crinkled, resting at my eyes, eager. And then I would stop, turn it all off, look at myself like I was someone else now, a stranger, someone who didn't live in this apartment, who didn't have to practice, who just *was.* I clicked the smile on, and off, and on, and off, like a lightbulb, or Morse code.

Dot-dot-dot, dash-dash-dash, dot-dot-dot.

—*

My thoughts come to me like startled birds. I don't know which way is up, or what time it is, or what is real and what I am imagining, because whatever I have been seeing is still there, and I know this from the sounds in the walls as I walk through the house. Drumming for entrance, drumming to get in. The commotion is deafening, and even when I manage to change, feed, swaddle the baby, even when I get her down, the house is loud. *Shut up,* I hiss. *Shut up.* The baby seems oblivious to it all, but the noise follows me into the bathroom, pattering on the wall behind the toilet. It follows me into the kitchen, a hollow, fragile sound as it moves onto the glass panes of double-hung windows from the 1890s. The walls of the house are the membrane, the drumming like an unsettling heartbeat.

I am on edge, always on edge with this sound. I try to play music over it, putting my headphones in as I pace, but it is relentless. The house is too hot with all these windows closed and drapes pulled. I feel as if I am suffocating, how on earth can I breathe, how am I supposed to continue on like this? I can't. I flee to the largest window; I pull the curtains aside and open it with both hands wide over my head. The night air rushes in and the relief is immediate. There is no one out here, just the stars, just the breeze. I inhale deeply, filling my lungs to capacity, ribs expanding. I pull a chair over to the window and breathe it in—slow, measured breaths like I am in shock and breathing into a paper bag. I lean over in the chair, head between my knees.

Finally, a chill sets in, I stand and close the window. I listen hard for drumming, for anything, but not even the baby upstairs stirs. Hands cupped around my ears; a nothingness rings. The house is quiet as a land mine.

Photo ID: I hold a lit candle in front of my face, smiling a grin that is too wide to feel natural. All of my teeth are visible. My hair edges the photo, diabolically messy. Darkness surrounds me but maybe, just maybe, do you think you can make out someone else there in the gloom?

What time is it?

I post it. A few minutes pass. I delete it.

—*

The phone rings. Emil. A FaceTime call. He wants to see me, or so he thinks. I answer. I look at myself in the small frame within the slightly larger frame containing Emil's face. I haven't seen my face properly for a long time. I am a wild thing, the room around me is dark, the hollows of my eye sockets illuminated by the phone's glow.

"Hey!" Emil says, so brightly that I have to wince. It is like unexpected sunshine pouring into a banquet hall, a table full of wilted flowers.

"Hi."

I am focused on my own screen still, I can't look at him in his cyber world, clean and orderly.

"I wanted to check in and see how you're doing," he says, with something new in his voice. "I spoke to my mom, we were thinking it might be good if I came home a little early."

I shrug childishly, like I don't care. Too late, too late.

"We got a lot done this week, even with the extra shots," Emil continues, filling in the silence I have left. "I'm thinking of getting the red-eye home on Saturday, letting the second AD take over, what do you think?"

He extends this like a prize, an early return, a hero swooping in with his cape to save the girl from the burning building, but the building is an inferno and the girl is toast.

"If that's what you want," I reply. Behind me, in the mirror of the screen I hold, I see the shadow person like an old friend, erect and upright. If I am afraid then my body is too drained to let me know it. I stare back at where eyes would be, I feel a shiver of connection xylophoning along my spine. I look at my own eyes, which are Lite-Brite alert. The right one feels like it's twitching.

"Can you see my eye twitching?" I ask.

"Huh? No," Emil says, confused. "Did you hear me? I said I'm gonna try to come home early."

What does he want, a medal? Prodigal son returning? I am in the underworld; he would have to venture further out than that to save me. He wouldn't survive down here.

"I don't know what you want me to say."

"I want you to say, yes, come home!" he snaps, and then immediately checks himself. "I'm sorry, baby. I'm worried about you, I thought you'd be happy to have me come home early."

"When you say early, what is it that you mean?"

I am feeling cruel, I let Edwina surge through my body.

"I was thinking of a red-eye on Saturday," he repeats. He is trepidatious, he knows he is walking into something but he doesn't know exactly what.

"Instead of . . . ?" I prompt, leaning forward, hand cupped to my ear.

"Sunday?"

"Not much of an early return, right?" I say, satisfied. "Don't do me any favors."

Emil pauses, searching my face. He is confused. He is trying to understand, trying to come to terms with the transformation before him. *Victoria Page will not dance the dance of the Red Shoes tonight, or any other night.* Something hardens in his eyes.

"I'm worried about you," he says, "and so is Dominique."

So, they've been talking about me. They've been whispering behind my back like I am a leper in my lepers' colony, in this dark house all alone.

"Wow, great to know you guys chat together when I'm not around to compare notes. So, she's spying on me for you? The cameras weren't enough? How often do you talk anyway?"

An errant wave of emotion moves through my head, knocking thoughts off tables, flooding me, but I keep it cool, I keep it calm, I keep it collected. The rage is cold, icy, treacherous.

"She says the house always looks dark when she drives by to check on you," he continues, ignoring my questions.

"Overhead lights are a sleep preventative, they restrict your natural melatonin production," I say, as if talking to an imbecile.

"Yeah, dark in the bedroom, sure, but, babe, the whole house? It's weird . . . What are you doing?"

Sitting here listening to you lecture me on something you know nothing about, I think, making co-conspiratorial eyes with the shadow in the background. If it could talk I know it would agree with me.

"I mean with your eyes, what are you doing?" Emil repeats, alarm rising in his voice.

"What?" I say, checking my face in the little window of myself to see what he is seeing.

"You're blinking a lot, like all the time."

He is studying me too, as if I am an imposter, a fake, *Invasion of the Body Snatchers.*

"My eyes feel dry," I say defensively, rubbing them.

"Okay, I'm officially getting worried. When is your next appointment with Dr. Lester?" Emil demands, a pen poised in his hand ready to take useless notes on a hotel room pad.

"I don't know, six weeks from when I gave birth?"

He jots something down. So studious. I could laugh, but I don't.

"So . . . in about a week?"

"Sure," I reply. The shadow is gone, and I feel a delayed sensation of fear. I think of the baby, small and soft and vulnerable. Is she safe? I know nothing about what the shadow is capable of, what it could do.

"Right after I'm home?"

"Emil, I've got to go."

I stand, thumb poised over the red disconnect button.

"Maybe you should call, move it forward. I'm going to have Domi or Buffy come by the house, so you're not alone."

The baby's cry punctuates his sentence for him, and I am suddenly frantic.

"I'm fine," I say, unconvincingly. "I've got to go. I have to check on her."

"You're not fine, Sofia. You're acting strange and you seem off. I can't remember the last time you smiled," Emil says quickly, aware I am about to hang up.

"Why don't you give Dominque a call? She has all the time in the world to talk to you," I say. I press the button. Good-bye.

—*

Amina has blocked me on social media. She still hasn't replied to my email but I can see she has read it. I draft another one. *Please,* I beg. *I need you.*

—*

I get the breast pump out. I don't need to pump but I want to hear the voice, I know it is waiting for me. As I pump four ounces of liquid gold straight from my right breast I close my eyes and listen.

Kill her.

Milk churns out of me in thick spurts, into the pump and down into the plastic jar screwed onto the contraption. I can fill one easily. I could feed two babies, maybe three, in my sleep.

Kill her.

Google says my milk can detect when a baby is sick and adjust its nutritional content accordingly. Can the baby taste my state of mind? Does she taste the metal of my fear? Is my madness bitter? What else am I passing on?

Kill her.

I wonder how I would kill Buffy. Would I do it in the dark, in her labyrinthine house? Strangle her in her sleep? No, I have too much rage for that, it would need to be angrier, one of her many decorative art pieces, the bowls dotted around the country house. The Chihuly, because Buffy has a real-life one-of-a-kind turquoise Dale Chihuly and there would be something poetic about bashing her skull in with it, the sea greens against the reds of her brains. Beautiful.

Buffy's death now plays in my mind on a loop, like black-and-white motion pictures—tied to a train track while I silently cackle like a good villain. Burned at the stake like a witch. Thrown off a cliff to meet sharp rocks below. Forever locked inside her clifftop home, starving to death while I watch through the windows. I could poison her. Pesticides in her tea. It's above Marta's pay grade to taste all of her food. I'd bring her the cup and saucer myself, my own milk in to sweeten it. Earl Grey, Darjeeling, chamomile.

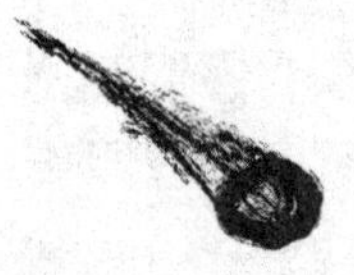

If I stand still enough, I am like a tree in the forest halfway up a mountain.

I stand still in the kitchen.

I am still in the hallway.

Thoughts come to me, forgotten thoughts.

I am reaching my arms out, stretching out for the sight of land. Is there such a thing as a fresh start? Can you truly begin again, on a clean sheet of paper, waiting for you to get it right? Trauma begets trauma begets trauma. Nothing clean, then, only our desperate desire to build again, to distance ourselves from the past. I manifest. I manifest what it would feel like to fly. I manifest weightlessness. I manifest an empty shell with a painted-on smile.

—*

Eddie is calling, leaving voicemail after voicemail. She calls even in the dead of night. Long meandering voicemails, sermonizing against my will. I hurl my phone across the room, and when I look up I catch a camera, winking its red eye.

—*

What if the act of pushing out a child, of physically pushing, started this whole thing, started it with blood and guts and shit and screamed retractions? A slingshot into a grim carousel of green baby poop and crusted nipples, hair matted, eyes black, nails brittle and bitten, leg hair like overgrown grass on a neglected lawn, wild and tall, nothing left of me. I'm just a tunnel. I'm just a portal for this child and then what becomes of me, this rattling shell, the last bullet in a cylinder, a game of Russian roulette, while the shadows twist up the walls with a dancer's grace, whispers in the night, long-forgotten bedtime stories my mind is crowded and I clean the child clean her and clean her, the baby, always dressed in fresh laundered clothes, fed from my own stinking body, milky like afterbirth. Brown flesh against her warm brown flesh just two little piggies in a butcher's window because someone will feast, somewhere.

—*

Emil texts me.

> We are worried about you

and then,

> Me and Domi.

I delete these texts. They blemish my pristine inbox. But I can't stop thinking about them talking about me, whispering in hushed tones even though I am not around to hear. I never told Emil about the bridge, or St. Raphael's, the hospital in New York. I knew all along that he wouldn't get it, what does a good boy know about sadness? About loneliness? What tragedy ever befell his life? But maybe Domi told him? Maybe one night late on the phone she had confided in him.

She's crazy, you know. She's just holding it together.

And he would have cried and she would have comforted him and what else do they talk about, when they are done worrying? Do they talk about being lonely, do they talk about what they've been up to, does the tone shift and change as they realize the page they are on, the tension between them? I shake my head, hard, like a tree shaken for fruit. This is wrong. I imagine Dominique driving past but not stopping by my house, as though I am something to be kept at arm's length. I am not well, and everyone knows it. They will take the baby from me soon, I am certain. Emil will come home and be flanked by Dominique and Buffy and they will advance upon me, concern knitting up their features, pretending to care.

And, as if she had been summoned, like I had cast a spell and drawn her here, Dominique knocks at the door, unannounced. It is dark outside, nighttime already, the hours jumbled and indistinguishable from one another. The night-light I bought and had delivered on a midnight whim fills the living room with a red glow like a Dario Argento film. I get to the door, baby pressed against my chest, her head at my shoulder. I do not open the door fully because I know she is here for the baby, I know she must have been texting Emil, they probably chat all the time, texting like traitors. She pushes past me into the house, taking it all in.

"Heyyyy!"

She draws the word out like she is talking to a crazy person.

"Heyyy," I repeat moronically.

"Can I hold her?"

Dominique points at the baby and for a minute I think of her taking the baby off into the night, away from me. *If she does that, I will kill her.* I dare her to. I am ready.

"Wash your hands."

Dominique dutifully does so at the kitchen sink, using the hand soap that has actual sand from the Black Sea in it, to exfoliate. I stand behind her, watching, making sure she does it properly. She manages to hold her questions in her mouth until she has the bundle of baby, holding her with more ease than I expected her capable of.

"It's so dark in here."

"I know."

"Can we turn on a light?"

"No."

"Okay . . ."

She looks around the gloomy living room, finds a place to sit on the couch.

"You could really use some fresh air in here. When was the last time you got outside?"

I ignore this, remain standing. I can't remember the last time I did not have the baby's weight against me, it feels weird. I open and close my hands, like jazz hands. Open close open close. I use my hands to massage the opposite biceps, fascinated by the lightness of my own arms.

"Sofia," Dominique presses, "we're worried about you."

"*We*? Who's *we*?"

I already know the answer but I want it confirmed, I want her to tell me they've been talking about me behind my back.

"Me and Emil. We've been texting."

"Oh yeah?"

I sound as if I am jeering and I don't mean to be but I can't seem to take the tone out of my voice. I crack my knuckles, one by one by one by one until all four fingers have been reset. Then I fold my easy breezy arms, slowly walk around the couch so that Dominique has to follow me with her eyes, turning her body this way and that to look at me.

"What do the two of you talk about?"

My voice is heavy with suggestion.

"Come on! It's not like that, babe, please. He thinks he should come home early; he thinks it's too much for you, all of this."

"Does he?" I laugh, a metallic bullet of a laugh that clanks off the walls.

"Yes."

Dominique shifts herself once again to meet my eyes. I am now stood by the window, looking out through the drawn curtains. It is brighter out there than I imagined, my eyes wince and I pull the curtain back, tight. The baby stirs against Dominique and she instinctively lifts a hand to pat her back to sleep. She is a natural.

"Maybe he could have thought about that before. Maybe he could have considered my needs before. It feels a bit *fucking* late now, doesn't it?"

I have never spoken to Dominique, or anyone, like this and she is taken aback. This wasn't how she expected this intervention to go, she thought she'd waltz in and shake me by my shoulders, have me whipped back into shape in no time, call her best friend Emil and tell him not to worry, the ship had been righted. The course had been corrected. Or else she was going to take the baby, take her back to Emil. Start a new, real family. Well guess what, Domi. You can't always get what you want. I am not going to make it easy for you.

I move once more, into her blind spot, watch her twist her neck to keep me in her eyeline. She is scared. It should soften me, this realization, but instead I feel myself solidify with power. I feel as if I could crush her larynx with one hand like Lex Luthor. It would be hard for her to fuck my husband with a crushed larynx.

"So, he wants to come home early. What is early when he's already been gone for three weeks? What does it fucking matter if he comes home with only days to go? It's too late, Dominique."

To emphasize my point, I tap my temples hard, hard enough to bruise. It feels good.

"Too late for what? What are you talking about?" Dominique has stood to face me, clutching the baby in the safety of her arms.

I smile. I usually tell her everything but, in this moment, I realize how little she knows. If I wanted, I could tell her about the faces I have seen stalking my house at night. I could tell her that sometimes I catch myself suddenly time-warped to another part of the house, digging in the dirt of the houseplants, looking for something. I could tell her about the astral projection, all of the intimate, strange scenes I find myself in, but I don't. There is a gulf between us now, an ocean that I have traveled. I don't want to go backward.

"Nothing. I'm okay, don't worry about it."

I grin, too wide, too many teeth, an attempted approximation at former Sofia.

"Don't worry about it? You don't seem okay at all. I know you don't want to talk about it, but . . . the last time you were like this, it didn't end well, remember?"

How dare she bring up the past like that! She seems to be finding her backbone, remembering what she came here for, I think to do something to scare her, like screaming as loud as I can or pulling out my hair but she is still holding my baby. I don't want Dominique to drop her.

"In fact, I'm wondering about taking you to the hospital. You need help, you need a break."

I am incensed now.

"The hospital? And then what would happen to my baby? *You'd* take her?"

"You need help. The hospital helped, before. This isn't healthy," Dominique pleads. She reaches out and places a cool palm on my arm but I refuse to allow it to subdue me. "You need quiet, rest. I think whatever was going on in New York is happening again, maybe brought on by postpartum? I've been reading up on it and lots of moms—"

"What do you know about moms?" I snap in an elevated whisper, speaking the unspeakable. I wrestle my baby out of her arms, Dominique puts up no fight. "You don't know shit about motherhood or being a wife. You weren't there with me in New York until it was too fucking late. You never came, Dominique! You promised me we'd be out there together. You left me, even after the hospital you left me to figure that city out on my own. You've been checked out from the beginning; I have been entirely alone."

My voice cracks and weeks of swallowed tears threaten to erupt. "Entirely alone," I repeat.

Dominique seems to think this is the time to approach me and I let her, she wraps an arm around my shoulders. Somewhere inside me is a person who wants to be comforted, wants to feel warmth and love from her best friend. That person is weak, and will not do what needs to be done if I let Dominique soothe me. I cover the mouth of this internal person, suffocate her and stuff her body down inside me. I shrug Dominique off violently, push her away.

"You need to leave," I say, using my free hand to angrily wipe the buds of tears from my eyes.

"I am not leaving you right now." She is resolute.

I recognize that it will be difficult to get her to get out, to get her to stop worrying about me unless I give her something, and I know exactly what she wants. This is my job, to anticipate what is needed and thanklessly serve it up. I take a breath, prepare to lie.

"Domi, I'm sorry."

I use her nickname, softly, make my voice small and harmless. I am a tiny, tiny mouse.

"I'm okay, I am just really, really tired. You're right, I need to rest. The baby isn't sleeping well so that means I'm not either, but I'm just going to set her down early tonight and get into bed and try to sleep too."

Dominique visibly relaxes as she hears the change of my tone. This Sofia she knows, this Sofia is the one who makes sense. Reliable and affable. The good girl.

"Are you sure?" she says, uncertainly. She wants to believe me, though, I can feel it. Even Domi hasn't seen the real me, the one I have unburied, she wouldn't like it if she did. I have to take it across the finish line.

"Yeah. I'm sorry I snapped at you, it's just . . . hard."

Dominique is nodding, and reaches out and rubs my back. It is unbearable but I bear it, the circular motions she makes with her hands are sickening.

"I can see that. It looks hard. You're doing an amazing job."

And then Dominique lies to me for the first time in our friendship.

"And you're an amazing mom."

I almost guffaw out loud. People really just be saying shit. For the sake of it. I suppress the laughter and instead reach for a grateful smile, which does it, and Dominique looks ready to leave. She thinks she did something here. She thinks that she intervened and fixed the unfixable, like it is that easy. It would be very satisfying to tell her she didn't do shit, that I am still a monster, but I don't. It would be very satisfying to just kill her, how easy it would be, but I don't. I am proud of my restraint.

"You should go. I have so much to do before Emil gets here. It'll be easier once he's home, and that's soon, like you said. Just a couple of days to go, I can make it."

I dodge Dominique's insistence of help and manage to bundle her out the door, into her car.

The thing with being someone people worry about is that the minute you are out of sight, the minute they leave your presence they forget. They forget because they want to, because it's not fun to always worry. It is easier to pretend that someone doesn't exist, to get on with your life, like when people ask me about my mother I tell them she is dead because in part it is the truth. I killed her character off a long time ago, I just didn't expect her to resurrect.

Again, like a sorceress, I evoke her. The phone rings on the kitchen counter and I don't bother to pick it up. I watch it ring, wondering. I think of Devon across the country, who I had always assumed was fine, and he probably assumed the same thing about me when in reality neither of us is, probably never will be. I want to blame Edwina, but perhaps it was me who ensured we can't be together ever again. We were torn apart, and maybe the pieces are too sharp to mend.

My dreams are back, I don't even have to close my eyes for them. They are full of blood.

The minute he comes in the door, I have decided, I will hit him. If I wait longer, if I let him talk, try to explain, I might forgive him, and I already know this is unforgivable. I touch my scalp, tender from my own fists, to remind myself I am capable of inflicting pain. The rolling pin seems easy, I don't know how many strikes it takes to kill a man but I have a little energy left, enough to do this and leave here, no more suffering no more waiting for someone else to help because then it'll just be me on my own, which is something I know how to do. I am empty.

Existing in the world is easy once you figure out the formula. Looking right is at least seventy percent of the battle. And then thirty percent is hiding the pain of being human, no one wants to see that. No one wants your grief or disappointment, no one wants your loneliness, no one wants the ways in which you are not who you imagined you would be.

My head feels empty, and I bet if I jump off a building right this minute, I could fly. I think about the Bronx, about New York before the hospital when I started seeing things, imagining that I was being followed. Bereft, I half worried, half hoped my mother would come and find me, comb the city for me. Hahahaha. I would see her on every street corner, my heart would lurch when I saw Witnesses at my subway station, I would walk around a dark New York, windows of houses and apartments illuminated, vignettes of regular lives continuing on as I stood outside, glued to the glass. I missed the organization, not in a warm and fuzzy way, but the structure, the routine of it. Without it, and I guess without my mother, I was out on a boundless unknowable ocean, wondering which way would lead home. At least with the scripture the answers were clear, you knew where you were going. The faces of strangers on the street became indistinguishable from one another; they could all be my mother. I would walk around the city in the milky morning lights, storefront shutters opening, rats feasting on the contents of spilled trash cans, and walk all the way to the water of the Hudson and feel a definitive pull, like it was calling me, the oblivion of the cold water was tantalizing, the feeling of sinking like a stone to the bottom, my last breaths escaping in bubbles above me. Eventually I found myself standing on the George Washington Bridge, a winter's wind in my face. I knew it would be easier to jump than to not, and there is no dazzling villain origin story here. It was dark enough that no one noticed. No stranger leaped out to rescue me, I didn't slip and have to swim to shore, I didn't die. I simply stepped down, and walked myself into St. Raphael's. But the promise of peace that the water held never left me.

I was weak then. My body is tough now, like armor. I have often wondered what would have happened if I had jumped, if I had let the shadows seep in, take over, take control like a sleeper cell, a double agent. I find myself muttering, half asleep half awake, where are you *where are you, I hate you I hate you.* Delirious. Fevered.

And if Emil were here, I could suffocate him easily, a pillow over his face two elbows either side. My body is sluggish and would make the perfect anchor, wrestling him down to the depths, fueled by hatred and exhaustion. The nights are endless. I don't remember much from them anymore—when I think back the evening hours are like found footage. Like a natural disaster being filmed on a nineties camcorder dropped on the ground in a moment of mounting panic and so all that is captured is half images, audio, blurs you can't quite make out: me skulking around searching for the smell, counting the knives out on the kitchen surfaces, pacing, talking, face illuminated by my phone in the gloom.

I call and cancel the cleaners; I want to be alone. I let dishes pile up, I don't change the sheets. I allow filth to accumulate. I find myself crouched in the corner of our massive bedroom, squatting on my haunches, and I am back on Instagram. It was a mistake to leave. I have decided that, in order to pay attention, to stay awake till Emil comes home, I will scroll through Insta stories, sound off. That way I can still keep an ear out for the shadow that I know will return. On every story I do heart eyes, and on the selfies I follow it up with an r u real. I send this with such a mechanical fervor that, the next morning when the sun is up, I am depressed by the rote replies that have gathered:

r u?!?

Coming from youuuu

Omg imagine looking like you and being a mom I should ask you the same thing 😍😍

One day our children's children will be wondering why we didn't live it up, why we were so scared all the time, worried about the end of the world. We should have been dancing, we should have been savoring. Instead, we worried about the asteroids and wildfires that would eventually kill us, worried about something we couldn't see. In reality it's too late, it's already happened. And when you accept that, you can accept your role in life a little easier. No more preaching about the end of the world; it's already here.

It is fucking nigh.

And there is an emoji for that. A flaming hot meatball blazing across the sky.

When I wake and look at my messages, the asteroid is what I have chosen to respond to the Insta stories. No more heart eyes, asteroid asteroid asteroid as far as the eye can see. And then—a crack in my ear, loud, like a plate pushed onto the floor. It makes me alert; I look around but nothing has changed. The room is still dark, shadows are still cast high but opaque against the walls from passing headlights. No shadow woman waits for me. Nothing is different but I feel something inside myself I haven't before. It is hard, shiny. It feels like the end of something, the bottom of something. I know that there is nothing left to dig. The crack was the sound of me hitting this thing, this final wall.

VI

First was Sekesu, our Caribbean girl.

Second came Della.

Third, Agnes.

Catherine was fourth.

And fifth was Catherine's daughter, Edwina. Edwina grew up far from the island her mother still called home, even though her mother had lived outside Jamaica longer than she ever lived inside it. The shadows followed her from Jamaica even after it was left behind because something happens to a person when the navel string to the motherland is stretched that thin, sometimes it can sever and leave you drifting, aimless. That was Edwina's mother. That's when the spirits tend to come, good and bad. Nana Catherine had first landed, pregnant and poor, on the East Coast but hated the cold. The promise of a good life taunted her, and she grafted her way west, baby in tow. When they got to California all of Edwina's mother's drive seemed to dry up and drift away.

Edwina's mother had always been a dreamy woman, uprooted and desperate to find something she couldn't put words to, but it got worse as Edwina became older and less dependent. She found her mother childlike in a way that made her feel carsick and vowed never to be like her. Edwina was the one who straightened things out, made sure bills were paid and school supplies purchased, her mother was like a sleepwalker that she had to take care of but be careful not to wake. Edwina was shaped by her mother, and in turn she would shape her own children.

Her mother fell in love every few months, and the men were always terrible. One night, Edwina had woken in the pitch-black to one of them in the doorway of her room, stinking of drink, unbuckling his belt. She had at first assumed he had simply walked into the wrong room, but when it became clear that he hadn't, she threw a glass of water at him, which shattered on his big dumb skull, driving him from her room. That was the moment she realized the depths of her mother's failings. It was clear to Edwina at a young age that her mother was not capable of being an adult. Late at night she would drink, and always drank too much, telling long meandering stories of Jamaica, of the beaches and the mountains and endless, endless trees. All types of trees she would list off from some lesson long ago, her voice honeyed from drink, each word overenunciated, like someone clumsily typing on an old typewriter, pecking for letters. She would talk of an island Edwina had never known, didn't care to know, as if Jamaica was her child, not Edwina. Edwina resented that place, because she was the one in front of her mother, couldn't she learn about Edwina, instead?

The point in the night when her mother started to call her Eddie was the tell that it was time to get her to bed, slip the shoes off her feet, hardened by long nights cleaning at the hospital, and tuck her in. Stinking of booze, her mother would try to embrace her, but by then Edwina ("Eddie! My babygirl, Eddie!") was sick and tired of it. Some nights her mother's drinking would take a dark path, although Edwina could never figure out quite what set her off. Those nights she would talk of a man Edwina assumed was her father, of those last few nights in her home country when something terrible happened, but Edwina would plug her ears, she didn't want to hear it. She was sick of the sentimentality, the pining for the past.

She found her faith early on, after her mother's early attempts at regular churchgoing fell off. She was a teenager in a run-down part of town, businesses that had been the mainstay for the Black community they had found in California were being bought out or burned down, the only parts that were relatively untouched were the churches. Edwina found the Kingdom Hall and made herself indispensable. She liked the no-nonsense of it, the clear, unambiguous lines to be followed. They planned and they preached, all in preparation for the end of days. Edwina liked having an expiration date, it felt like safety. When she met the person who would become her husband, she assumed it was divined by Jehovah himself, this good, upright citizen. Spineless maybe. Boring definitely, but Edwina had had enough of excitement, and of men full with spines.

The food of her motherland had been peppered throughout her childhood; her mother could always be counted on to find the nearest Jamaican restaurant, few and far between as they were in those days, calling herself an island girl with pride. Edwina felt superior in her heart, haughty even, at the idea of being first-generation American. Her part of town was mostly Black renters, worn out but at least she wasn't in the South, no one was getting lynched. Of course, it wasn't just the island girl in her that made Edwina other. There are things you cannot scrub. There are shadows you cannot ignore, no matter how you turn your head.

And Edwina tried to ignore it for a long time, the call of this shadow. She thought of it as an intruder to her thoughts and treated it as such, pushing it out of the door like a spurned lover. But then she had her second child and it was harder to keep pushing. She would catch herself staring out the window feeling a chill when she thought of how her mother would do the same thing. Edwina was a strong woman, from a long line of strong women. All that pushing, all that straining.

Her mother went back to Jamaica, back to her home. Catherine had to leave for her own well-being, but she never stopped writing Edwina, telling her the important stories of their family, stories she felt Edwina should know, that could help her. She begged Edwina to come back, to bring the children, to feel the earth of their land beneath her feet, but her mother died without ever getting a reply. The lessons this life has to teach are not always fair, but they must be learned anyway.

Edwina only really knew how to tell Bible stories, stories where the meaning is hidden and you have to sit with the scripture to understand it, really understand it. She believed those who want true enlightenment must come to terms with the marrying of these two concepts, of the invisible and unattainable with the imminent and immediate material. Just like the raising of Lazarus from the dead, the raising of Jairus's daughter, we must also have faith in the impossible becoming possible. Edwina didn't speak plain, preferring the words of the Bible, and her daughter grew bigger and more beautiful and less patient with Edwina's temper, her preaching, her paranoia. And then Edwina cut the navel string once and for all, burning all of her mother's letters. But burning doesn't always mean the end, it is merely a transmutation of energy. Edwina would eventually learn this lesson, but by then both of her children, and her husband (who suddenly grew a spine) would have left, unable to stand it. She was left alone, haunted. As Job said, "Naked I came from my mother's womb, and naked I will depart." Except Edwina came to realize we aren't naked; we are cloaked in a history we cannot outrun. There is a pain and a loneliness that, like the scriptures, needed to be sat with, instead of pushed by.

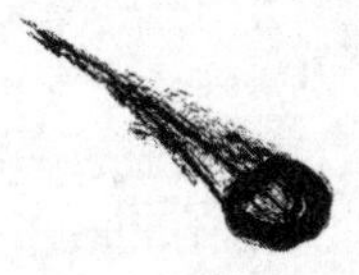

Home stretch, a text from Emil reads.

I delete it.

—*

Lying down in my bed, flat on my back, matted hair sponged out around me. The baby is in her nursery today, in the crib, an experiment because I need space to figure this all out. I rewrap my robe around me, the phone is heavy in my pocket as I lie on top of the covers. I do not want to be weighed down. I let my lids flutter against the darkness of the room, frightened to fully surrender to sleep. There is something I must see; I feel it on a cellular level, my pores alert.

I begin to dream. A wetness laps my feet. The ocean, I think, without looking up. The sky is dotted with foreign birds, and warm earth against my back. Low mangroves behind me. I scamper into the woods, up and up and up without a break until I feel my lungs will give out. Safe in the trees, high above, on a mountain. If I stand still I can hear this mountain whisper to the next: *listen, listen.* A game of telephone being played, if only we could hear it.

And then I am someplace else, something terrible has happened and I scream to a crowd of impassive faces, my own face illuminated by torchlight. Fire against my skin, melting to the bone. I scream and I scream and I scream and I am upright in bed in the house, tears against my cheeks, which are still, impossibly, hot. I leap up and head to the shower, the whispers still in my ears. Rinsing off in cold water, I realize the sound is coming from me, from down below. The horror begins to shift into curiosity and, like weeks before, I grab a hand mirror, spread my legs. The sound of speaking continues, and as I look down at my pubic hair it is different, it is a head of kinky hair and the head looks up and its eyes, not black but brown like mine, look at me, and it hisses, "Listen."

I drop the mirror and it shatters on the tile floor, right as my phone chirps in the pocket of my robe that I hung on the bathroom door. I get up, still naked, and I answer it. I do not let my mother speak.

"Where are you?" I say.

"I'm coming," I say.

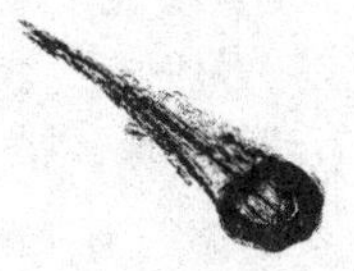

"Sofia, it's your mother calling.

"I've always told you stories, because they are important, they help us understand. Sometimes the truth is unbearable in its raw form, unpalatable. Stories are the things we make up to reframe those truths. Nothing is ever like how it is in the fairy tales, is it? But maybe if I had begun with 'Once upon a time,' things would have been a little easier. But what is time? Is it moving forward or is it actually very, very still? Weighed down by piles and piles of stories on top of one another, never growing in height but staying the same size, a life on a life on a life on a life. Moving through the murk and mire of our ancestors, weaving our lives into theirs until, sometimes, some rare times, they merge. And we are them and they are we. It's always been this way. Are you just Sofia, pioneer, new woman, no need for anything or anyone? Or are you everything that came before you, and everything that will be?

"The question has always been, if the time is always now, who are you?

"I'll try you again later."

I need to go back to the wreckage, dive down deep, because maybe something can be salvaged. Maybe there are answers. My hands tremble as I search for the car keys, I look down at them and they shake, blood in the veins so close to the surface and I could tear the skin with my bare teeth, one wrist after the other. I call a taxi instead, strap myself and the baby in the back as the car takes the well-lit streets of my neighborhood on a journey across the Bay to the dark, potholed ones of my childhood. When we arrive, I stand out on the street outside my mother's apartment block with the baby, car seat mooring me. An inky blue sky shifts above promising darkness, there is no moon and no streetlights. I check the address I wrote on my phone as she told me, not far from our old apartment. I try to orient myself but I am lost. I turn and there she is, illuminated by the light from inside of her apartment, standing there at her window like a lighthouse. I allow my legs to walk me toward her, toward the person I have been running from for fifteen years.

Storm clouds frame her apartment block, gray against indigo-lavender blue. A bruised sky, voluminous with clouds. The air feels thick and close. The smell of burning is in the air, and I shudder at the thought of my dream, the feeling of being burned alive. I climb the stairs toward my mother's door, which she holds open, expecting me to walk through, which I do.

Edwina is older than I remember her. The expression is the same—a mouth turned down at the sides like a military made bed—but something is different around the eyes. She seems calmer. Her hands take mine, although I am reluctant to give them. They are rough in my hands, a deep brown skin wrinkled by age and dish soap from cleaning other people's houses for too long. The sound of our skin touching is like ribbon being pulled through the pages of a book. She looks at me long, as if reading my face, and then does the same to the baby in the car seat, using one tentative finger to stroke her cheek as she sleeps.

"She is a beautiful baby," Edwina says, voice hoarse. She ushers me out of the narrow hallway into a small, dimly lit living room. The view out of the two thin windows is not dissimilar to the one we had growing up: power lines crossing over one another, becoming one in the waning half light. I nod dumbly, sitting myself and the baby onto a faded floral print couch I recall from my childhood.

"I am glad you came," continues Edwina, sitting in a nearby folding chair meant for beach excursions. "I've been calling."

"I know."

"Well. I'm glad you came," she repeats, tenderly. Her voice sounds even. Something flutters within me, something I haven't felt for so long it takes a minute to remember what it is. Hope. It is hope. On a cheap coffee table between us is a blackened stack of letters, and immediately I know that these are whatever is left of my Nana

Catherine's. The sight of them shakes me, the answers to the past three weeks, to a lifetime of questions, are close, within an arm's reach.

"Mommy." I whisper the words I haven't uttered since I was a very small child, feeling the last tendrils of Sofia reach out to the woman who has done nothing but push me away. "I don't know what is happening to me."

"I know. I was frightened too. But you've got to face it, girl."

Her face is thinner, cheekbones high as I remember but hollowed out, eyes tired. The hair peeking out from beneath her bonnet is flecked with gray, her housedress clean but faded. She cracks her knuckles one by one by one, like she always did. Craving her touch, I reach out for her hand because, it turns out even after years of distance, even after so much pain, so much stifled desire, I just want my mom.

Before I can touch her, I sense something has followed me here and is in the room with us. I stand up too fast, causing the baby to cry out, eyes wide, and I scoop her up protectively. The shadow is here, shimmering like it is a multitude. I can scarcely catch my breath, the familiar fear returning. A boundary has been crossed; it has never left the house before, but here it is. A gecko skitters across the ceiling above me. I open my mouth to scream but Edwina stands too so that she is between me and the shadows, because now it is not one but five of them, and my mother locks eyes with me.

"It's all right, it's all right."

She strokes my arm, not breaking her gaze. I settle, and so does the baby.

"I know you haven't been listening to my voicemails, but you'll come to understand in time. Lord knows it took me long enough. I was listening to the wrong voices."

Edwina speaks like it is an apology, but because I have never once heard my mother apologize it confuses me, it does not compute. The shadows shift in the subdued light of the living room, and I can almost make out faces. They look like my mother; they look like me. The floor shifts beneath my feet, I am tipping I am turning I am upside down. I wrap my arms around the baby, who hasn't noticed the shift of the universe.

I see Eddie inhale deeply, then pause. She looks me squarely in the eye. "There has always been something following us."

And then the past the present the future merge on top of me. I am buried.

A voice that sounds like my mother's whispers to me: *Our stories are the ones that we have told each other, over and over again, from village to village, from one continent to the next. Stories that only survived on the tongue, because anything else could have been discovered and destroyed. (Although tongues can be cut out too.)* And then I see it, as if it is all coming into focus for the first time.

I watch as the shadow goes from eldest daughter to eldest daughter, collecting echoes as each daughter dies. A palimpsest of history. The letters contained stories of the past, a paper chain that led back to one original sin. We cannot turn our backs on our roots, we take them with us whether we want to or not. And if ignored, it only makes the past angry. I see these dead ancestors at my door, desperate, waiting for me to comprehend. What does this have to do with me? Didn't I make my life over, build better for my child than I ever had? Isn't that enough?

Just as quickly as I disappeared, I am back in Edwina's cramped apartment, my mother looking at me expectantly. Even the baby is looking up at me as if waiting, unblinking and knowing. The shadows are vivid now, no longer patchy but solid beings, driftwood come to my shore. My hands tremble as I bring them to my face and rub my eyes, incredulously. My eyes roll back into my head as it all comes spiraling into a constellation I can begin to understand, stars in alignment.

But it's too much, my breasts feel full and urgent and I need to get home, I cannot be here. I get up out of my seat, dazed, ready to leave.

"Sofia! This is a moment of revelation! Remember Jacob, his encounter with Jehovah was called an apocalypse? But it wasn't the end of the world. It was the end of what he couldn't see. You must do this too! Witness the revelation! You must listen! You never *listen*!" My mother lectures, a bite to her voice, and a little of her old rage is visible. It repulses me, it pulls some unseen trigger and history repeats itself again as I prepare to leave my mother's house, breathless, reaching for the door. Edwina's hand on my shoulder stops me, she spins me around, looks deep in my eyes.

She opens her mouth, comes close so that I can feel her breath inside my ear, and says, "Let me tell you a story."

VII

The way my memory works these days, I have to get them out before I forget, that's why I've been calling you. I worried I would forget.

There is one more way-back ancestor I haven't told you about. She was a warrior, a great sorceress who could not be contained by the history books. Many lies permeate about who she was and what she was capable of, but I shall try to give the truth to you now. She was known as Ma Ro, she was a first generation of a new Jamaica, the new island. Ma Ro's people were born of a cruelty that will never in our lifetimes be paid for. Stolen from the shores of their home and brought in ships to the islands, as you already know, as your ancestors have already told you, and so I will not horrify you with details. The passage was treacherous and deadly and to make it more bearable, Ma Ro's people had whispered tales of a race of underwater children with fins and gills, iridescent scales like the finery of royalty, borne from the many pregnant women thrown overboard. These stories were told with the hope of freedom, the hope of escape, the hope of another reality beside our own, but different.

Ma Ro had the power to move her mind outside her body, and could wander down into the plantations of Seaman's Valley or Golden Vale or any of the others without being seen, without even leaving her bed. It was said that this is how she knew when the British were planning an ambush, what they were plotting. Despite the whisperings on the island by enslaved and white people alike, Ma Ro's obeah was wielded with kindness, for the most part. She didn't worship one God but rather the unseen, that which is still to be revealed. Healing, divining, helping crops to grow. Of course, Ma Ro murdered many, many British soldiers. But murder, it could be said, was the wrong word. Perhaps the correct word was executed, terminated. Their deaths necessary because of the horror, the pain, the bloodshed, the excruciating separation that your people have already told you tales of, and so I will not repeat here. It is enough to tell you that Jamaica was known throughout the Caribbean as the cruelest of enslavements. Brutality for brutality's sake, a death rate that far exceeded the birth rate. This is why Ma Ro killed all of those British redcoats.

But blood is still blood, no matter how you look at it, and someone will have to pay for it, sooner or later. Stories were told among the greatly outnumbered white people of Jamaica that Ma Ro was a bloodthirsty witch, and these lies the British lieutenants also told to their troops. These were the lies they told to justify what they did next. They killed her baby, sliced it like soft bread.

A Judas led them to the child and killed those who cared for it, leaving the baby like an offering for the British. Some crimes are never paid for, like the crime of what happened to the Taino people of Xaymaca for example, so many of whom were slaughtered long before Ma Ro was born. They had loved the land first, cultivated and nurtured it, lived by the stars and by the tides, learning the swells of the ocean, the calls of the birds. All that humanity, all of that knowl-

edge, eradicated off the island to make way for an imported workforce. But you know this. The land knows this. Some sins cannot be forgotten.

This agonizing theft, the irrevocable grief of it all, was what eventually shattered Ma Ro. Her mind split clean in two like a plate breaking, and she took her remaining eldest daughter and some of her followers and went deep into the jungle, high up into the Blue Mountains where they say she became feral. Stories continued about her existence out in the jungles and in the trees, waiting; a shadow person, a demon, an otherworldly. Sometimes with a mother's face, sometimes with that of pure darkness, an endless black pit of despair gaping at her chest.

It was told that she made a family up there of followers and kin, deeper in the jungle than even the villagers would go. Her ancestors would have been gifted as she and her daughter were, and cursed by a grief too gargantuan, too insidious to ever get over without a true reckoning. Loss was everywhere in those days; it permeated the air. Stories of those underwater miracles endured, shaping a pain such as ours into magic, because that is all that is left when you squeeze all the hope, all the strength, all the joy, all the life out of a people. The magic, the power, sustains. Choke it down, let it fill you. Let your nasal passages transform into gills, let your useless hands, that hang like so, turn into fins. Let that noose around your neck become a net you can swim from. Move through the ocean with ease, evolve, swim.

Despite her transformation Ma Ro was still incredibly powerful, and she found the men who had dismembered her child's tiny body. She found them and she and her followers did the same to them. They tore them apart with their hands, because they could, because when the rage goes and all that remains is a cool resolution, that is what you can do. If you corner a person there is no limit to their wildness. The

British searched high and low for her, tormented and tortured anyone thought to be in allegiance with her, but most were too afraid to follow Ma Ro into the woods to hunt her for her crimes.

It was the obeah that enabled Ma Ro to commit one last act of generosity and ransom sacrifice for her people, although none are around to tell if this truly happened or not, but what Nana Catherine wrote is this: She walked out of the woods and right into the barracks of the men she had murdered. She was seized immediately; they couldn't believe their good fortune at capturing the one who could inspire countless acts of vengeance in her name.

There was no mystery in what they would do to Ma Ro. They enlisted the help of a slave owner crueler than most, who would go on to burn his slaves alive on the eve of their emancipation. They took her to the slave owner's plantation, for they knew word would spread among the enslaved that the obeah woman was dead, and with her, the white men hoped, the chance at any more rebellions. They piled wood around her like a pyre, adding sugarcane stalks for extra malice because sugar burns hot and quick, snapping against the skin, and the smoke from its burning can be seen for miles around. The air was soon thick with an unforgettable saccharine scent, flesh and crop melting together.

They say the women of Ma's mountain villages watched as she was burned. That they left their sleeping bodies safe in their beds, faces painted white with clay as was the custom for such death rituals, and traveled like stardust to do all they could do: watch and witness. So that as she too turned to stardust she could join them, and the resistance could splinter and go on and on into the future, into freedom.

It is said that when Ma Ro succumbed to death, the white spectators wanted their souvenirs in the form of her bones to brandish in the faces of the enslaved, proof of their power to kill a woman thought more than mere mortal. But they only found ash and hardened chunks of coal, which they took for their mantel, for the type of after-dinner conversation sure to make the ladies faint. And when they abolished slavery on the little island of Xaymaca and told the Black people there they were free, the lumps of coal were still kept, passed hand to hand to hand until the owners had long since forgotten what they kept them for, only knew that they were precious.

And then life moved on and some things changed and some things didn't, but it is said that Ma Ro's duppy still walks the mountains. The magic remains in her lineage, in us; it is fertile soil for some of that old magic from long ago, when such things were the only real hope. What happens to all the anger burning in the past if no one is there to put it out?

And that is where we come from, you and me. These shadows need us, Sofia, to bear witness as the villagers did, to sit in our grief and feel it. All that pain and suffering we have all been shunning, all that history we turned our backs on. Remember: Ma Ro did not cry to her gods or her maker, did not beg for mercy, but instead called the names of her children, over and over like a garbled prayer, eventually swallowed up by heat and carried away on the embers through the night sky.

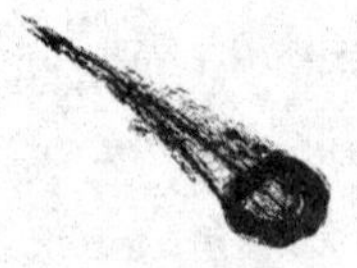

My head spins, and something within me is clear-eyed with revelation. I know that I must go home and so I reluctantly leave my mother, who looks drained, as if telling that last story has taken everything out of her. I get a cab back to the new neighborhood. I ask the driver to stop when I am still several blocks from my house because I need to feel the air. I feel the urge to call my brother, to tell him what I know, but it is too late and he is not ready. Life will be different now; I can feel it. My mother's stories echo in my head, I feel drunk off it, I can smell pepper pot soup and bananas and fresh mangos, the juniper trees in the sun's heat.

I can't help but wonder what else could be told to me, if my mother hadn't burned the rest of those letters, if there had been more. I walk swiftly home, somehow getting there sooner than I expected, as if time has bent back on itself, as if I really never left. I round the corner to my cul-de-sac, the air thick, and a hooded figure is making its way toward me through the still night air, determined walk making it clear that it is meant for me. Fear left my body back in my mother's apartment, I do not falter in my steps. I must confront it, I must close this portal, I must complete this ritual.

"Sofia?"

"Who are you?" I say in a too-loud voice. I feel the baby stir next to me and I rock back and forth on my toes.

"Sofia, Emil called. It's Buffy, I'm here now."

She removes the hood of her raincoat and my face must betray my disappointment because she briefly looks hurt before continuing.

"Come inside; you'll catch your death out here. Emil asked me to wait with you until he comes back. I brought you a lasagne."

I pause, uncertain.

"Come on, now, dear. That baby is too small to be out in the elements. Come on."

Like a sleepwalker being returned to bed, or like a lost sheep herded, I allow her to lead me back to the house and inside, as promised, there is a lasagne on top of the stove. The smell of it triggers forgotten hunger in me. My stomach rumbles in response, I haven't eaten a real meal in a long time.

Peeling off her raincoat, Buffy starts to fuss around the kitchen, getting plates and cutlery out for the food I know Marta made. I take the moment of preparation to go upstairs to the nursery. I undress the baby I clean the baby I redress the baby I feed the baby I rock the baby. It physically hurts to set her down, to be apart. I clutch at my chest. Dizzy, I grip the side of the crib in the dark room, my eyes drift in and out of focus. My heart rate is speedy, I do my deep breathing to calm myself, to center myself. My eyes begin to adjust and spot the shadow, or shadows. They line the room, shoulder to shoulder, edges blurred like smoke rising from warm bodies. They are here but the fear has gone. I know them, and they know me. A blazing trail of stars across a sky, telling a story only we can continue.

I head downstairs, my army of ancestors like wings at my back. In the kitchen my mother-in-law prepares a meal for me. She has her own stories, well-documented stories of her kin, family trees that are easily traced back. Her foundation is known and solid. I look at Buffy as her mouth moves, telling me something about something. I am not listening, not seeing.

"I saw my mother today," I blurt, watching her for a reaction. My ancestors murmur encouragement.

"Your mother?" Buffy asks, confused. She thinks I'm an orphan. Eddie didn't even come to our wedding.

"Yes."

"And," Buffy begins, searching in her basket for ingredients, "how is she?"

"Did you know she's Jamaican?" I say, ignoring the question. My ancestors hoot.

"Warrior heritage," one of them whispers, accent lilting. I think she says this only to me, but Buffy replies.

"I didn't know that. How interesting," Buffy says. She would like this conversation to end, she plucks a knife out of the rack and begins to chop cucumbers for a salad, peeling the green skin first, exposing the watery flesh.

"Why do you say interesting when you don't actually care?" I shout as she chops. Chop chop chop. "You know nothing about us, or where we came from and you have never cared to learn."

"Sofia," Buffy starts, setting down the knife, fatigue lacing her voice. "I don't think those type of details should matter, do you? I don't see color. Black, white, yellow, purple, it's all the same to me."

She pauses. "And we have the most important thing in common now." Buffy has a self-satisfied smile plastered on her face. My eyebrows rise. "We are both mothers."

I snicker. The ancestors join me. It's cruel and I know it, but I can't stop, I feel feverish, infected, lightheaded.

"What's so funny?" Buffy's face is red, flustered.

"Well, you didn't really raise him, did you?" I snap. "What does mothering mean to you? Emil was raised by nannies, just a bunch of nameless nannies. He told me. You hired people so you didn't have to do the dirty work. You don't know anything about motherhood."

"Emil has it wrong, I'm afraid." Surprised, I look at her. Her eyes are downcast, but she speaks with such certainty, robbing me of my *gotcha* moment. I'm confused. The ancestors are too, and they quiet down, take a step back toward the walls. I falter on my feet and Buffy grabs my elbow with her bony hands.

"Sit down, you need to eat. You're skin and bone. Eat while your baby sleeps."

I nod dumbly, grateful to be told what to do. Buffy puts the lasagne back into the oven to keep warm and I sit at the French country kitchen table, bought for more than it was ever worth at the Alameda Flea Market. Dominique and I got up at five A.M. to go, wandered around till we found it, bought champagne afterward to celebrate and drank it from the bottle. Buffy sets a plate in front of me and I eat ravenously, like someone just come in from the woods, because I haven't in weeks.

Buffy sits at the head of the table, naturally. "I'm sure that's what Emil told you, but I'll tell you the real story." There's a slight pause as if Buffy is deciding if she can share this, if it is okay. My silence as I shovel food into my mouth, famished, gives her permission to continue. "We tried to have a baby for years. We married young, like all of my friends. I met John in college, he proposed . . . It was what you did in those days. I was twenty-two. I thought it would all come so easy but it didn't."

I listen, keeping my fork moving, hardly tasting it but feeling the lasagne's fortifying effects immediately.

"No one told me it could be heartbreaking, watching all of my girlfriends deliver happy, bouncing babies. We had three miscarriages early on, and one stillbirth at eight months. I think the stillbirth was what broke John, he never really recovered. Emily, we were going to call her Emily." I nod, encouraging her to continue.

"We had the nursery painted, we were ready, and then they couldn't find the heartbeat and I had to give birth to her anyway. I labored for ten hours, and then . . ." She trails off. I know how this ends. A husband who held his dead child in his arms and never felt alive ever again. How can you after such pain? That loss would haunt you forever.

I swallow. The food is stabilizing.

"Buffy," I whisper, "I'm sorry. I didn't know."

"No one does. When Emil was born I think I experienced some sort of deferred grief. I couldn't stand to look at him, I hired those nannies so I could be sure he would be well cared for. One was Black. She might have even been Jamaican. Definitely Caribbean but I can never tell, you know, with the accents. Anyway, I focused on my silly little hobbies; tennis, the club, philanthropy. It was easier than looking at him. I regret it now, of course. I missed so much."

Buffy grits her teeth, struggling to compose herself, she won't allow herself to cry. I have the realization that all of her sharpness is her armor, holding in the rot of grief. She touches a perfectly manicured hand to her temple, lightly, like a clairvoyant.

"We never told Emil about his sister."

"I'm sorry. I can't imagine . . ."

"I think you can, Sofia," she says plainly, getting to the root. "I watched you when I was over the other day. Something's not right, and you won't accept help. Hiring someone isn't a sin. You could even get a Black nanny, if you liked. Plenty of them over from Haiti these days, poor things."

Despite her revelation, Buffy is still Buffy.

"Emil should never have left you alone like this."

This admission, this verbalizing of all I have been burying, tugs like hands pushing something out. Water springs from my face, rivers of tears down my cheeks. It is more than I can bear. The ancestors weep too, because they know this grief. Buffy places a hand on my head and briefly I am a child again, small and wronged and desperate to please. She keeps it there until my breathing slows, my head bowed, snot and tears dripping.

The ancestors seem placated by Buffy's candor, and they are calm. My stomach is full and the exhaustion held in my body suddenly feels unavoidable. I want to sleep.

"You must be exhausted," Buffy says matter-of-factly. "I'll watch the baby while you sleep. When Emil comes home we can talk about staffing."

I stand up, more stable than I have been in weeks but still woozy.

"I can help clean up," I say, and I pick up the kitchen knife used for the salad.

"No, dear, that's fine, I can . . ." She doesn't finish her sentence.

I look down, and the knife is in her abdomen, as if someone pushed me into her. I have sliced through fat and tendons like a butcher block piece of meat, it feels as if her innards are pulling me in. Blood bubbles up around the blade; it's unbelievable how quick it all happens; I almost laugh at the ridiculousness of it all. Buffy's mouth makes a small *oh* sound and she puts her hands on top of mine and pulls it out. My hands shake, the blade shines red. Buffy is paler than I imagine a person can get. I pick the knife up, as if I can undo it. I shake my head, no no no no no, but it's too late, it's been done.

Now

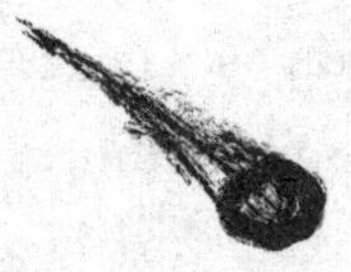

There is something very satisfying about doing the worst thing you have ever done, could ever do. A leveling-out. A new low. Of the deadly sins, this is the worst. Nowhere possibly could be lower, I've reached the limit of the horrors I am capable of. I've done it.

That feeling lasts approximately eight seconds and then I panic, I look at the hand holding the knife and it looks like someone else's. Buffy's hands hold her stomach like a crucial part of a dam; blood is geysering up like a fresh spring between her fingers and I couldn't stop it if I wanted to. The ancestors fade back into the walls, into the shadows, like they were never there. This is all wrong.

Buffy crumples to the floor; the blood was the only thing holding her up. I look at my hands and they are gruesome, dripping long strands of crimson that decorate the wood. I try to wipe them off on my clothes but the blood is almost creamy and I cannot get them clean. In every true crime story, there is always the witness who says, "I never knew there would be so much blood," and you think, sure. How much blood could there be? But when you are standing there, knife in hand, over the body of the person you just stabbed, you realize how right they were. More blood than seems possible to fit into the average human body. With that much blood you'd imagine we'd all be beefy full-to-the-brim bodies, juicy blood puddings, waterlogged with blood. A pinprick and it would gush out of us, big waterbed-type bodies. I drop the knife. It audibly splashes; I am standing in a puddle. Buffy is motionless; a panicked noise escapes me. I must undo this. My head is filled with a deafening noise, and then there is a silence that is almost as piercing, sharp, a high-pitched tinnitus. I should clean. Yes. I get a bucket, towels. My house socks are absorbing blood like a sponge, my feet bathing in the warmth of it.

I am splicing between time and space. I am in the vicissitudes. I feel calm. I've done something awful and there is no fixing it. The shadows shimmer, the end of the world has come to meet me here at the end of my tether. I pick up the knife again, it almost slips in my hands but I hold it tight, thinking about what to do next when, behind me, I hear the front door click open.

The baby begins to cry from upstairs as Emil's keys turn in the door. Of course, tonight of all nights, he is punctual for the first time in his life. There is no stopping it. Buffy groans on the floor next to me, I crouch to observe her ragged breathing and to my relief she's not dead, I haven't killed her. I am not a murderer. This should bring clarity, I should know what to do next but I feel I am balancing on an apex of horror, I can't seem to get equilibrium.

"Sofia?" Emil's voice wavers.

I turn around. Emil is dressed in a light rain-spattered trench coat, hair slicked back, keys in hand. He hesitates, taking in the scene, and then he screams a scream I have never heard before, his voice joining with the baby's disembodied cries.

"Mom?" he sobs, eyes wide in horror, rushing toward her, knees in the blood that immediately suckles up his jeans. He turns to me, taking in my face as if he has never seen me before in his life. "What did you do?"

His crying is desolate, as if he cannot comprehend. I stammer but no words come out. Buffy speaks his name and Emil's eyebrows rise in hope. She is whispering to him and I lean in, desperate to hear.

"An accident," she moans, blessedly. I am so relieved to hear her talking, it is the most beautiful sound.

Emil pulls out his phone and calls 911 while I stand there, an imbecile, unspeaking. I can't breathe, I put my hand to my chest and try to focus, raspy inhales getting faster and faster. I want the ancestors back; I want my own mother. Suddenly Emil is next to me, sitting me on a stool in the kitchen, telling me to breathe. He grabs towels and presses them to his mother's stomach, he mutters to himself, "Okay okay okay okay." His suitcase is abandoned in the foyer. I think of taking it upstairs, of unpacking it.

The bleeding is slowing, and in no time at all the paramedics arrive, rushing through the foyer. They brush past me to Buffy, who is repeating "accident, accident" on every wet exhale. Upstairs, the baby's screams twist up an octave in mounting frustration. Confused, I leave the paramedics working on Buffy, make my way to the stairs, socks soaked with blood. My footsteps sound like they are walking on moss, soft and damp.

Emil heads me off before I can ascend, stepping toward me with the same precaution he would take toward a wild animal.

"The baby is crying," I say.

Emil's eyes dart in the direction of our steps. He seems unsure of whether he should soothe me or go upstairs. His face is drained. I stare at him like a changeling, or like Jacob in the might of Jehovah's great revelation. He shakes his head almost mournfully. "No, Sofia, she isn't." But then, second-guessing, he turns and sprints up the stairs to the baby, perhaps realizing she could be hurt. Finally, my legs come alive, and I follow, taking the steps two at a time. He is in the nursery between me and the crib, and as I approach him, he grabs her and cradles her close. She wakes and begins to fuss, her murmuring crescendo-ing into a loud cry as she realizes she is not in my arms but those of someone who is a stranger to her. He looks the baby over, searching. I am offended. Someone who has just stabbed her mother-in-law should probably not be, but I am.

"What is going on?"

"Emil. I would never hurt her."

He is relieved but still shook. "What is going on?" he repeats, almost begging. I am not sure I have ever seen him this frightened.

"I just needed it to stop."

"What to stop?" he pleads, his eyes red.

The baby is arching her back in hunger now. Emil is struggling to hold her still.

"Can you just give her to me?" I say, taking a step forward as Emil takes one back, bumping into the crib, betraying his fear. My outstretched hands are bloodstained.

"Not until you tell me what the fuck happened! What did you do?"

"Calm down."

He's been off on some fake set and I've been in real life, he knows nothing, he's no help, he's nothing.

"Calm down?" he yells, causing the baby to silence for a moment. "I walk into my home to my mother bleeding on our kitchen floor and you're all fucked up, and you want me to calm down?"

I look around for my ancestors, I need them to tell me what to do next, but there is only Emil, looking at me with a face of mistrust and how can I blame him? I am both inside and outside my head, uncertain of where my reality went. I have to tell him the truth.

"I've been seeing things."

"The intruder? Yeah, I know, you told me this already," Emil yells impatiently. The baby is quiet in his arms as if she knows something is coming. I run my fingers through my hair, it is coming out entwined around my fingers, thick strands of tight curls.

"The shadows . . . I think they are ghosts of the past. I think they need me to do things."

Emil is approaching me like I am a rabid dog.

"What are you talking about? What things?"

"I think they are the ones that hurt your mom. I think they pushed me into it."

He pauses, and then with concern dripping in his voice he says, "Sofia."

Just *Sofia.* Simple as that but it does it, that's it, that's the safeword. I crumble to the floor, it is too much, it is all too much. Vignettes play in my head like a movie, but which were the real ones? Where have I been, what have I done? I think of the security cameras.

"Check the tapes," I whisper from beneath my disheveled hair. Emil looks up at the cameras, remembering. He hasn't inched away from where he is rooted. He is afraid. "You can log in and check the tapes, right?"

"I think I need to call Dr. Lester. I think you need help. I can't do this right now, I have to . . ." Emil's tone has shifted, a flat affect, he looks down at the baby, and then to the door, which leads to the staircase, which leads to the foyer, which leads to the kitchen where his mother is bleeding, tended to by paramedics. "I have to help her."

"Please," I beg, "I have to see."

Emil puts the baby back into her crib and somehow she settles down immediately. Of course he found it easy; it's always so easy for him. We go back downstairs and Emil watches as the paramedics work to stem the bleeding. Buffy smiles weakly; she will survive. The paramedics need space, one of them makes a garbled call over the radio at his shoulder, runs back to the ambulance to get more supplies.

Emil looks at me with disbelief as he moves to unpack his laptop. His bloodied hands tremble as he flicks it open on the kitchen counter. He clicks something on the desktop, leaving dark stains on the keys, and it springs open to a window of various security cameras. I don't even remember having this many installed but here they are on the outside of my house in the backyard the hallway the kitchen. I have been surveilled from all angles. He didn't trust me even from the beginning. I push this betrayal down, because this means I will finally get proof of my visitors, convince Emil that this is real.

"I don't see anything," Emil says, pressing the fast-forward button, causing the gloomy black-and-white image of a house to spring to life. Even in fast-forward the house is dead quiet. I feel dejected. I was so sure I would see someone or something in the darkness with me but there's nothing just empty hallways and unlit windows. But then suddenly something flickers in the corner of the image of a hallway.

"There!" I yell, startling Emil next to me.

Emil clicks, enhances, like an episode of *CSI.* We watch the figure move furtively in the corner of the screen hooded and dark, the shadow person made flesh. Now I know it was real now I know I am not crazy. I take control of the trackpad and click through the other cameras, fast-forwarding. I watch the shadow person pace my house, speaking things I couldn't listen to, that I can't hear now, even in the black-and-white video. Emil tenses beside me. An intruder has been in his house, moving his things, stalking his family. A dangerous intruder, capable of God knows what. He is lucky that I protected our child from it all, that in his absence I have become a hardened person, what my father would have called a tough nut. It was them, not me, that hurt Buffy. But what Emil says next changes everything I know to be true, shattering my newfound enlightenment.

What Emil says next is:

"That's you."

I bring my face inches from the screen to find that he is right. I am the one on the camera, lithe and primed, in one security camera window I am violently smacking my hand over and over again with a paperweight, in another I am steady with scissors, snipping at the baby's unworn clothes. I am the one hiding things around the house, furtive and fearful. And then I watch myself open the window of our bedroom wide, I see myself step up and look down, the outside calling me. I push Emil's hand off the laptop and out of the way, I scroll forward in time on the video to another night, another wide-open window, stepping up to face oblivion. I am teetering on the edge, moments from the recent past are unrecognizable to me.

I watch myself, two-dimensional and monochrome, moving from room to room, from windowsill to windowsill, with a jerkiness I do not recognize. I watch myself pull out clumps of hair that I shove indiscriminately into drawers and pillows and plants. I knew that I had been hollowing myself out for something, that I was making a path within me, but I had no idea what I was creating. It seems too complete a metamorphosis to have been isolated to these past few weeks, maybe I have always had this shadow within me even back in New York, maybe this has always been the final destination. Like mother like daughter.

I know I should feel something about making my husband scared in his own home, of creating a crime scene, but nothing comes to me when I reach for it. I only feel a sort of remorseless cold chill inside me that lets me know whatever was left of the old me is dead.

"Okay, all right," Emil mutters, resolute. "I am going to take out my phone and call Dr. Lester, okay?"

The lasagne is still in the oven, burning. The smell of charcoaled meat billows out of the oven and seeps into the walls, travels upstairs, gets into the crawl space. It'll never come out; it'll always smell like burning. He is talking slowly, as if I have suffered a head trauma. The paramedics have also stopped their work, they seem aware of something I am not. I rub my eyes like a cartoon character. If the person on the security footage is also me, then who am I? I falter on my feet and grab the counter, but I am uncertain it is even there, if what I am grabbing is even solid.

—*

I should have heard my mother earlier. After all of the damage she inflicted, I thought she had nothing left to give me, but she had a final warning about the vengeance of ancestors ignored. The ancestors weren't angry, they just needed me to listen. Perhaps if I had listened, Buffy's pain could have been spared, but maybe resolutions are always bloody, perhaps you cannot reconcile the pain of the past without a taste of it in the future, metallic on the tongue. I hear my mother speaking to me, her breath once again close in my ear:

Our story must be continued, Sofia. These tales are our road maps for survival. We must listen, we must stand still and hear them so that they may live. So that we may live. Remember the story of Jacob? The apocalypse that Genesis talked of was not what you think. The word apocalypse *comes from the Greek, and it doesn't mean the end of the world. It means disclosure. An uncovering.*

We are creatures who want to walk toward the light instead of the darkness, and you have your light, Sofia. Walk toward her.

—*

In this house that I have made an endless night, the bedroom illuminates, staccato, in red and blues. Emil and the paramedics confer downstairs; I won't be alone with her much longer. The door is barricaded, chair wedged beneath the door handle, closing us in like a private club of two. I feed her one final time and set her in the crib that Emil and I built together what feels like a lifetime ago. The baby is settled, dressed neatly in a sleeping onesie, wrapped in a clean swaddle. There is something so comforting about her neatness, her mere existence is a feat.

I kept her alive, I think. I did it. I am doing it. She looks up at me and for the first time ever, a crooked baby smile works across her face. A spit bubble, perfect and clear, is blown from her lips. My heart explodes, a room within it opens and blooms. I reach down and allow her to grasp my finger tightly. The world is crashing down around me and if the meteor comes let it be hot and let it be fiery, let it cleanse and purify because the end is nigh but she is here, this seed, this sapling reaching up toward the heavens. She is mine and I am hers. This is all there is. Blue and red light from outside the window mottles the ceiling, a Technicolor camo print spreading above my head.

I look into her face and there she is, all smiles and coos. I scoop her up as if for the first time, nestled in my arms as if she has always been here. My daughter, the eldest daughter of the eldest daughter of the eldest daughter of the eldest daughter of the eldest daughter, the outline of the future against the imprint of the past. Layers upon layers of women peeling back to show this face, this perfect face, hair black like my brother's. She looks at me with eyes that are the exact same shade of brown as mine. Something settles; all of the questioning of the evening, of the past few weeks, recedes, leaving only certainty pulling like an undertow.

I look at her like I am shipwrecked and she is home, and finally, finally I say her name.

Acknowledgments

It takes a village to raise a child, it takes a village to write a book.

To my village, the parents and caregivers and nannies and babysitters and teachers in my community that I lean on—Sarah Rainey, Robyn Greene, Laura Whelan, Emily Bell, Robin Semmelhack, Amy Davis, Elizabeth Durney, Mary Dooley, Denise Gage Collins, Dana Duncan, Suzanne Garcia, Sarah Seitchik Sebastian, Kailea Fredrick, Charlie Vaughan, Kate Sheehy and her jumper cables, Lizzi Kitaen Sanchez, Shelly Romero, Janet Gardner, Ryann Nordahl, Lily Verdone, Beth Green, all the WoW, Courtney Reiman, to name just a few. Thank you for picking up my children, feeding them, watching them, soothing them, laughing with them, helping me raise them, bringing me coffee, listening to me. I need you; I love you. Special thanks to Andrea Tomkins, who consistently and effortlessly steps in to help whenever she can sense I need it.

Particular thanks to Ashley Austin and Jessica Marasa, community members and dear friends who have propped me up and held me down more times than I can count. And Marissa Puget, a champion of Eirinie Carson and a fabulous mother and artist.

To my Stephy, my Stephanie Tataryn. They don't make them like you anymore; a warrior of a friend, a force, you have read everything I have ever written and still ask for more. Time spent with you is some of my most treasured. May every artist find their other half who nourishes and, on occasion, when it is needed, tells them to *shut the fuck up and write.*

Thank you, Hedgebrook and My Hedgebrook Huns, Vesna, T Kira, Tamar, Katie, Sarah. Five women who, at the crucial point, stopped me and said *you are worthy, you belong* and saved both me and the book from certain peril. Thank you. Our two weeks in the Whidbey woods changed me.

Thank you to the Hambidge Center and the NEA for my two weeks in the Georgia woods, where I reconciled much of this book, and also went just a tiny bit mad.

Thank you to the Awesome Foundation for the funds you graciously gave me that allowed me to take the course by Dr. Joy DeGruy. Thank you for sharing your knowledge on post-traumatic slave syndrome and the epigenetics of trauma.

To the Virginia Center for the Creative Arts for space and time and introducing me to Dionne Irving, author and mother and fellow member of the Jamaican diaspora. Your stories allowed me to access my birthright, my Jamaican heritage. Your humor and intelligence and skill with a pen encourage me more than I can say.

To Daesha Devón Harris, Saratoga Queen and an artist of the highest caliber, thank you for always taking me seriously.

To Meghan Sadler for her artistic opinions and skill, thank you. To Laxmi Hussain for her adherence to a deadline, her beautiful art, and her blues, thank you for this cover. You were the most perfect pairing for this book.

To the other writers and authors who supported or inspired me,

Savala Nolan, Nana Kwame Adjei-Brenyah, S. A. Cosby, Raha Jorjani, Margaret Wilkerson Sexton, Kai Harris, Malkia Devich Cyril, Jungwon Kim, Renée Lertzman, Vijaya Nagarajan, Michelle Cliff, Marlon James, thank you for your work and your words.

To Shirley Recinos-Bull for sharing your lived experience, thank you.

To Steve Pairman for answering "how much blood is too much blood," and to Beatrice Fisher for answering questions about postpartum and live births, thank you both.

To the Mesa Refuge and Kamala Tully for a fertile soil and the chance to write on the very edge, and the time you generously furnished me with so that I might dig into my final edit with editor Lashanda Anakwah, whose tender, kind annotations kept me from leaping off a cliff several times during the draft process. Thank you for making me laugh, relenting when needed, pushing back when needed. You showed me just what a great editor can bring to a manuscript, I appreciate you.

Tim Wojcik, who always indulges my panicked *is this maybe all shit* texts, who is probably so grateful his phone doesn't allow me to send him voicenotes. Tim is a phenomenal writer and agent; his dogged assuredness and fierce advocacy kept the Good Ship Eirinie afloat. Don't quit on me coz we have work to do, and I promise to try to move my communications over to email exclusively (jk).

Thanks to the Center for Healing and Liberation, namely the work of Victoria Santos, Sayvannah, Ashley, and Cristina, which ensured I spent the most magical days in the woods with Black women and femme people on the island of Whidbey in 2023, and then gave me the same gift in 2024 at Commonweal in California. The work you do is essential.

To Dmitra and all at the Black Therapist Fund in Sonoma

County, which provides free therapy to Black people in Sonoma County, boy oh boy am I grateful to you, and also to Karen Daley, my treasured therapist and Hakomi specialist, thank you for your time and your care.

To Ambreia Meadows-Fernandez—our future is bright with you.

To my mother-in-law, Jeannie, who is absolutely nothing like Buffy. Thank you for welcoming me into your family and your traditions so seamlessly all those years ago. I think myself lucky to be one of the few who truly adores their mother-in-law. I love seeing so much of you in our girls.

To my father-in-law, Will, who, the minute he heard of this book selling to Dutton, began telling everyone he knew—thank you for being the proud father I never really got to experience as a child. It feels good having such an honest, kind, pragmatic man in my life, who knows how to do things right.

To my beloved, Adam Alexander Carson. Your capacity for understanding, for adjusting, for atoning, for mending, for healing, for loving, knows no bounds. The evolution of you facilitates the evolution of me, and round and round. You are nothing like Emil and I am so happy to be raising our children together. You are a champion of me and my work and believe in my success when I cannot.

To my daughter Selah, whose birth was the catalyst for this book, thank you, my angel. Much of this book was written with you on my body, even now as I type this you are laying your four-year-old head on my shoulder, asking me what I am doing. I am making things for you, baby.

To my daughter Luka. I am inspired on the daily by your artistic nature, fashion sense, and kindness. You are one of a kind, our kid, and I am so glad I get to witness your growth. I love you more than words can say.

To my own brother, Nick aka Uncle Nick Nick, reeeeeeal badman, thank you for the advice, thank you for your read on the character of Devon. I have been your champion since you came out the womb, I think you're funny and crazy smart and spending time with you feels like home to me. I love you so dearly. You are a wonderful father to my beautiful niece Kaziah and a fearless partner to our beloved Poppy. Big tings a come.

To my mother, Edith, who remains the smartest person I know, whose intellect and brilliance and readiness at the end of the phone line keeps me going, thank you. I love you, Mumski, and I simply could not continue without your support.

I am the eldest daughter of the eldest daughter of the eldest daughter of the eldest daughter of the eldest daughter of the eldest daughter of the eldest daughter of the eldest daughter of the eldest daughter. Thank you to my grandmother Anne, great-grandmother Joan, Edith Sr., Isabella, Mary, Teresa, Teresa Sr.

And finally, to the trinity of ancestors I carry at my back: the grandmothers I am named for, Anne and Sophia, and Larissa, whose encouragement of my writing is felt now, even all this time after their deaths. I feel you with me. You told me *more,* and I promise, it is coming.

About the Author

EIRINIE CARSON is a member of the Writers Grotto in San Francisco and a frequent contributor to *Mother* magazine. Her work has also appeared in *Literary Hub*, *Notre Dame Review*, *Mortal Magazine*, *Electric Literature*, *Sonora Review*, and others. *Bloodfire, Baby* is her first novel.